To Sam —

POO

AND UCKS

A NOVEL BY JOHN BRUNI

www.strangehousebooks.com

Beware the dick! Enjoy! [signature]

StrangeHouse Books
An Imprint of Rooster Republic Press

www.roosterrepublicpress.com

Poor Bastards and Rich Fucks

ISBN-13: 978-0692378670
ISBN-10: 0692378677

To Kevin Strange and Don Noble, two guys who took a chance on a collection of short stories from a guy they'd never heard of before.

PROLOGUE

1

Steve McNeil tossed his head back and felt cheap whiskey burn down his tongue and ignite his belly with a comforting warmth. Not enough to soothe the demons that lived in the wrinkles of his brain and the chambers of his heart. Not enough to drown the devils and anxiety that cavorted in the darkest depths of his guts. Not enough to peel his skin away and reveal a new person beneath. But he hoped it would set him down the path to forgetting about himself, if only for one lonely night.

Lenny came by and filled his glass again. Not just a couple of fingers, like any other hole-in-the-wall bar; Lenny poured whiskey up to the brim. He knew how his customers liked it. Steve nodded his gratitude and stared at the amber fluid. He thought about his life as a reverse exorcism. He poured the liquid spirit into his body and waited for it to possess him.

He knew the others in Lenny's Tavern, but not as friends. Not really. They were just acquaintances drinking away their remaining lives. They drank, waiting for their livers to quit on them, or maybe their hearts. They recognized each other as society's cast-offs, so far in the hole that they couldn't even acknowledge each other.

Not that Steve minded. No, he liked being alone. He'd been alone for what? A year? It couldn't have been that long, could it?

It didn't matter. His uncle had always joked about how everyone died alone. Steve had made peace with this uncomfortable truth. Maybe he could even find comfort in it. But he doubted it.

He sipped again and glanced to his periphery. A digital read-out of the time ticked away, second by second, at the very edge of his sight. He looked up and saw a notification of how much he had left on his credit chip. He had all the time in the world, but he didn't have much money in his account. Not enough to afford the booze it would take to put him down into the merciful arms of slumber.

Fuck.

After all this time, he'd finally run out of money. He knew he'd spend the last of it here. By the end of the month, he'd be kicked out of his apartment. At this point, he wouldn't be able to move into even the most flea-bitten motel on the Sleaze Strip.

He tried to envision himself living on the streets with his hand out. How many bums had he rousted in his day? How many times had he brought homeless drunks downtown? This time next month, he will have joined their ranks. Just another alcoholic homeless guy. Another filthy face in a sea of the destitute.

He took another drink and found that he cared less and less about it.

"Holy fucking shit. Steve Mc-fucking-Neil, as I live and breathe."

Steve turned his head and saw a man he'd never seen in Lenny's before. A light blue circle formed around the stranger's head, and after he buffered for a moment, a name popped up next to the guy's face: BOB WHITEMAN. That sounded kind of familiar. The icon next to the name asked if Steve would like to know more.

Yes.

Several social media sites popped up in Steve's left eye, and he saw pictures of Bob's life. Mostly whoring and drinking. Playing cards. That sort of thing. He flicked on Bob's LiveStream and saw himself staring back. The image jarred him too much, made his stomach do a couple of flips. To save himself from losing the precious whiskey he'd imbibed tonight, he banished the stream.

"Shit, don't tell me you don't remember me. It hasn't been that long."

Steve blinked, trying to place him. Bob stood maybe five-ten and had a hell of a gut on him. He weighed maybe 240, but much of it had enough definition to suggest he could kick an ass or two, if needed. He wore a shirt that said PUSSY SATISFIES and ragged jeans over a pair of scuffed boots, heavy enough to stomp a head if the issue came up. Steve placed him at forty-five years of age with a shiny pate starting to show between the graying hairs on his head. A light scruff of whiskers covered his jowls, not doing much to hide a second chin.

"It's me. Bob Whiteman. We used to drink together all the time."

Déjà vu. A bulb went on somewhere in the recesses of Steve's booze-addled mind. And then, he hit it. Back when he'd been on the job, he used to drink with a lot of his fellow cops. Just hanging out, talking shit about the scumbags they'd had to deal with that day. Maybe a card game here or there. Bob had been among them. Not a cop, just one of the guys who hung out at the same bar.

He flipped through the records of his own social media and found some footage from back then. He froze the video and superimposed it over Bob's face. Sure enough, they matched. Bob had more hair back then, and it had been darker, but the images were otherwise the same.

"Bob," he said.

"See? You *do* remember. How the hell are you?" He held out his stumpy hand. Short, but beefy.

Steve took it, and they shook vigorously. Both had four red spots on the sides of their hands when they drew away from each other. Only then did Bob pull up a stool and sit next to him. Lenny came by, and Bob ordered a beer. "And one for my old friend here."

Lenny filled a couple of mugs and put them down on the bar. He wandered away and stared off into space. His eyes flicked back and forth, evidence that he'd busied himself with reading something online.

"Jesus, Steve. It's been a long time. What have you been up to?"

Steve gritted his teeth, committed to lying without even thinking about it. "Nothing much. Same shit as always. What are you doing around here? I thought you only drank at the Red Hand."

"Wow, that's a name from the past. I haven't been there for a while. How are the guys doing? It's been ages since I saw them."

"I . . . they're fine." He suppressed his LiveBlog, on the off-chance that Bob had tuned in to it.

"Good to hear. I've been trying to stay out of trouble. Not always successful, of course."

Steve laughed. "You got business in this neighborhood?"

"Yeah. Thought I'd stop in and catch a beer, and look who I found." He gestured a hand to Steve before downing half his drink in one go.

Soon, the beer flowed, and the more they drank, the looser their tongues became. Before long, Steve let his façade drop, and if he'd been sober enough, he would have been horrified to hear himself unburdening his woes onto his old friend.

He told Bob about what got him kicked off the force. About a quiet night and a dark alley, where he'd found a young man, gakked-out of his mind, beating the shit out of a woman who later turned out to be a fuckslinger. About how he'd given the punk back more than he'd ever given. About how the youth had turned out to be the mayor's nephew. About the crucifixion the media had given him as a power-crazy cop. The dots connected to form a picture of Steve living on the last of his money, a pussy hair's length away from living on the streets.

"Holy fuck, Steve. I had no idea."

Steve sniffed. He hadn't cried in a long time, and now he felt on the very verge. His eyes burned, and he pretended to rub at them out of tiredness. "I guess you haven't been watching the news, then."

"You know me. I don't give a tin shit about what's happening in the world."

They sat in silence for a moment. Behind his closed eyes, Steve looked to the left and saw how late it had gotten. He thought about all the drinks he'd had with Bob, and his stomach froze over. No way did he have enough left in his account to cover his end. Lenny would probably let him slide, but he didn't want to have to resort to that.

"Last call!" Lenny said.

The other patrons lined up to the bar, eager for one more round before they had to take to the streets and crawl back into whatever hell hole they called home. Father O'Riley held an empty glass in his trembling, liver-spotted hands. John Kroger, who had to be over a hundred years old, gripped the edge of the bar as if he were afraid he'd fall over. Ted Bentley, who still wore the car accident that had killed his baby daughter around him like a shroud, stood by their side, trying to get his empty glass in front of the others.

They all ordered doubles.

"What do you think? A shot to round out the evening?"

Steve nodded, unthinking.

When the others had been served, Bob ordered a couple of shots, and when they got them, they clinked the glasses together. "To the future," Bob said. "It's more fucked up than you can possibly imagine."

Steve thought he detected an extra dose of bitterness in Bob's voice, but he didn't object to the toast. They drank fast and hard and clunked their glasses on the bar upside down.

Lenny came by with his chip device, both of their bills loaded and ready to be paid off. Steve nearly choked when he saw how much his was. He'd spent more than double his remaining amount.

He knew Lenny would be okay with him promising to pay later. The others asked for this favor all the time. Old man Kroger would walk out of here tonight without fulfilling his transaction. Why not Steve?

Bob must have seen something on his friend's face. "I'll pay for both."

"You sure?" Lenny asked.

"No," Steve said. "You don't have to do that. I can—"

"For old time's sake," Bob said.

"I can't. I won't accept charity. It's—"

"Enough. I think I owe you from back in the day, anyway. Consider us even."

Steve felt the urge to argue the point, but he simply couldn't remember if he owed Bob or not. A part of him—a weaselly part he didn't like—knew for a fact that *he* owed *Bob*.

He didn't stop Bob from running his left hand over the chip reader.

"Now that that's settled," Bob said, "you look like you could use a ride home."

"I'll be fine." Steve stood up, and when the world shrank away from him, he began to doubt his statement. However, the booze had indeed possessed him, and he could never admit being wrong, not even as he leaned against the bar to keep on his feet. Already, he felt the blackout creeping across his mind.

Bob looked into Steve's eyes. Twin blue circles analyzed them and came back with some kind of medical term Bob didn't know. Also, an estimated blood alcohol content of 1.9 appeared. It asked if he wanted to call 911.

No. He banished the system and said, "Come on. My van's right out front. It'll be no problem."

Steve opened his mouth to object, but his numb lips decided to not help him form the words.

Bob helped steady him, and the two of them walked past the other poor, desperate bastards, all nursing their final drink before their nightly hibernation from their selves began. Only old man Kroger looked up and nodded.

Outside, Steve leaned up against Bob's van and waited for his friend to unlock the door. Bob accessed the van's security system, and when it asked if he wanted the door unlocked, he said, *Yes*. The rear door slid open.

"In you go," he said.

Steve stumbled, and Bob had to help him get into the back. At this point, he knew Steve wouldn't be conscious for very long. He debated not using the needle after all, but he knew he had to play it safe. Richard Coppergate paid him very well to play it safe, and although he led a questionable life, he always considered himself to be a professional.

He slipped the needle from his pocket and thumbed off the protective cover. All he had to do was stick it in Steve's ass, and that would be it. His obligation for this night would be over. Yet he held back. He'd never had to do someone he knew before. He actually liked Steve, and unlike everyone else in this rotten city, he actually believed the story about how he'd lost his job.

Fuck it. If he didn't do this, he'd never be able to work for Coppergate ever again, and that motherfucker paid better than anyone else Bob had ever known.

"Sorry, Steve," he said.

"Huh?" Steve collapsed in the back seat, face down on the cushion.

Bob stuck the needle in and depressed the plunger. Three seconds later, Steve didn't wonder anything anymore.

Bob stood there for a while, staring at Steve's unconscious body. He thought about all the horrible shit Coppergate had in store for the poor bastard. Granted, there was always the possibility that Steve would come out on top, but that rang false even to Bob. The only people who ever came out on top were Coppergate and his rich fuck friends.

He slid the door shut, and then he climbed into the passenger seat. The driver—a long-haired, bespectacled man with an impressive set of buck teeth—glanced over at him. He didn't say a word.

"Let's go, Tim," Bob said.

Time paused, and in the glance he gave to the backseat, Bob could see the frustration and remorse his partner felt building up inside for so many years.

"Fucking go, would you?"

Tim's regret folded into him like a pair of bat wings. He pressed his thumb into the ignition. The van roared to life, and after a moment, the track in the road caught on the undercarriage and carried them out into traffic at a brisk 30 mph. Neither spoke again for the rest of the ride.

2

Neither Bob nor Tim saw the man a half-block away. He stood in the shadow between streetlights, and he had seen everything as Bob had herded Steve into the backseat. He'd seen the needle. He'd seen the van glide away into the scuzzy night.

Jimmy Monaghan couldn't believe what he'd just witnessed, but he knew he had to tell Jack about it right away. He forgot about the quick pint he was planning on having at Lenny's. Instead, he climbed into his own car and let it drive him back to his apartment at top speed.

The car parked itself, rattling into his reserved spot. He popped the door open and jumped out as it finished the process on its track. The car closed behind him and shut itself off, locking all entryways. Jimmy slapped his hand on the key plate just outside the building, and as soon as he heard the lock disengage, he rushed in and up the stairs to his own apartment. Just outside the door, he accessed his online security system, and he waited until it recognized his social security number and granted him access into his place.

He didn't waste time kicking off his shoes or shrugging out of his trench coat. He rushed to his tech station and stabbed a cigarette in his mouth. As his unit powered up, he squeezed the end of the cigarette, and it ignited in a gentle glow of SafeFire. As soon as calming nico-fresh filled his lungs, he riffled through his pill drawer until he found the one he needed. He popped it in his mouth and dry swallowed it, waiting for the wifi to kick in. Then, he cut off his LiveStream. Even though it couldn't follow him into the 'net, he didn't want to take any chances. There were too many freaky drugs out there, and they were capable of almost anything.

His consciousness ate through his face, and he soared into the 'net, where he shot through social media and pirate sites and streaming products until he found himself in his very own corner of the virtual city. Here, he had access to all of his technology, where messages and updates waited for him from all of his friends and fans. They clouded his vision over with flashing lights and icons and other various notifications, so he pushed them all away and stepped through to his contact list.

Then, finally, he found Jack LeCroix, and he sent a message to him and waited. Soon, the pill took over and melted the virtual landscape around him. The city dripped in waves, as if he looked at it through a very old, sun-distorted window. Jimmy left the 'net behind and entered the world that exists beyond tech and flesh. He felt data flow through him like energy as he abandoned tangible reality. Yet even here, he felt vulnerable, and not just for the empty body he left behind in the real world. No, even here, where form gave way to energy flow, he didn't feel safe. Zeroes and ones rushed through him in a constant stream, images broken down to cold numbers, and yet he felt more alive than he ever felt in the real world.

His digital flesh gave way to a cobwebbed network of nerves, and he sent out psychic pulses from his mind, seeking out his companion. He detected Jack logging on from his cabin in the middle of nowhere. He felt his friend dissolving through flesh and data until he'd joined this metaworld, rushing through space that didn't seem to exist. Soon, Jimmy saw Jack's gossamer shape approach, gliding through nothingness; far away, yet so very close.

"Jimmy." Jack's voice, smooth and ephemeral, eased from a closed mouth deep into Jimmy's skull.

Jimmy breathed fire, and it swept its way around the two of them, a burning wall against anyone who might want to spy on them. Such a device could never be 100% perfect, but whoever tried to break through it would have their work cut out for them.

"It's happening," Jimmy said. "We got the fuckers."

Though he couldn't see it, he could feel Jack's eyes growing wide, even though in the corporeal world, they were separated by maybe fifteen miles. "How?"

"Steve McNeil," Jimmy said. "You remember him?"

He could see a halo of information swirl around the bundle of nerves that served as Jack's brain. Soon, an image of Steve McNeil formed from the ones and zeroes. "You wrote a column about him."

"Right."

"It didn't work. Your friend still wound up getting kicked off the force."

"Perfect fodder for Coppergate's game."

Jack saved the information about Steve and accessed another program. "What happened?"

"I actually saw the fuckers kidnap him right outside Lenny's. Check it out."

He gave Jack access to his memory, and soon his friend watched video footage of the incident. Jack paused it at the moment just after Steve had been shoved into the back of the van. He cut the image of the kidnapper's face from the video and enhanced it in another program. As soon as he could see the guy's face clearly, he ran it through the police wiki and came up with a name: Bob Whiteman.

"He sound familiar?"

Jimmy shrugged. "I don't think I've seen him before."

"Arrested for whorehopping, back when that was illegal, and a few battery charges. Nothing ever stuck. Even though he hasn't had a job in ten years, it would seem Bob here manages to get out of everything. He must have friends in high places."

"He's got to be working for Coppergate. This can't be coincidence."

"Let me access his LiveStream. Hold on."

Jimmy watched as Jack's energy wrestled with a bundle of data, shifting and struggling, almost like a fighter. Finally, he stopped and said, "Nothing. That can't be, unless he works for the government. Or . . ."

Jimmy nodded. "Right."

Jack slipped and changed, almost into a worm, as he tried to follow some path Jimmy couldn't see. After a moment of churning and twisting, Jack reformed, his nerves glowing, twitching like an electrified mouse. "A pathway can't disappear. It can only be disguised. I just looked for others vanishing in just the same way, and I think I'm on to something. There are six others matching the same pattern. No more."

"Then, this is it."

"Yes."

"Can you trace the others? Maybe we can cut these fuckers off at the root."

Jack trembled, as if a breeze had run through his ethereal form. "No. This is a professional job. I've never seen anything like this. I'll need some time."

Jimmy grimaced, and even though he had no face to betray his impatience, his aura flashed and gave him away.

"I know," Jack said. "It sucks. But—"

"Let's just go to Coppergate's place and raid it. Nail them in their own den of affluence."

"We need to play this cool, Jimmy. If we make a mistake, we're fucked. Well, maybe I'd be fucked. You, I don't know. They can't afford to get rid of a journalist. But they'd feed me to their fucking gargoyles."

Jack didn't need to tell him that. Still, he burned to get these fuckers. Jimmy had been after them for five years, ever since he first caught a whiff of the game from a drunken police officer. Now, this close, he felt like flinging caution into the garbage disposal.

"Just give me time. I need to try to hack their LiveStreams. Maybe I can trace them through Steve's. If I can do that, we're in business. In the meantime, why don't you stake out Lenny's?"

Jimmy knew the theory that as soon as Coppergate had briefed his contestants, he had the collectors drop them back off where they had first been captured. Maybe he could catch this Bob Whiteman in the act and—

"No," Jack said. "If you take them, Coppergate will know someone is on to him. We need to be incognito. Shit, man. You're a journalist. You can do that, right?"

Well, journalism hadn't been about being incognito for quite some time. No, these days the fifth column stood more for whoever could speak the loudest. But Jimmy didn't subscribe to that train of thought. His heroes in the industry were long dead, and they would be considered too subversive for today's audience.

"Right?"

"Right," Jimmy said.

"Good. Now give me some time to figure shit out. If you need me, you don't have to come here. Just call me. Or come out and see me at my cabin."

"But—"

"No one is watching us. I'm off the grid, for the most part, and you're just the court jester the powers-that-be use to keep the people in bread and circuses. They know you'd never do anything to kill your cushy job. Just enough to make your audience think you're on the edge."

Jimmy wished Jack wouldn't put it like that. It made him feel low, kind of like he brushed his teeth with Uncle Sam's pecker. But Jack had the score right.

"Come on, man," Jack said. "You know what I mean. Don't get all pouty on me."

Jack's energy flickered, and Jimmy knew the drug had finally dissipated in his system. His body had probably just sweated out its remnants. He ran on fumes. "All right. I'll contact you as soon as I know something."

Jack's nerves blacked out, and the fire boiled away into nothingness. Jimmy felt himself falling through data streams again as the digital flesh of his avatar slithered over his energy. Bones firmed his body up, and he could feel his own weight crash down on his consciousness, pulling him back to the earth, tethering him back into the virtual city of his computer.

Then, he forced himself back through the wifi connection into his body. His eyes snapped open. He looked to his left and saw the time readout; only a minute had passed since he'd left reality. He shut down his system and snapped another cigarette to life. He sucked down SyntheSmoke and chased it with a tug of bourbon from a nearby bottle. When he exhaled, he seemed to release all the tension in his body.

But his teeth still ground tightly against each other, and he wanted nothing more than to hug himself until the sensation passed.

It never would.

He removed his shoes and molted from his sweaty clothes as he headed for the bathroom to the shower. Chilly water cut across his flesh, reminding him that he no longer wandered the metaworld, and he scrubbed the day from his pores. He thought about Steve, about where his friend might be, and about what he might be able to do to help the poor bastard. Even as he dried himself off, he knew that anything he had to offer to Steve would be a long shot. Yet, it was better than nothing.

Jimmy got dressed, and he took one more drink to fortify himself before he set out to the streets, to what he hoped would be the culmination of five long years of investigative journalism. To what he hoped would be the end of a terrible game. To what he hoped would be the crushing blow to a group of rich fucks who thought they were above the law.

He had high hopes for Jack LeCroix, but he didn't have a lot of faith in himself.

CHAPTER 1

The limo hissed along its track down the street like a predator, shadows creeping across its waxed, black body and shining chrome. The tinted windows reflected flashing lights and the faces of fuckslingers and mutants as it eased past the filthy islands lining the polluted rivers of pavement. The city howled with sin and crime, shaking buildings and souls, but the inside of the limo remained quiet.

Edward Bridges liked it that way. He glanced out at the needy, desperate faces staring back at him; some with disdain, some with desire. He tried to remember what it was like to be among their number and found that he couldn't, even though he'd been homeless only a year before now. Wealth suited him so well he couldn't imagine what it had been like without money. Survival was merely something you asked the cook to whip up for you. Even though he owed this luxury to pure happenstance, he felt like he'd earned it with blood. Surely enough, he had.

He reached around the woman's bobbing head and grabbed a bottle of whiskey from the mini bar. Back in the old days, he would have been happy with common rotgut. Now? He settled for nothing less than a five hundred dollar bottle of Kentucky's finest. He plunked two ice cubes into a glass and poured in a couple of inches of amber spirits. Normally, he drank it straight, mostly because he didn't really have any obligations to attend to (he had billions of dollars, who did he need to stay sober for?), but tonight, he knew he had to stay fairly straight. He would be up for at least a couple of days without sleep, so this would have to be his last glass of booze for a while. From here on out, he would have to rely on the vials of cocaine he carried with him at all times. Sure, he could probably find a variety of crazy drugs promising to do all kinds of things, but Edward liked to be old school. Coke would get the job done.

The fuckslinger hit a good spot with her tongue, and his body tightened. "Damn, woman. Do that again."

He felt her smile around his shaft, and she complied. He moaned and took a sip from his drink. Whiskey burned down into his belly, turning it into a furnace. He closed his eyes and moved his hips.

Something tapped on the window, and Edward noticed for the first time that the limo had come to a halt. His driver stood outside, and behind him stood the Wingate mansion, rising up like a castle in the background.

Edward looked down at the blonde hair flowing down his legs like golden waterfalls. "Come on, baby. You gotta hurry up."

She said something with her mouth full. The hum made him suck his breath in and clench his buttocks. Getting there.

He tossed the whiskey back and put the empty glass in an armrest cup holder. With his hands free, he let them sift through her hair, wrapping his fingers in her beautiful tresses until his grip allowed him to push her head up and down. Quicker. Quicker.

Showtime. He convulsed in her mouth. She tried to pull away, but Edward held her head in place, waiting until every drop of his satisfaction oozed out of him. She wheezed through her nose, and as soon as he released her head, she reached for a glass.

"No," Edward said. "Swallow it."

"Nn-nh." She picked up the glass, but Edward lashed out, knocking it from her hands. It thumped on the carpet but did not break.

He grinned so hard he could feel his lips crackling. "What the fuck do I pay you for? Swallow it. Cunt."

She looked at him, panic in her shifting eyes. Her lips—once painted thickly with lipstick—pooched, desperate to spit out his seed, but she didn't dare do it. When she didn't gulp it down, he grabbed her jaw to keep her mouth closed and pinched her nose shut. She moaned and tried to slap his hands away, but he held firm against her quivering face. She tried to hold her breath, hoping he'd see her determination and decide that she was too tough to bully, but the viscous fluid in her mouth made her want to gag.

She didn't even make it a minute.

Edward released her and patted her on the head. "Good girl."

Cowed, she asked, "Can I have a drink?"

Edward nodded. He watched as she poured a glass to the brim with hard liquor and quaffed it like a pro in three gulps. As she did this, he accessed his account and prepared the transaction. A hundred for the blowjob. No tip, though. Fucking bitch should know that the customer is always right.

They used the chip reader in the back of the limo to complete the transaction, and the driver let him out. Edward emerged, letting his cock drop back into his fly, zipping up as he stood. He told the driver to take the girl back to the Sleaze Strip, and he approached the Wingate mansion.

The building sprawled across what must have been a half-mile at the least, surrounded by well-manicured grass and bushes. Some of the topiary had been shaved into the form of animals. Lights illuminated every feature, reducing dark beauty to stark exposure. In the center of it all stood the giant front door, easily twenty feet tall, inlaid with an elegant gold—*real* gold—pattern. By each side of this door stood two guards in ornate cloaks that went down to their feet. Rapiers hung from their belts, though they were much more adept at using the semiautomatic weapons slung low under their shoulders and out of sight. Circles popped up over their faces, but Edward dismissed them, not caring to know who they were.

"Good evening, Mr. Bridges," one of them said. He enunciated his words perfectly. Until Edward had become rich, he didn't think anyone could do that without affecting an English accent. "You are expected, sir."

The guard opened the door, allowing Edward to step across the threshold and into the opulence of Charles Wingate's home.

The butler walked swiftly toward Edward. "May I take your overcoat, sir?"

"Sure." He let his coat slip down over his shoulders to his elbows, revealing the sharp black suit beneath. The butler eased the coat the rest of the way off and brought it to the closet.

"Mr. Wingate is waiting for you in the parlor, Mr. Bridges."

"Thanks." But to Edward, it was an empty word. It had no meaning, not even when he'd been homeless. Its appearance in his speech only stood testament to force of habit, something beaten into him by his boring and preachy parents.

He made his way down the hallway, enthralled by the echoing sound of his own footsteps. Nothing quite matched the sound of good shoes clopping down a resonant corridor, and he still couldn't get over it. It struck him as a very rich sound.

When he got to the parlor, a voice rang out immediately. "Edward! Come in, come in! Good to see you!"

Charles Wingate advanced toward him, holding his hand out. Edward tried not to grimace as he took the offered hand and pumped twice. Charles wore strong cologne, and wherever he went, he left its odor like a vapor trail. He wore a smoking jacket and held a loaded pipe in his left hand. His silver hair swept back like a bird's wing, thick and lustrous despite his fifty-five years.

"Good to see you, too."

"Hello, Edward." This from William O'Neill. Edward couldn't believe the guy still had that stupid pencil line mustache resting lazily on his upper lip like a fecal smear. Also, his hair had thinned noticeably since last year. Back then, it had looked pretty nice, hair that Edward had even envied a little, but now, large patches of his scalp shone through his slicked-back dark hair.

Edward thought that if he ever started balding, he'd do something about it. He had ten billion dollars at his immediate disposal, to say nothing of the vast billions he had invested in various places. All of that money could ensure that every hair on his head stayed where it belonged. William had no excuse for letting his own go.

Edward shook William's limp hand and grimaced. It felt like he'd just handled a dead animal.

William turned to a young man Edward didn't recognize. "I'd like you to meet my son, George. George, this is Edward Bridges."

George stood at about five-nine, compared to his father's towering six-four, and he definitely didn't have his father's hair. George's stood out in all directions, greasy and tangled. Pimples stood out like lights on his pale flesh. If not for his gray eyes and aquiline nose, Edward would have thought William's wife had been cheating on him.

When they shook hands, Edward grimaced yet again, appalled to learn that George had inherited his father's grip. Edward remembered when he was a kid, and his father had taught him that when you shake a man's hand, you look him in the eyes, squeeze hard, and pump. A man who didn't do the same couldn't be trusted.

"And," his father had added in hushed tones, "the guy might be, you know, one of . . . *those* types." His hand tilted back and forth.

"Nice to meet you, George." Although he didn't much like the look of the kid. Young George did not appear very comfortable in his suit. He fidgeted, probably not used to such garments.

"George is going to inherit my business when I pass on," William said, "so I thought he'd like to see what goes with it."

Edward forced a smile on his face. "You'll love it, kid." Even though George looked like he might be twenty-five. Edward himself only had thirty years under his belt.

Edward reached into his suit coat and slipped out a gold cigarette holder, from which he removed a single, virgin white rod. Edward put the cigarette in the corner of his mouth before squeezing the end and breathing sweet, safe, soothing SyntheSmoke.

Charles handed Edward an ashtray with the face of the President on it. Most of it had been smudged away, as if the maid didn't clean the ashtray properly. He flicked the first clump of environment-friendly ash off into it and settled into one of the chairs.

"Anyone else here yet?"

"Hello, Edward."

Edward turned to see Richard Coppergate had just made his entrance, or at least what was left of him. The word "old" simply didn't apply to someone as ancient as Coppergate. He sat hunched over in a wheelchair, which looked more like a rolling throne. The wheels aside, it could have belonged in an old English castle. A lever on one armrest stood out, which he used to steer himself.

Coppergate didn't even look like he should have been alive. His real teeth were long gone, but he'd had them replaced by implants. They were all cold metal, and they were each filed to a point, like a cannibal's. His hands, gnarled and liver-spotted, hung off the armrests of his wheelchair, and his long, yellow fingernails stretched out like claws. His shriveled head looked like a jaundiced prune, wisps of hair hanging from the back like a cloak of cobwebs. His eyes, though, were the worst. He'd lost his sight back in 2178, but such a rich man didn't have to put up with such trifling matters as blindness. He had his eyes removed and replaced by the best optics technology available. He had better than 20/20 vision now, but he'd requested no eye color, no pupils, nothing. His eyes were pure white orbs hanging above his bulbous nose.

As gnarled as Coppergate looked, Edward couldn't think of anyone scarier or more intimidating.

Behind Coppergate's wheelchair stood a young woman in a dark suit carrying a suitcase. Edward knew from experience that it contained the old man's legs. Not his real legs, which he'd lost in 2164, but the robotic ones he'd had custom made. In his old age, Coppergate rarely had the energy to use them, but on special occasions, he'd push aside the blanket that covered his lower half, and he'd latch the robot legs onto his stumps. This display usually disgusted Edward, and he hoped he never had to see it again.

As for the young woman, she stood only a half-foot taller than Coppergate sat, and her stout body betrayed her thick muscles and all the strength they entailed. She moved Coppergate from bed to chair, from chair to toilet, and so on. She also, as Edward understood it, bathed Coppergate and wiped his ass. Edward supposed she was decent looking, but he'd never want to fuck her. If a woman looked like she could kick his ass, he didn't want any part of her. Another of his father's rules.

"Hello, Richard," Edward said. He didn't move to shake the old man's hand. He considered it a blessing that Coppergate hated to be touched by other men. He didn't want to find out how dry and leathery the old man's hand would be.

The others made their salutations, and Richard said, "It's good to see you all." His low and shaky voice crawled over Edward's ears like a dying spider.

Coppergate turned his blank eyes on Edward. "Welcome to your first year in these proceedings."

"Well, it's my second," Edward said. "It's just this time, I'll be on the other side of things."

Coppergate nodded. "Quite right. I do hope you enjoy yourself. There are not many people like you."

"I know." He thought about Samuel.

Coppergate turned to Charles. "Has anyone else arrived yet?"

"Martin and Elizabeth are in the observation room," Charles said. "Shall we?"

"Of course," Coppergate said. He hit the switch on his armrest, and the wheelchair crept forward. Everyone followed him, the paupers after their prince, and when they entered the observation room, they found the other two sitting, waiting. Neither of them talked to each other, but that surprised no one. Elizabeth and Martin didn't have a lot in common.

Ah. Elizabeth Drake. Despite her beauty, she could be just as nasty as Richard Coppergate. Her light blue, almost colorless eyes never seemed to blink, as if she were a corpse. She never seemed to move anything at all. Even her face was usually blank, the picture postcard of eternal boredom. Her perfect figure hid behind a power suit, except for her incredible legs, which topped out at a mini-skirt that must have cost her thousands of dollars.

These proceedings were usually men only—not even wives were allowed—but Elizabeth was the exception. She had more money than all of them combined, except for Coppergate and Samuel, and she had a taste for blood.

God, how Edward wanted to fuck her. He'd tried many times, but she always shot him down. She liked strong men, men who could kick ass for breakfast and fuck like mad for dinner. Edward didn't fit either of those categories.

He remembered a time when the two of them had been waiting for their limos outside of a posh restaurant after an excellent meeting. Coppergate had been with them, but he wanted to stay for a late business dinner. As

Edward and Elizabeth waited, a junkie with a gun approached them, demanding their money.

Elizabeth laughed and used some martial arts moves that Edward hadn't even seen in movies. When the mugger's arms and legs had been twisted beyond recognition, she took the gun and shot him six times in the chest. She laughed as she did this.

Yeah, Edward had no chance of getting up her skirt.

Martin Taylor, on the other hand, didn't seem to have much of a taste for anything, not even when he sat in on these proceedings. However, like Elizabeth, he was different from the others. Whereas everyone else was white, Martin was black. Nobody seemed to have a problem with that, except for Samuel, who had a problem with fucking everything.

As for Edward, he would never be entirely comfortable around a black man. His parents, while they weren't obviously racist, had been closet bigots. They never said the dreaded n-word, but they used to talk about Them when they were around like-minded people. Growing up, Edward had picked up on that. He never treated Them poorly, but he would never be truly okay with Them, even though he'd hung around with a lot of Them throughout most of his adult life.

Edward approached the large, stoop-shouldered man and said, "How's it going, Martin?"

Martin shook his hand. "All right."

As he greeted Martin, Edward noticed Elizabeth get up and approach Coppergate. In her calm, lifeless voice, she said, "It's wonderful to see you, Richard."

Coppergate showed off all of his metal fangs. "I always find your presence spiritually rewarding."

Elizabeth bent over, her lips puckered. Coppergate, who didn't mind the touch of a woman at all, lifted his head up to offer a clear target. Edward looked away from the horrible display, but he still heard the smack as her lips pressed down, then pulled back from Coppergate's withered cheek.

Edward felt a little sick. The booze had kicked in a little, and that didn't help. His bladder felt a bit tight, so he said, "If you'll excuse me, I need to use the facilities." Ordinarily, he would have said that he needed to "take a piss," but Coppergate hated vulgarities. Coppergate, above all the others, was not a man to fuck with.

"You know where it is, I'm sure," Charles said.

Edward nodded, and he left the observation room. The echoes of his footfalls, which had so enthralled him earlier, now comforted him. It would be nice not to have to see Coppergate for a while.

He stepped into the bathroom, and he locked the door behind him. Just in case. For the most part, he didn't care about the others walking in on him. However, having Coppergate do so, as irrational as the thought seemed, would have been terrible, kind of like standing naked in front of a hungry lion.

Edward unzipped his pants, and his heart nearly gnawed its way out of his chest. Blood stood out on his dick in a ring, and he couldn't help but think that someone had tried to bite it off. Then he remembered the fuckslinger and her lipstick, and he grabbed a tissue to wipe it off.

He broke the seal, and when nature's call had been answered, he went to the mirror and looked at himself. His blue eyes were bloodshot already. He'd put on a few pounds since a year ago, so his face seemed puffier than usual. That was okay, though; back then, he'd been too skinny.

He reached into his pocket and withdrew one of the vials of coke, pondering whether or not he should do a line yet. After two seconds of consideration, he tapped out two thin rails and snorted them up each nostril. His circulation kicked up a couple of steps, and he washed his hands. He whistled a tune as he did so, eager to get back to the others, to start the game.

He dried off his hands and stepped back out into the corridor. On his way back to the observation room, he passed through the parlor, where he ran into a middle-aged man, about fifty, with a gray handlebar mustache resting on his upper lip and his balding hair cut fairly short, almost to the length of a crewcut. He grew it out long on one side of his head so he could comb it over a scar that ran the length of his head from just above his ear to the back. Edward smiled, taking satisfaction in the fact that he'd caused that scar. He'd marked this man for life.

For being fifty, though, the man's arms were as big as tree trunks, bristling with well-cultivated muscles and veins. Samuel Maxwell Barnabas III had nearly as much money as Coppergate, but he spent most of his time away from his business. He enjoyed hunting, among other sports, far too much to spend his days languishing in a suit behind a desk.

Unlike all the others, except for Coppergate, Samuel had earned every penny of his fortune. Everyone else had inherited their wealth, and Edward himself had won his first billion dollars from these very people.

"Eddie," Samuel said.

He hated being called Eddie. It made him sound like some kind of sitcom jock, or a barfly in the background of a cop show. Eddie was dead. He was Edward now. But he knew he had to play ball with this guy. "How's life treating you?" he asked.

"Fine, fine. I can't wait to see the group Charles put together this year."

They entered the observation room, and for the first time, Edward looked through the one-way glass to see who they'd gathered so far. There were only six of them. They needed one more to get this ball rolling.

All of them were unconscious except for one. Odd. Usually they were all out cold by this time. The one who sat up stared out into space, as if he were watching a TV program no one else could see. His gentle brown eyes remained stationary behind his thick, blocky glasses. His short, slender form didn't move except for a slight chest movement caused by breathing. Though he looked harmless, Edward felt slightly unsettled by the guy's posture. No normal human being could sit so still and passionlessly.

Samuel had gone directly to Coppergate, and while they conversed, Charles's butler took drink orders from everyone else. When George asked for a soft drink, William said, "Why don't you bring him a whiskey, neat?"

"Dad, I—"

"It's time you learned to act like a man. Men drink whiskey."

"But Mom said—"

"She's not here. I am."

When Edward's turn came up, he considered going with water, thinking it would be best to stay away from anything that might make him sleepy. Instead, he decided he wanted something to even out the coke, so he asked for a double whiskey, intending to nurse it for a while.

Samuel asked for a beer. "Nothing fancy, either. Just bring me whatever."

Coppergate didn't drink. Instead, he sipped at a bottle of water his assistant provided. Not that he had an issue with alcohol, but he hadn't survived as long as he had by putting garbage into his body.

To take up the time, Edward picked up an InfoPad that contained the dossiers Charles had put together of their guests. Edward downloaded this and flipped through files leisurely and thoughtlessly until he came to one.

He blinked. Looked up through the glass at one of the unconscious forms. Looked back at the tablet. He reverse-pinched the screen in his mind, and the picture of this one expanded until he knew he was right. Double-checking the name sealed the deal. Barry Taylor. Martin's son.

"Martin?"

"Hm?"

Edward held up the InfoPad as soon as he found Barry's picture again, so his companion could see it. "Did you know about this?"

Martin sighed, nodding.

"And you're okay with this?"

"I don't have a son."

"I . . . um—"

"Don't worry about it. I certainly don't care."

"But . . . he's your *kid*."

"Not anymore. Not since he pulled that stupid stunt."

Edward opened his mouth to say more, but he knew how pointless it would be. Once one of these guys made up their mind, that was it. No compromises. Nothing. Part of him wanted to know about the "stupid stunt" Martin referred to, but he knew he'd get no answer. His companions were all free with other people's information—especially those in the next room—but their own? They'd die before divulging anything personal. Half of them didn't even use their LiveStreams.

The butler came back with everyone's drinks. When Edward picked up his, he sipped at it. The desire to gulp it down hovered near the back of his mind, but he didn't want to have to go back to the bathroom for another snort from his vials. That would look bad, and it wouldn't last him through the night. Instead, he swallowed the tiny sip in his mouth and let it warm his insides.

While the others conversed among themselves, Edward glanced over the occupants in the observation room. He easily picked out Martin's son, since he was the only black guy in the room. He rested on the floor in a heap, his raggedy clothes puddled around him like a dirty, full-body halo. His mouth gaped open, showing off his rotten, jagged teeth. The fronts were missing on the top and bottom. He barely had any hair, and even though the dossier said he wasn't even fifty, he looked eighty.

Next to him sat a guy that looked even dirtier than Barry. He had a mop of greasy hair covering his facedown head. His trench coat, spotted and stained, covered a stick-thin body and flowed out behind him like a cloak. His face sported lesions all over it, and blood seeped through his pores, revealing his disease. Edward thought he'd seen the guy before, back in the old days, but he couldn't be sure. The dossier said his name was Wayne Richards. Didn't ring a bell, but then again, he never really knew anyone's name on the street.

He smiled when he saw the woman next to this guy. Stacy Bartlett. Fuckslinger. She certainly had the body for it. Nice ass, which he could almost see spilling out of the super-tight jean shorts. Small but perfect tits. Long blonde hair. Perfect. Edward would fuck her up, down, left, right and sideways. He found it hard to believe she was only fifteen years old.

Edward knew for sure he'd seen the next guy in the room. Steve McNeil, former cop. Got kicked off the force for brutality a while ago. No one would miss that scumbag.

Edward nearly did a double-take when he saw Laura Bard. The dossier said she called herself Skank, and it sure showed. She only had a band of hair from one temple, around the back of her head, to the other temple; like an old man, except her hair was purple. Two horns jutted out from the sides of her forehead, and between them were tattooed the words FUCK YOU in dripping-blood letters. A tattoo of a bat flapped around on her skin, moving from her head, down her back, and up her arms. Her fingernails were grown out to claws, and she wore rings that had razors on their edges. Then, he realized that she had six fingers on both of her hands. The scarring at the base of each betrayed body modification. Edward squinted his eyes and saw, through her barely open mouth, that some of her teeth were missing. Pulled, no doubt, to fit in with the current punk style. She looked like a jack-o'-lantern from hell.

The last one in the room sat up at the table, the only one conscious. That had to be Toby James Munger. Also unlike the others, he wore nice clothes and seemed pretty clean. His blocky glasses covered up dull brown eyes, and he simply stared ahead, waiting for everything to begin.

Edward shuddered. The guy gave him the creeps. He knew why Charles had chosen him, and he figured Toby would do an excellent job.

The door at the back of the observation room slid open, and a team of doctors entered, pushing a wheelchair with the final contestant in it. They carefully picked him up and brought him to the table, where they leaned him forward, since he still hadn't regained consciousness.

In the moment before his face went down on the table's surface, Edward noticed that this guy was beautiful. He didn't like to fuck guys, but if he had to, he wouldn't have minded doing it with this one. He also dressed pretty well, and his short blond hair twisted around, sexy even in his unconsciousness.

Edward didn't remember seeing his file, so he flipped through the dossiers in his head until he got to the final one, showing off the guy's face.

Another fuckslinger, but this one serviced his own sex, too. Samuel Maxwell . . .

Holy shit. Samuel Maxwell Barnabas, IV. He went by the name Randall Marsh, but now that Edward knew the truth, he could see a faint resemblance between him and his old man.

At that moment, Samuel looked up from his conversation with Coppergate and saw the new arrival. At first, he smiled, excited to see who else would be competing tonight. Then, recognition lit his face, and his brow furrowed. His nostril flared, and he almost grunted like an animal.

He whirled on Coppergate. "You think this is going to stop me?"

"Calm down, Samuel," Coppergate said. "As I understand it—"

"I asked you a fucking question." This time, spittle flew from his lips and dotted Coppergate's raisin face.

Coppergate recoiled at Samuel's expletive, but it looked more like a matter of style than actual surprise. His assistant patted his face dry with her handkerchief. "I don't think it necessary—"

Samuel grabbed the arms of the wheelchair and brought his head down to Coppergate's level, their faces mere inches apart. "Answer me, you goddam cripple!"

Coppergate's eyes snapped down into slits, and he bared his fangs. "Take care, Samuel. You are dancing on a gossamer tightrope, and I will not hesitate to destroy you, if need be."

His assistant drew her gun from inside her power suit, and she pointed it at Samuel's face, directly at his left eye.

Samuel didn't flinch. "You don't seem to understand. That thing in there isn't my son. And it's not going to stop me from the hunt." He released the wheelchair and slumped onto the couch, his arms crossed.

Coppergate's assistant put her gun away.

Elizabeth took the chair next to Edward. "This just got interesting." She sat so close that her soft voice tickled at his face.

"I don't know if you noticed, but Martin's son is in there, too."

She ignored him, staring at Randall Marsh. "He's a cute one. Too bad he's not like his father."

Had she fucked Samuel? He knew she'd had a thing with Coppergate, but Samuel? Who else in this room had she fucked? Did that mean that she might—?

"Uh, you'd fuck him?" he asked.

"If he wasn't a faggot."

Wow. Even a nasty, ugly word like “faggot” sounded like honey from her. Something fluttered in the front of his pants.

“So.” She placed a hand on his thigh, high enough to almost pinch the head of his dick. “I take it you brought something tonight.”

“Something?” As if he didn’t know what she meant.

She tweaked her nose. “I wouldn’t mind sneaking off with you for a toot.”

“Sorry. I don’t have anything.”

Her head tilted sideways, and she rolled her eyes. “Come on. The white smudge under your nose says otherwise.”

Shit. He wiped at his nostrils and found white on his fingers. He licked them clean.

“I know a way I can pay you back,” she said.

This piqued his interest. Maybe he’d finally get his turn at her now. Just as he opened his mouth to give his assent, Coppergate said, “They’re waking up.”

Edward glanced into the observation room and saw Wayne’s head starting to rise. Behind him, on the floor, Barry shuddered, and his feet twitched. Stacy moaned, rubbing at her face.

“Later,” Elizabeth said.

Edward nodded and waited for the game to begin.

CHAPTER 2

Yelling. Steve McNeil's eyes creaked open, and bright light stabbed through to the back of his skull. Groaning, he straightened up and nearly fell off his chair. The fuzzy world swayed around him, and he wondered how much he'd had to drink last night. The swirling miasma in his guts tried creeping up his throat, but he swallowed it down. This had to be the worst hangover he'd ever had.

But something seemed off. He looked at his surroundings and discovered that there were other people in the room with him. Most of them looked like they might be homeless, and their sweaty pork stink wafted over to him. His gorge nearly gave up the ghost. They all yelled at each other except for one guy; this one sat quietly in the corner, observing the whole mess. He didn't register amusement, nor did he seem put off by the behavior of the others. Instead, he just existed.

Who were these people? Where the hell was he? This place had an odd ER waiting room feel to it, but there were no nurses or offices or anything, just a sliding door behind him and a giant mirror in front of him. He tried to remember leaving Lenny's last night and couldn't quite get there. He went to access his LiveStream, but every time he did this, he received the same message over and over: THE SYSTEM IS TEMPORARILY DOWN. PLEASE TRY AGAIN LATER.

"Some government cocksucker kidnapped us! They're going to do all sorts of fucked up tests on us! Maybe fiddle with our buttholes, or something." This from a black man whose breath somehow managed to out-stink his body odor. His eyes rolled slightly, indicating some kind of unbalance.

The others ignored him. The blonde-haired woman—no, she couldn't have been legal, so she had to be a girl—held up her hand. "I think this is something else. I remember the guys who got me. They said they wanted to do a three-way, and they transferred enough money for it into my account. I figure we're here for some weird orgy."

Then, Steve remembered Bob Whiteman. He flashed back to last night and distinctly recalled heading out to Bob's van. Then, he remembered feeling a jabbing pain. A needle. "Hey," he said, "do any of you remember being drugged? With a needle?"

The blonde nodded. "That's how they got me."

"Me, too." This from the good looking guy. "The ones who got me said they wanted to do a three-way, too."

"So, are we all fuckslingers here?" the blonde asked.

"Fuck no," the punk said. "I fuck for free."

Another homeless guy—this one with horrible marks all over his skin and a constantly bleeding face—spoke up. "I don't do anything for money. I don't even have a chip. I traded it for a bottle of hooch, what? Last year, I think?"

"I'm a cop," Steve said. "Well, I used to be. The guy who got me didn't want sex at all."

"Same here," the homeless guy said.

"Then what the fuck are we all doing here?" the punk said. Even though she'd practically yelled her question, her voice quavered, showing the fear beneath the bravado.

"I'm seeing a pattern," Steve said. "We may not all be fuckslingers, but I can assume that society won't miss us much, if we went missing. Am I right?"

No one wanted to admit to something like that. Only the homeless guy with the bleeding face nodded, and he wouldn't meet anyone's eyes when he did. Still, no one objected, not even the creepy guy with the glasses.

Steve turned to him. "How about you? What do you do?"

The guy said nothing. Instead, he glanced at the mirror.

Steve looked that way, too. Then, he realized he'd been too busy thinking about the situation instead of his surroundings. He felt to a moral certainty that someone stood behind that mirror watching them. Scientists? Maybe. He didn't think it was the government, but someone clearly wanted to learn something from this.

Just as he opened his mouth to voice this idea, they all heard a loud click, followed by a whirring sound. The mirror slid aside, revealing a window, through which they could all see their observers. There stood two women and seven men. One woman, despite her beauty, looked cold and dead, except she didn't seem to know it. The other could have been built from rock. The men looked rich enough to pay someone to wipe their asses and chew their food for them, but the old man in the wheelchair stood out from the rest. He barely looked human with his pure white eyes, jaundiced head, gleaming metal fangs and grotesque claws.

He flicked a switch, and the intercom crackled. "Welcome, friends," the old man said. "Hello, Toby James Munger, Stacy Bartlett, Wayne Richards, Skank Bard, Randall Marsh, Barry Taylor and Steve McNeil." As he made each announcement, his soulless gaze switched to the face the name belonged to. "You are all wondering why you're here. Before I get into that, I want to tell you each something about yourselves."

"Fuck you," Randall said. "I want to get the fuck out of here now. I don't care about whatever pitch you're going to make."

"Patience, Mr. Marsh. I feel no need to remind you that you're among my captive audience and therefore have no choice but to listen."

Randall opened his mouth to refute this, but looking at the door behind him—solid steel—he knew he couldn't just walk out of here.

"I just want to know one thing," Stacy said. "Are you going to let us go?"

"Of course," Coppergate said. As if it had been the most obvious thing in the world. "But before you go, there is some information I feel that it would be beneficial for you to know."

Randall picked up one of the chairs and brought it down as hard as he could against the window. He felt a terrible jolt go up his arms, and the chair did nothing more than bounce off the glass. He felt the urge to try again, but when he saw Coppergate's amused smile, he knew it would do no good. Instead, he flung the chair aside, where it clattered against the wall and to the floor.

"Now that that's been settled," Coppergate continued, "we'll start with young Toby. All you own came as a result of thievery. No one has ever helped you in any way, not even your father, a farmer who worked you like a hired hand instead of a son. Of course, he feared losing his government subsidy more than he loved you. The only time he spared for you was used for disciplinary measures. He never had praise for you, only punishment. When you left home, you began your life of crime. You squat in a dilapidated building that used to be an abortion clinic, but you've always wanted to live in a 'classy' place. You are in dire need of money, correct?"

Toby drew his head down in a half-nod. He remained silent.

"Stacy, you were born to a life of prostitution and desolation. Since the age of ten, you have been selling your body to help your mother pay the bills. When your mother—"

"That's enough," Stacy said. "I know all of this. I sure as shit don't need to hear it from you."

Coppergate smiled. "Then suffice it to say, you are also in dire need of money. In fact, I see a doctor's bill in your possible future." He pointed a tree branch finger to her pelvis.

Stacy looked down to see a sore had recently appeared on the inside of her thigh, visible to any who looked for it. It matched the dozen or more that dotted her pussy and asshole. She quickly crossed her legs before anyone else could notice. How could his blank eyes see so well?

"Wayne, you have been living on the streets for quite some time. To lose your parents to a car crash, your home to the bank, your money in the name of survival and your health to your various diseases in such a short time, that must have been quite unnerving."

"To say the least." Wayne uttered a humorless laugh through a sneer.

"Need I say how much you require money?"

This time, Wayne barked. His laugh petered out into a soft chuckle, and he shook his head. "Money don't mean shit to me now. I'm probably not going to be alive this time next week. I'm in the final stage, in case you couldn't tell." He wiped fresh blood from his forehead and looked at his slick, red hand.

"Bleeding pores, painful lesions, uncontrollable diarrhea, insomnia, cold flashes and pustules on the genitals. I believe the street name for it is the Red Death."

"I'm surprised I made it this long," Wayne said.

"It is commonly known to be incurable," Coppergate said. "What if I told you that there actually *is* a cure. It's very expensive, but it exists."

All mirth suddenly disappeared from Wayne. "I'd call you a liar."

"I wouldn't be too quick to dismiss my statement." Coppergate sent the medical information from his tablet to Wayne's social media.

It flickered immediately into Wayne's vision. He glanced over it, but he couldn't make much sense from the medical jargon. The pictures seemed to be pretty convincing, but anyone could put this thing together. It didn't take a genius in this modern age to fake documents of this nature. He flicked his eyes, dismissing the file to his trash folder. Now, he looked at Coppergate, trying to access his PeopleFinder. A circle formed around Coppergate's head, but a message popped up: YOU DO NOT HAVE ACCESS TO THIS PROGRAM AT THIS TIME. PLEASE TRY AGAIN LATER.

Fuck. He looked away from the old man only to see a familiar face through the glass. He blinked to make sure he hadn't been mistaken. Nope. The guy dressed better now, and now he had good grooming habits, but Wayne knew him for what he really was.

"Is that you, Ring-Piece Eddie?"

Edward fumbled in his pocket, looking for his cigarette case. "You talking to me?"

"Yeah, you."

He lit up and blew SyntheSmoke out at the glass. "My name's Edward Bridges, not Ring-Piece Eddie." Even though his reddening face betrayed him.

"No, I know you," Wayne said. "You and me, we used to drink rotgut together under the el."

Elizabeth turned to Edward. "Ring-Piece Eddie?"

"I don't hang out with filth like you," Edward said.

"My ass," Wayne said. "I couldn't mistake that face, but it looks like you hit it big. What the hell happened?"

"He was in your place once," Coppergate said. "That's all you need to know for now."

"Why the nickname?" Elizabeth asked. A ghost of a smile flickered to life.

Oh shit. Edward's mind raced. "I, uh, used to steal rings off people, like some pick pockets, you know?"

"Like hell," Wayne said. "Why don't you tell her the real reason, Eddie? Or are you trying to fuck her? Am I right? You getting lucky?"

Edward clenched his jaws, acutely aware that he'd been ready to curse in front of Coppergate. He forced his rage back down. Instead, he said, "Listen, you'd better shut your mouth."

"Are you trying to fuck me?" Elizabeth asked. Her eyes remained as calm as a pond on a humid day.

Flustered, Edward struggled to find words. "No, I . . . I just don't—"

"We called him Ring-Piece because he sold his ass to get by," Wayne said. "It was fucked up, because he's straight, and he never had to resort to anal before. At first, he got this big red ring around his asshole, hence the nickname."

Edward pounded the glass with his fist. "Shut the fuck up! I swear, I'll fucking kill you, you filth-ridden fuck-faced dickcheesed horsefucker!" Spittle flew from his lips and dotted the glass. He didn't notice the scathing look Coppergate gave him, nor had he noticed the string of curses from his own mouth.

"Well, you showed me your ass, man. It's not my fault."

Samuel bellowed with laughter as he stood and approached Edward. He clapped Edward on the shoulder. "Looks like our friend Eddie here's a fudgepacker! Just like that piece of shit in there." His humor died as he nodded to his son on the other side of the glass.

Randall did not look very surprised to see his father. He didn't even say a word. He crossed his arms and fumed in silence.

Samuel didn't notice. "So, Eddie! How's it feel to have someone stick it in your ass?"

Edward couldn't see through the cloud of rage hanging in front of his eyes. He whirled on Samuel and threw the hardest punch he could. He felt his knuckles connect with Samuel's cheek, and the middle-aged man went back a couple of steps, but he didn't seem to have felt it.

"You even hit like a faggot," Samuel said. "If you hadn't had a gun last year—"

"Fuck you," Edward said.

"That will be all from you, Edward," Coppergate said. "There is no call for coarse language. Also, we have more to discuss with our guests. I suggest you sit down and behave yourself."

Only then did Edward realize the extent of his language. He felt his stomach drop out and wondered if Coppergate planned on chiding him more later on. Maybe even do more than chide. His heart convulsed as he headed to the couch, not daring to look at the old man.

Samuel watched after him, his fists bunched up, restrained only by the fact that he felt hitting Edward would be kind of like hitting a woman.

"Nice seeing you, Ring-Piece," Wayne said. He retreated to his own chair.

"How do you know all of this shit?" Skank asked.

"I have decent researchers," Coppergate said. "Not that I need them for much. Everything I know about you, I learned from your social media. Nothing is secret from anyone, and you simply volunteered it all. Speaking of which, let's speak of you, Ms. Bard."

"Call me Skank."

Coppergate grimaced. "Very well. Skank." The word tumbled from his mouth like a turd. "You once had plenty of money; or rather, your parents did. However, you chose to leave your abusive and neglecting parents and their money for a punk lifestyle. This choice left you poverty stricken. Imagine how you could live better with an abundance of money."

"Fuck money," she said. "I don't want it. Look what it did to my parents. Mommy lost herself at the bottom of a pill jar, and Daddy was twisted enough to fuck me when I was eight. If that's the joy of money, then fuck it and fuck you."

"Tell yourself whatever you will, but everyone desires money. Everyone."

"Not me."

"Yes, even you," Coppergate said. "Without money, you would not be able to attend the music shows you so adore. Nor would you be able to buy your precious music without money."

"I sneak into clubs," Skank said. "I steal music from the store."

"Yes, why don't we speak of the music store at which you work? You have a job, which is defined as work for compensation, and in these modern times, compensation comes in the form of money."

Skank didn't say anything to this.

"Randall," Coppergate said. "Or should I call you Samuel?"

"No," both father and son said in perfect harmony. The moment didn't last for very long, but for its brief existence, it radiated beauty. Their voices sounded the very same at the root, the only difference being the elder Barnabas's gravelly voice.

"Randall, then. I don't think we need to discuss your past, but in light of your solicitous practices, you are in desperate need of money, as well."

Randall didn't say a word. He didn't even acknowledge Coppergate or Samuel.

"Barry. I doubt you would understand any meaningful discussion."

Barry snorted. "Try me, nigga'. I know all about all your CIA plans for my man, Jack."

Martin turned away from his son, covering his eyes with his hand.

"Hi, Daddy," Barry said. "Always knowed you was with the CIA. You sold me out, motherfucker!"

Martin joined Edward on the couch. Edward hardly noticed.

"With money, you could no doubt find your friend, Mr. Kennedy, and you would be able to protect him," Coppergate said.

"If you ain't already killed him," Barry said.

Finally, Edward couldn't take it anymore. "What's with this CIA garbage? And who is this Kennedy guy?"

Coppergate didn't even look at him. "Just read the dossier."

Edward rolled his eyes, but only because he knew Coppergate couldn't see him.

Coppergate turned to the last of the captives. "Steve, you used to be something good."

Steve rubbed at his temples. "Skip me. I don't want to hear it."

"You were a good cop, which is something rare in this world. And yet, when you played the hero, what did it get you?"

"Fuck you."

"You got a crumbling apartment, which is a month away from condemnation. Not that you'll be there when it happens, of course. You're out of money."

"Listen, if you're going to kill us, get it over with. I'm sick of this shit, I've got a hangover, and I really don't need to see that gnarled turd-face of yours, okay?"

Coppergate's smile vanished. "You have not been brought here to die, Mr. McNeil."

Samuel snorted. "That's a matter of opinion."

"Tell that to Nutsack," Skank said. "Your fucking lackeys killed my boyfriend."

Edward stopped himself from asking who Nutsack was. He didn't think he could stomach saying those particular words in that particular order.

Coppergate ignored her. "You have all been brought here for the chance of a lifetime. By now, you will have noticed that you don't have access to the 'net, that you can't get any of your programs to work. That's because we have cut you off from the rest of society. Some things will be restored, but not your LiveStreams. From here on out, you'll broadcast to an intranet, which only we can view."

A portion of the wall shimmered and pixilated, showing off seven screens all with different angles of the same room. Wayne waved a hand in front of his eyes and saw it appear on the wall.

"Why would you do this?" Steve asked

"Because you, my friends, are going to be our entertainment for the next day, perhaps less," Coppergate said.

"Entertainment?" Wayne asked.

"There is nothing wrong with your ears, Mr. Richards. How would you like to receive a billion dollars?"

"I would love it," Stacy said. No hesitation.

"If what you said about the cure for the Red Death is true," Wayne said, "I'd like it, too."

"Damn straight," Barry said.

"I wouldn't say no," Toby said.

The rest remained silent. Stacy, in a moment of levity, said, "Who do we have to kill?"

"Each other," Coppergate said. He chuckled, and it turned into an outright laugh as he watched the seven people trying to figure out if he was joking or not. "No jest. In a short while, you will all be set free where you were found in the city. From that moment on, you shall use whatever resources you have to find and kill the other six in your group. The one remaining person will get a billion dollars."

Steve couldn't believe the sheer lunacy of this. "What if we refuse?"

"Attached to your spinal cords, at the base of your skull, is a small time bomb, which I am now activating." Coppergate pushed a button, and everyone simultaneously reached to their necks. They each heard a beep somewhere deep inside of them, even though they could barely feel the incision the doctors had made in their skin.

"In twenty-four hours," Coppergate continued, "if there is no clear winner, the survivors will be destroyed. I suggest you use your time wisely. Any questions?"

Wayne stood up. "Yeah. Is this how Eddie got his money out of the blue? He won this . . . this game of yours?"

"Yes," Coppergate said.

"What about the rest of you?" Stacy asked.

"No," Coppergate said. "The rest of us are old money, so to speak. In the past ten years, no one else has won."

"The bomb got the others?"

Coppergate smiled again. "That would be telling. Now, in the interest of time, we're going to have to bid each other adieu. Good luck, and may the festivities begin."

He pressed a button, and the room filled with gas. A couple of screams rang out, and Skank flailed around, trying to hold her breath, but they were all out in a matter of seconds.

CHAPTER 3

Edward watched as a team of doctors entered the room—their faces obscured by masks—and hauled the unconscious contestants out of the room like they were moving furniture. He rubbed his eyes, remembering when he'd been in that position, and the acrid taste of gas seethed in the back of his throat. If felt like someone had wrapped a plunger handle in sandpaper and tried to ram it down his esophagus. He swallowed, trying to banish the sensation, to no avail.

Samuel clapped a hand down on Edward's shoulder, causing him to jolt slightly. "Sweet memories, eh, Ring-Piece?"

"Fuck off."

Samuel chuckled, but his humor sounded bitter and empty. "Time to get ready for the hunt. Have fun."

He then turned his back on Edward, swaggering toward Martin. "I'll kill your kid first. If you want me to, that is."

Martin didn't look up from his shoes. "It doesn't matter to me."

This time, Samuel howled with genuine laughter. "Nice attitude. I almost like you. I'll catch you later, Marty." Then, he went about his rounds, saying his goodbyes before heading to his limo outside.

Edward sighed, glad to watch Samuel leave. He looked through the glass into the other room, which now stood empty. The vents shuddered and pounded, hard at work clearing the air.

"Are you enjoying yourself thus far?"

Edward turned toward Coppergate, who had spoken, and nearly gagged when he saw the old man. Coppergate's gnarled hands gripped the armrests of his wheelchair while his assistant held his dick in one hand and a bedpan in the other.

In complete contrast to Coppergate's shriveled body, his dick stood out vibrantly, full of vim and vigor. He grew them from his stem cells and DNA from porn stars. The average life of one of his dicks was half a year. They tended to turn a bit greenish after three months, but he managed to keep them from rotting completely for a bit longer than that. The one his assistant now held looked fresh, the best of his transplants yet, despite the nest of scars where pubic hair should have been. The assistant had no trouble aiming ten inches of thick, flaccid cock at the porcelain pan. Red-tinted urine flowed from one to the other.

Edward didn't know how she could stand doing that, but he figured she bathed him and wiped his ass, so it couldn't be too bad. She kept a poker face, so at the very least, she was used to it.

Still, he averted his eyes to a painting on the wall. He thought it might be a Monet, but he didn't know art that well. "It's pretty good, being on this side of the game."

"I suggest you enjoy it," Coppergate said. "I don't think it will last very long this year."

"But Samuel—"

"It doesn't matter. One way or another, the numbers will be whittled down rather quickly. It should only be a scant few hours."

"If you say so."

"Nevertheless," Coppergate continued, "no matter how short this year's game will be, I'm confident that it will be the most exciting we've had in a long time." The urine stopped flowing, and his assistant shook him dry before covering up his nakedness.

Out of the corner of his eye, Edward saw that Elizabeth had been watching this whole grotesque display with a smile on her face, yet when Coppergate's member was hidden, she looked away, almost disappointed.

"It would be a bit more exciting if we could gamble, like in the previous years," Charles said. "I'm afraid that without money on the line, it will be dreadfully boring."

"Why not bet?" William asked.

Charles looked at William as if he'd said something about giving his fortune to charity and then living off the land. "What good will it be to bet on a fixed game?"

"I know, I know," William said, "but that still doesn't take into account other factors."

"Such as?"

"It's altogether possible that the fix might not work. You know how nasty, resourceful and cunning Samuel can be."

"The files he has have been doctored," Charles said. "When a hunter like Samuel doesn't have all the information, he can't very well expect to succeed, can he?"

"Samuel's smart, though."

"Smart be damned! What, do you want to make a bet against the fix?"

William laughed, but his voice sounded broken, and he couldn't meet Charles's eyes. "Let's not be hasty. All I mean to say is, maybe this won't work. Maybe we can make a few wagers after all."

Edward's head pounded slightly as they continued the argument. He rubbed at his temples and barely noticed it when Elizabeth leaned toward him. "Remember what we were talking about?"

He sighed. "Look, I'm almost out. I only have a couple of vials, and one of them is almost empty. We have a long way to go before this game is over."

"You're full of shit," she said.

He shrugged.

"Fine. I'll let you see my tits."

"What am I, in fucking high school? I've seen tits before."

"You haven't seen mine."

"Tell you what. You let me fuck you, and I'll give you a whole vial for yourself."

She withdrew from him, her eyes aflame. "No deal."

A part of him wondered if maybe he'd fumbled this one, but fuck it. If she wanted the coke badly enough, she'd come around. The two of them, along with Coppergate, watched William and Charles argue, while Martin sat in the corner, still looking at his shoes, and George sat next to him, polishing his greasy glasses with a sweat-stained shirt tail.

"Consider this," William said. "Instead of betting on who will win, why don't we bet on who dies first?"

"Samuel already said he'd kill Martin's boy first," Charles said. "What good is that?"

"Maybe one of the other contestants will find another of the group first."

"And maybe Samuel will stay home tonight. William, that's ridiculous."

"It'll give us something to do."

"Fine. In that case, I'll bet that the ni—the black boy gets killed first. I'll be nice and make it a mere hundred thousand. Anyone want to take that bet?"

Martin didn't even flinch.

"A hundred thousand?" William asked. "Why not make the first bet a gentleman's wager? All things considered."

Things started getting heated between them, and Edward closed his eyes, hoping the slight throbbing in his temples would go away. He remembered back to a year ago, when he'd been a contestant in this game, and he tried to remember the other people he'd been competing against. As with this year, there had been plenty of homeless people and fuckslingers, but no one really stood out except for the circus strongman.

Edward remembered that back then, it had come down to just him and the strongman. Samuel had been taken out of the picture by then, since he'd caught the hunter by surprise with the .22. He'd shot Samuel in the head, except he should have checked to make sure he'd done the job right.

At the final hour, the strongman had come lumbering out of an alleyway with murder in his eyes. Edward remembered his butthole clenching in terror, despite the fact that he still had almost all of his bullets for the gun. He'd fired every single one of them, and they'd all found their mark in the strongman's chest . . . except the giant still staggered toward him.

In the end, the strongman had broken Edward's right arm and three of his ribs before Edward managed to jam the barrel of the gun through one of the strongman's eyes, where the sight scrambled enough of his brains to kill him.

Even though he'd been a finalist, Edward hadn't killed anyone to get there. The strongman had been his first, but when he discovered that his act of murder had won him a billion dollars, his heart soared with elation. He hadn't killed anyone since then, but he knew he could, if he needed to, especially if the financial stakes were high.

Charles and William came to an agreement. The wager would, indeed, be a hundred thousand. Charles had Barry, and William had an innocent bystander, which was a safe bet. Every game had its share of accidental deaths.

Before long, the dark screens on the wall flickered to life, one by one, and the rich fucks settled in to watch as the poor bastards started their journeys through their various filth-ridden worlds, meeting with pimps, fuckslingers, the homeless, and a cast of hundreds more.

CHAPTER 4

1

At first, Stacy couldn't move, not even to open her eyes. The gas had rendered her completely motionless, but it hadn't taken away her consciousness, not entirely. She knew she'd been dropped in the alley where the kidnappers had first picked her up. She could feel the cold pavement against her bare flesh. And she could hear two assholes talking as they stood over her.

"That's a hot piece. Young, too."

"Take those off."

She felt their clammy hands yanking down her shorts, and the cool breeze of the evening air chilled her bare pussy. Hard pebbles bit into her buttocks as she tried to lift her arms up, to fight off her assailants.

"Dude! What the fuck are those?"

"I've never seen anything like that. What do you think they are?"

Ah. They'd seen the sores. Maybe she wouldn't be violated after all. She found it shocking to think the only thing that would save her from being raped would be her disease.

"Well, I'm not fucking that, man. I like my dick too much."

Silence. Then, the other guy said, "We don't have to fuck her with our dicks. We could do other stuff."

Oh fuck.

"Like what?"

Stacy heard metal scraping across the pavement. It stopped when it reached the area between her legs. One of the guys laughed. "Think this'll fit?"

"No way. That's . . . don't do that."

"Come on. I know this chick. She's a fuckslinger. She don't care what goes in her pussy."

"I don't know. That might kill her."

Stacy strained to open her eyes, desperate and afraid to see whatever they were talking about. She thought if maybe she could see it, it wouldn't be so bad. Just knowing would help. The vagueness made her sick.

"So what? She does nothing but take dick from dawn till dusk. No one's going to miss her. Besides, I want to see how far I can get this thing in."

She felt freezing metal touch her labia, and if she could, she would have shivered. She begged a god she didn't think existed to stop them from doing this to her. Pain shot through her pussy as it started entering her, popping some of her sores as it went.

"Aw, man! That's fucking gross! Stop."

"Nah. The pus'll help us get it in further. It's, like, lubricant."

The darkness of Stacy's vision cracked slightly, and she could see two foggy forms standing over her. One of them held a very long piece of metal, but she still couldn't tell what it was.

She tried to talk, but she could only manage a small squeak.

"Dude, I think she's waking up. We should get the fuck out of here."

"Stop being such a faggot. I almost have the tip in."

Finally, Stacy felt a scream painfully crawl from her throat as her eyes popped wide open. She sat up, blinking the blur from her vision.

"Oh shit! Run!"

She heard the metal object clank to the ground as the two would-be rapists ran as fast as they could away from her. Only then did she see what they'd been trying to stick into her, and she shuddered.

Between her legs rested a forgotten damaged piece of the road track. It was about six feet long and as thick as the average forearm with a curved, hooked end, which rested almost against her pussy lips. She didn't want to think about what would have happened if they'd succeeded in getting the hook into her.

Dazed, she looked around for her shorts and found them in a pile of garbage. She took a moment to evaluate her dripping sores before pulling the shorts up. Casting her mind back to before she'd been kidnapped, she remembered her last john of the evening. He'd been a fat mouth-breather with a pigtail dick. She'd insisted on fucking with the lights out, so he wouldn't notice the sores. Now, she didn't think anyone could miss them, not even a blind man.

Fuck. That old bastard hit the nail on the head. She needed money to deal with this shit. She had no doubt that her pussy would rot and fall out if she didn't get this taken care of. She didn't want to think of that.

Instead, she had to figure out how she could find the others and kill them as quickly as possible. She flicked her vision to the side and saw the time. She also saw a countdown clock, which she assumed those rich fuckers had put in her. According to this, she had about twenty-two hours and change to go.

She felt a sudden anger come over her. Not at the rich people who had kidnapped her, or even at the guys who had tried to rape her with a piece of road track. No, she suddenly hated the others, the ones who had been kidnapped with her. She felt hungry for their blood and wanted to hunt them down so she could get her prize . . . but she had no idea on how to do it.

She tried to access her social media, but then she remembered what the old guy had said. Some programs were back, but others wouldn't open. She couldn't even access her online map.

Did she know anyone who could help her? She certainly didn't have friends, unless you counted Susie, a cross-dresser from the Sleaze Strip, or maybe Don, the guy who had dicks for fingers and liked to fuck himself with them for money. But they were more like acquaintances.

Well, there was King James, but he would demand a hefty price for his aid and succor. Maybe, just maybe, it would be worth it, though.

Stacy stepped forward, but when her open sores scraped up against the rough material of her shorts, she felt a nearly crippling pain. She pressed her hand against her crotch, and this helped out a bit as she made her way home.

2

Once Stacy made it to her apartment, she went to her bathroom and cleaned herself up. She didn't have much by way of medical supplies, but she had enough to stop her sores from dripping, and she used a couple of pads to cover up the worst patch, so she'd be able to walk without hurting too much.

She took a moment to look around her apartment, a studio with a bathroom small enough to be a closet. The paint curled and cracked on the walls. Every time she turned on the lights, roaches scattered for their hiding places. Even though she'd lived here three years, the urine-stink of the previous owner still lingered. She thought about the billion dollars again, and it only solidified her desire to murder the other contestants.

She dressed in her most provocative outfit—but one that wouldn't betray her health issues—and set out for King James's place, bracing herself for whatever she'd have to put up with in order to get what she wanted.

When she'd first started working the streets on her own, King James had wanted to take her under his wing. She didn't want to work for a pimp, so she told him to fuck off. He didn't take rejection well, so he beat her ass and threatened to cut off her whore nose, but when she let him fuck her a few times, he figured they were even.

King James ran fuckslingers and drugs, but she figured it wouldn't be out of the question for him to be able to get a hold of a gun on short notice.

She arrived at the hotel King James owned, and when she tried to get past the front desk, a couple of guards stopped her.

"I need to see the King."

"So do a lot of other folks," one of them said. "Get your skanky ass out of here."

She'd expected as much from this guy, so much so that she didn't feel offended in the slightest. "Tell him Stacy Bartlett's here. He'll want to talk to me."

The guards exchanged a glance. The first seemed bewildered, but the other one must have recognized her. He nodded, and the first one said, "I'll tell him. He says no, I'm booting your booty to the gutter."

He left, and the other guard kept an eye on her. They didn't speak as they waited. Stacy saw the blue circle on the guy's face and his ID, and she felt grateful for the return of that particular program.

The first one came back and said, "You in luck, girl. Follow me."

The two of them went into a service elevator and took it to the top floor. After that, they went down a long hallway to the door at the end. Just before they entered, the guard gave her a pat-down. His hands lingered a bit too long on her tits, giving them a gratuitous squeeze, in case she'd hidden a gun behind her nipples, but she didn't mention it.

Only then did he let her into the King's chambers. As she entered, she saw King James hanging upside down like a bat from a bar attached to a wide doorframe. Straps around his ankles held him in place as he swayed back and forth, his tiny dick jutting stoutly out from a patch of thick pubic hair. A woman stood on each side of the threshold. The one at his back—a horned girl with demon wings and three tits—massaged his entire body with careful precision, and the one at his front—who had fangs and three snake eyes—recited poetry from a big black book while jabbing her long fingers into three of her four pussies right next to his face.

"Good evening, Stacy." He spoke in a deceptively cultured tone with a faint British accent. Almost in the same breath, he turned his head to the woman behind him, and his voice dropped back into the gutter, completely without accent. "Jerk my pipe, cunt. You know how I like it."

The woman reached around him and clutched at his member. It barely poked out of her closed fist. She also stuck two of her fingers deep into the King's asshole, matching thrusts with strokes.

"To what do I owe a visit from such a cherubic innocent as yourself?" King James asked.

She took a deep breath. "I know your time is valuable, so I won't waste it with pleasantries. I'm in the market for a gun. Can you get one for me?"

He smiled, but it didn't look natural on his face, not the way he hung upside down with the pasty, doughy flesh of his double chin trying to ooze around the rest of his face. "What would a fine bitch like you want with a piece?"

"I just need the gun, all right?"

"Cool. What kind?"

That question kind of surprised Stacy. She didn't know much about guns. All she needed was something that would fire a bullet when she pulled the trigger. "I don't know. A good one, I guess."

This time, King James laughed. "How much you got?"

"That's going to be a problem. I don't have much money. I only have a hundred bucks."

"A hundred? That ain't gonna' get you shit. The cheapest I got's worth five times that."

Stacy felt her face drip from her skull. If they cost so much, why did every poor kid on the streets have one? She sighed. So much for that idea. Maybe she could find something she could use as a club. She thought back to the piece of road track she'd almost been raped with, and she thought it would do well at cracking skulls. Maybe—

"Stacy, darling. I have a proposition in which we all come out a bit more happy."

She knew this would happen. She'd desperately hoped it wouldn't, but then she thought about how much money she'd have by this time tomorrow. She could buy her way out of any deal with King James.

"You sling your ass for me for, say, a month, and we call it even. Cool?" His face elongated as his dick convulsed. Semen rolled down his belly like spilled milk, and even though he hung upside down, it pooled around the fuckslinger's hand. Glazed jelly. Then, as if his orgasm hadn't just happened, King James said, "That is, provided you're not going to use said shooter to relieve a bank of its money, or something equally foolish. You ain't gonna' do something that stupid, huh?"

Stacy gritted her teeth, but she tried to play it cool. "Nothing like that. But if things work out, I'll be able to pay you back tomorrow."

"Bitch, you for real? Don't you play me. The only way this shit's gonna' work is if your ass belongs to me."

Fuck. Maybe a million dollars would change his mind tomorrow. For now, she had to go with it. "Two weeks. I can raise more than five hundred for you in two weeks."

"Three."

She could easily lie, but she didn't want to make it seem too easy. "Two. That's my final offer."

King James ran his tongue over his teeth and sighed. "Very well. Two weeks. But you'll be working your ass off."

"You know it," Stacy said. "When do I get my gun?"

"Moonbeam, darling. Put down the book and retrieve one of the .22's from my closet."

Moonbeam removed her glistening fingers from inside of herself and put the book down before following orders. Stacy glimpsed what looked like an armory in the closet before Moonbeam grabbed a gun and brought it out to King James.

"Give it to her."

Stacy took the gun. "What about ammunition?"

King James grinned so wide she could see every single tooth in his mouth, all in perfect condition. The upper teeth were gold. "Three weeks, sugarcooze."

Stacy's nostrils flared. "That's not fucking fair. Gimme the fucking ammo, all right?"

"Three weeks. Then you get heat for your heater."

"We had a deal!"

"I know," King James said. "Call this another deal, you wanna'."

Stacy wanted to kick him in the bare nuts. That would turn that insufferable smile into a frown. Her hands clenched into fists at her sides, and she could feel her face ignite with rage. Still, he had the women, and though they were nearly naked, she knew they would have weaponry hidden on them somewhere.

She had to remind herself that she'd been lying to get her temper back in line. "Three weeks it is. Just gimme the ammo."

King James laughed. "Go on, Moonbeam. Retrieve madam's ammunition. Three clips, one for each week she'll belong to me."

When Moonbeam handed them over, Stacy put two clips in her pocket. The third, she began to slip into the bottom of the gun. King James cleared his throat. "I wouldn't do that just yet, Stacy, darling. Not in my boudoir. You might make the ladies nervous, not to mention the ill effect your actions could have on me." The women produced derringers from the backs of their panties.

Stacy put the last clip with the others and slid the gun down the front of her pants. "When do I start?"

"Whenever your business has been concluded," King James said. "No later than next weekend."

"All right. Thank you, King James." She turned and walked out. On her way through the lobby, the two guards took time from their busy schedules to watch her ass as she left the building.

3

Stacy stood outside the hotel for a moment, feeling the weight of the gun just above her pussy. She fingered the butt, wondering how she would find the others. As she thought, she slipped into a nearby alleyway so she could put the clip in the gun. It only took her a moment to figure out how the pistol worked.

She knew the cop would be trouble, so she'd have to hope someone else managed to nail him. She didn't know much about the creep, but he looked pretty smart. She'd have to put him off for later. The others? They might be easier. She could probably find them all out on the Sleaze Strip. Fuckslingers and homeless guys should be easy to take care of. The punk might put up a fight, but so what? Stacy had firepower.

She stowed the gun away and stepped back out into the flow of fuckslingers and hustlers, keeping careful watch on every face she passed, hoping the blue circle would show her the info she wanted and fast.

4

She spent about a half an hour wandering down the Sleaze Strip. She saw a few familiar faces and stopped long enough to say hi. She didn't stay long enough to explain her situation, though; she didn't want to lose much time.

All the regulars put in an appearance. The guy with a lizard arm, who liked to cut it off so people could fuck the stump. It would grow back by the following night. The guy with a bunch of tiny dicks hanging from his crotch, waving like seaweed at whoever looked. The guy who took pills to make his legs fall off so he could beg. She ignored as many as she could.

She almost made it back to civilization when she thought about going home for a short while. Her heels ached, and she really wanted to change into something a bit more practical, now that she didn't have to put on a show for anyone. The night air chilled her mostly exposed body.

Just then, as she walked past an alley, she saw someone across the street. The blue circle popped up. Wayne Richards. An alert also appeared, warning her of the Red Death and that she shouldn't have sexual contact with him, nor should she get his blood into her circulatory system. Wayne stood there, almost casually leaning against a building, conversing with a stooped over old guy. Even though he stood mostly in shadows, Stacy could see the blemishes on his red-slicked face.

Her heart went rabid in her chest. Before, the thought of killing someone seemed doable, especially with such high stakes. Now that she found herself in that moment of truth, doubt settled in. Could she really put this guy down?

One way to find out. She eased into a crowd of fuckslingers as they moved across the street. This would hide her away from his view until the last second, but would she be able to kill him in front of so many witnesses?

No, fuck the witnesses. This was the Sleaze Strip. They'd be too busy worrying about getting into trouble, themselves.

Stacy slipped away from the fuckslingers and went into the alley nearest to where Wayne stood, his thoughts no doubt on the cool billion dollars. She didn't see the old guy anymore. Good. She pulled the gun out, and its metal cooled the sweat on her palm. She peeked out of the alley and aimed the gun at him. It shook, and she had to use the wall to steady herself.

She stood like that for a while, wondering why she hadn't pulled the trigger yet. The guy would probably thank her, considering how far along he was with the Red Death. Then, she thought about how the old man in the wheelchair had talked about Wayne's past. Did he really deserve to die like this?

Fuck him. Remember the billion dollars. All you have to do is put a third eye in his forehead, and there will only be five people between you and your wildest fantasies.

She breathed her tension out and tightened her finger on the trigger until it fired, sending a bullet off to her target.

CHAPTER 5

1

When Wayne Richards woke up, his ass felt cold and slimy, as if someone had slipped refrigerated marinara sauce down the back of his pants. He knew the feeling well, over this past month. Although he couldn't smell it yet, he knew he'd shit himself while sleeping again.

He couldn't get used to the sensation, no matter how many times it happened. He sat up, still feeling numb from unconsciousness. It took him a moment to get his fingers moving, as if they'd fallen asleep when he'd been out. He had to find a park pond or a water fountain and wash himself and his pants as best as he could.

He forced himself to stand, and he felt the slime ooze down the backs of his legs. He groaned as the stench hit him. Rotten egg, trash and gasoline. Never had the smell been that bad before. Maybe he wouldn't live to see tomorrow after all.

The thought jogged something loose in the back of his brain. He suddenly didn't remember passing out here. No, something had happened to—

Memories flooded back. The old man in the wheelchair, the fuckslingers and the others, the billion dollars.

The cure for the Red Death. Could that be real? If he had the billion dollars, could he really be cured?

He wiped at his forehead, and his hand came away slick with blood. In that moment, he knew he'd take any chance at all to clean his system of this horrible disease. It wouldn't solve all of his problems, but if he didn't have the Red Death, maybe he could make a comeback. Maybe he could get a job and start being useful again.

He thought back to his childhood, to his parents, to how easy life had been with money, and he wondered if he could have all of that again.

But could he kill those other people to get it? He didn't know. He'd never done anything like that before, not on purpose. Sure, in high school, he'd been a violent bastard, and there had been that one incident, but now? He couldn't throw a punch if someone helped him.

His dripping shit reached his socks, and he knew he'd have to table that particular thought for the moment. First things first: he needed to clean himself up. He duckwalked down the street with the rest of the drunks, homeless and fuckslingers, heading for the nearest park he knew, hoping he'd get there before his shoes got fucked up.

2

The park wasn't on the Sleaze Strip, but it was pretty close, close enough for Wayne to get there in about a half an hour. He bathed here the most, since they had the best fountain. The structure stood five feet deep in some points. Noble statues—Greek gods?—towered over it as water cascaded from their mouths. Lights illuminated their faces and their eerie cataract eyes.

Wayne stripped down to the skin, tossed his soiled pants and socks into the fountain and climbed in after them. The cool water soothed him immediately, and he felt the urge to sink beneath the surface and just let himself go. In the blazing lights beneath his feet, he could see flakes of brown coming away from himself.

He ran his fingers over his ass in quick strokes and then scrubbed his pants and socks with his bare hands. When his clothes were as clean as they were going to get, he dropped them out of the fountain and waited, hoping they would dry quickly. Not likely, in the cool night air, but he wanted to at least give it a chance.

He lowered himself until he could sit on one of the rocks below, feeling the waterfall cascade over his ruined face. He moved his feet through the pennies and nickels below him, the only money left in this cashless world, kept only for wishes. He wondered how many of them he treaded on. How many wishes would come true, and how many would become bitter disappointments? How many were cries for help and miracles?

In his youth, he would have never thought he'd have wound up like this. Not as he played football for his high school, not as he fucked his way through all the cheerleaders in the back seat of his father's car, not as he . . . not as money got him out of every problem he'd ever gotten himself into.

He thought about one man in this moment, as he often did: David Nelson. Wayne had never believed in any higher power, but David Nelson made him think that maybe karma existed, after all. Of all the horrible shit Wayne had done in his life, he regretted what he'd done to David Nelson most, and he wished with all of his heart that he could take it back.

Would he still be here if not for what he'd done to David Nelson? Probably. But all the hardships he'd experienced since then had shown him how wrong he'd been back then.

No, back then, he'd preyed on the weak. The guy with the glasses? The kid who couldn't catch a ball worth a damn? People who looked differently than anyone else? He thought about all the names, the racial epithets, the homophobic remarks, that had all been a part of his regular vocabulary back then, and he shuddered.

David Nelson had been black, the only black student at his high school. Ordinarily, that would have made him a target for Wayne and his football friends, but when he started dating a white girl, that upped the ante pretty far.

Wayne never considered himself a racist . . . provided black people kept to their own, everyone would be happy, right? But no, David Nelson had to stick his black cock in white pussy, and Wayne felt he had to do something about it.

One night, as David Nelson walked home after a date with his girl, Wayne and his friends cornered him. They'd only meant to beat the shit out of him, and they'd certainly done that, but then he talked back to them through a mouth full of blood and broken teeth. Wayne kicked him in the head a little too hard, and then the high school had lost its only black student.

Wayne's father greased the right palms, and he and his friends got out of a lot of trouble. Everyone congratulated him on what had happened, but even back then he knew he'd done something wrong, and it tormented him. He tried to bury it in alcohol and one-night stands, but David Nelson always came back and haunted him in his loneliest moments.

One of those one-night stands had rewarded him with the Red Death. She didn't show any of the signs, but in the early stages, she didn't have to.

He wiped at his forehead and saw that his hand only came away with water. The bleeding had stopped, at least for now. But when he looked down, he could still see the horrible lesions on his chest, a constant reminder of his dying body.

As he sat there, thinking about David Nelson, he knew he couldn't kill the others. He couldn't add to the nearly overwhelming weight on the back of his neck. But maybe, just maybe, he could make up for what he'd done by saving some lives. Maybe—

"Jesus Christ, buddy! What the fuck do you think you're doing?!"

Wayne looked across the fountain and saw a cop standing there, tapping his nightstick in his hand. He looked ready to hand out a wood shampoo.

"Good evening, officer. I know this doesn't look good, but—"

"Get your filthy, homeless ass out of the fountain, get those clothes on, and get the fuck out of here, got me? Or do I have to bash your fucking head in?" He pointed the nightstick at Wayne.

In a moment of fury, Wayne felt the urge to leap out of the fountain and tackle the cop, pummeling his face with punches, but he knew his ragged body would never muster the energy for something like that. He'd only get his skull cracked. Besides, he reminded himself, he wasn't a violent man anymore. He had to stay calm.

"I got you, officer-sir." Wayne climbed out of the fountain.

The cop's eyes widened when he got a glimpse of Wayne's naked, lesioned body, then they narrowed in disgust. "What the fuck's this shit?" He waved the nightstick at Wayne's chest.

"The Red Death," Wayne said. He pulled on his damp pants. They were cold, but at least they weren't cold and slimy.

"Red Death? Ain't you got no sense? What if kids got into that fountain and came back looking like you, huh?"

The Red Death didn't spread by mere contact. It had to be sexual contact, or his blood had to enter another person's system through a large open wound, but Wayne thought it would be better to not contradict the officer. "I'm sorry."

"You'd better be, you fuck. Go on, get out of here. Don't let me see you back here again."

"Yes, sir."

Wayne put on the rest of his clothes, tied his shoes and walked away, feeling the cop's gaze burn on the back of his neck. The feeling consumed him so much he nearly bumped into a statue. The marble base suddenly filled his vision, and he halted just before he ran into it. Looking up, he saw an angel, wings spread out far, an hourglass in one hand and an outstretched sword in the other. The stone blade pointed at Wayne, and the angel's black eyes stared down into his own. He felt suddenly judged, and the decision had been eternal damnation.

"You're going to die," a voice from behind him said. "Very soon."

Wayne whirled around to see a skinny little middle-aged man, his grin a black rictus, lacking front teeth. The bum pointed his supernaturally long finger at Wayne, mirroring the angel above. If not for the burning light in his eyes, Wayne would have thought him a walking corpse.

But no, he knew Old Shit from the streets. Like Wayne, Old Shit would probably not be here next week. Cancer. It showed in his skeletal body, which stooped over as if hung on an invisible hook.

Old Shit cackled. "Sorry, son. Saw the way you were looking up at this fella, and I had to fuck with you a bit."

Wayne turned and started walking away. Old Shit shuffled, but he managed to keep up. "Come on, Wayne. You know me. The Reaper's got his finger on me, too. You gotta' have a sense of humor about these things."

Wayne wanted to tell him to fuck off. Instead, he said, "Would you please leave me alone?"

Old Shit stopped. "Sure. Okay. Sorry I bothered you."

Wayne watched him pull a tattered pack of cigarettes out of his pocket. The old man lit up and took a puff. He hacked it out almost right away. Wayne knew that SyntheSmoke was supposed to be safe, yet he thought maybe someone who had lung cancer probably shouldn't smoke. Then again, by this point, what did it matter?

Old Shit staggered away and sat down on a park bench. Wayne considered walking away again, but the more he thought about his predicament, the more he realized he needed help. Old Shit was a smart motherfucker. Word had it that he used to teach at the university. If anyone in this rotten, dying world could help him, it would probably be Old Shit.

Wayne sat next to him. "Sorry about that. I've got troubles."

"We all have them. Smoke?"

Wayne shook his head. "You mind if I use you as a sympathetic ear?"

Old Shit grunted. "I'm not much good for anything else. Might as well give me a try."

Wayne took a breath and unloaded on Old Shit, telling him everything from the moment he'd been kidnapped until when he just woke up with his fecal pants. Throughout the story, Old Shit smoked constantly, stopping only to occasionally hack out a bloody piece of his lung. Ordinarily, something like that would cause Wayne to stop, but they both knew their own respective scores.

Finally, after the story, Old Shit said, "So that's what happened to Ring-Piece. I thought he'd just died."

"Me, too."

"That means these guys are serious about that billion dollar offer," Old Shit said. "Something to consider."

"What about the cure for the Red Death? You think that's real?"

"Hard to say. Rich people have privileges the rest of us don't have. But I lean toward yes. You never hear about one of these moneybags motherfuckers ever getting the Red Death, do you? It's always one of us poor bastards."

Wayne nodded. It made sense, but he still didn't put too much faith in the idea.

"You think you're going to kill these others to get that money?" Old Shit asked.

"No. I can't do anything like that."

"Then what do you have in mind?"

"I don't know." But that didn't strike him as true. He remembered back to his youth, before he'd even started going to school. He'd watched a lot of westerns with his father, all of them from a world long forgotten with actors at least two hundred years in their graves, but one recurring theme ran through almost all of them: the good guy, tough and tall in the saddle, would ride into town and get rid of the bad guys, who tended to be rich and well-respected in their communities. All his life, he'd wanted to be that good guy, fighting evil wherever he drifted, saving the communities the bad guys fed off of like parasites. He never understood the irony of that, considering how many scrapes his old man had bought their way out of, and somewhere in his teenage years of bitterness and depression, he'd lost that dream. He couldn't pinpoint exactly when he'd become a bad guy—bad guys were always the heroes of their own stories—but knew for sure that redemption existed. It *had* to.

Now? He looked anything but tough, but what did that matter? Maybe here, at the end of his life, he finally had a chance to be the good guy. He couldn't piss that away, could he?

"Actually, I do have an idea," Wayne said. "The only problem is how to do it."

"You can always go to the cops," Old Shit said. "You know Eddie's name. That should get you the rest of his friends."

"It wouldn't work. Come on. I'm homeless, and I'm dying from the Red Death. Those guys are rich beyond my wildest dreams. Who would you believe?"

"What about your LiveStream?"

"I don't have a chip. They couldn't ID me like that. Why trust footage from someone who technically doesn't exist?"

Old Shit nodded. "True."

"Besides, the cops are probably in their pocket, anyway. Remember, this isn't the first year they've done this. But I do have some allies, provided they don't want to kill me."

"You mean, the other contestants?"

"Yeah, except I don't know how to find them."

"Describe them to me again."

Wayne did, and when he'd finished, Old Shit said, "It seems to me that the easiest ones to find would be the two fuckslingers. You could probably find them on the Sleaze Strip. From there, if you manage to get on the same team, you can probably figure out how to find the others."

"That's a big if," Wayne said, "but I guess it's worth the chance. I need them on my side. What should I say to them, if I find them?"

Old Shit pitched the burned out butt of his cigarette to the ground, where it would biodegrade by tomorrow. "Tell you what. I'll go with you. I'm good at talking people into things. I had a 95% passing rate in my classes, you know."

Wayne smiled. "Thanks a lot, man. I really appreciate this. I'm sorry I was an asshole earlier."

"Think nothing of it, Wayne. Those of us blessed enough to be doomed should stick together."

3

A half an hour later, they made it to the Sleaze Strip. Despite the late hour, it still bustled with activity. Wayne and Old Shit had to go extra slow to make sure they saw every face as they passed. The blue circles offered no important info. About halfway down the Strip, Old Shit paused. "Hold up, Wayne. I have to get rid of some excess baggage."

Wayne nodded as he leaned against the wall. Old Shit disappeared into a nearby alley, where Wayne could hear him unzip his pants, then the resulting patter.

A minute later, he could still hear the steady stream hitting the ground. "Jesus, man. How much longer do you have to go?"

"I'm almost done," Old Shit said. "Hold your horses."

"Is that normal?"

"For me, it's either a ten minute leak or a slight sprinkle."

"Thanks for the imagery."

"You asked."

Another minute later, the stream started petering out. Just when Wayne thought it was almost over, it became strong once again. "How much did you have to drink today?"

"I got some coffee from a restaurant that was getting ready to throw it out. A whole pot full. I also got my hands on some rotgut."

"If you don't finish soon, my head's going to explode. Literally."

"Don't say literally if you don't mean literally."

Fuckin' teacher. He looked at the countdown. 21 hours plus. "It's pretty literal, Old Shit."

Finally, Old Shit's deluge of urine stopped, and he emerged from the alley.

"It's about time, old man. I thought I'd have to leave you for—"

A loud crack echoed down the Strip, and Wayne's face felt suddenly wet. His vision filmed over with crimson. At first, he thought the Red Death had come back with a vengeance, but then he blinked the haze away and saw Old Shit on the sidewalk, his head jetting blood just like the naked and noble gods of the fountain shot water from their mouths.

~

"Ha!" William shouted. He looked at Charles and shouted again, "Ha!"

"This is stupid," Charles said.

"Pay up, Wingate." William held out his left hand, waiting.

Charles rolled his eyes and held his own left hand over William's. He accessed his bank account and transferred the money over to William. "I shouldn't even give this to you."

"A gamble is a gamble, a debt a debt." As soon as he received confirmation of the transfer, he smiled and turned to his son. "I hope you've been paying attention, George."

"Sure," the young man said. "Uh . . . why?"

"Because this is an important life lesson. No matter how distasteful you may think it, you must honor all wagers. Right, Charles?"

Charles sneered. "Don't forget the other lesson. The one about being a gracious winner."

William ignored him. "Care for another wager? A million says Martin's son gets killed next."

"No bet."

"Come on, Wingate. Be a sport."

"No bet."

~

Though Wayne could hear screams all around him, he couldn't pay them any mind. He heard a few more shots, and a couple of fuckslingers around him fell, crawling for cover. None of the chaos mattered, though. His world filled with the image of Old Shit's death. He'd been willing to help Wayne, and now he didn't exist anymore. He hadn't even known the old guy's real name. What would go on his tombstone? He hoped it wouldn't be Old Shit.

Wayne fell to his knees and touched Old Shit's shoulder, feeling blood soak his own fingers. "Oh God, man. Don't die. Please, don't die." Except he knew Old Shit was gone already.

Tears cut through the streak of blood on Wayne's face. He remained hunched over the corpse until a shot ricocheted off the wall behind him, mere inches from his head. He instinctively ducked and rolled into the alley. Only then did he realize that whoever had fired those shots was aiming at him.

He didn't know how many shots had been fired, but he thought the shooter might be reloading. He peeked out from around the corner and saw a familiar face hovering over a gun, trying to pull the clip out.

Stacy Bartlett, the blue circle informed him.

Stacy had killed Old Shit.

Stacy.

Wayne screamed as he charged out of the alley, around the building, and toward Stacy's cover. As he approached, she managed to find the lever that shot the clip out. She could see Wayne getting closer, so she dropped the clip and scrambled for the next. Her fingers shook so badly that the fresh clip fell to the ground to join its predecessor.

She had no time to grab it. Wayne slapped at her hand, knocking the gun away, skittering down the alley. She roared as her other hand pulled back in a punch.

Wayne blocked the attack with his arm, and his own hand went back. For a moment, Stacy looked like Simone, one of his girlfriends from back when he'd had a real life. The only time he'd ever hit a woman was when Simone accidentally hit his car with a shopping cart, putting a dent in the driver's side. Wayne had reared back and slapped her as hard as he could. She bled a little, yelled, and walked out of his life. Still, it had been a gruesome incident, and it haunted him, not quite like David Nelson, but at least in the same direction. He'd sworn to never hit a woman again.

But he couldn't stop his hand from coming down on Stacy's face, not in a slap, but in a punch. Stacy yelped as she fell back, holding her inflamed cheek. A yell caught in his throat as he realized what he'd just done. Sure, she'd just killed a friend, but, well, he couldn't think of any rationalization for his reluctance to attack her, other than how his father had always taught him that hitting a woman was wrong.

"Asshole!" Stacy yelled. She brought her foot up and planted it into Wayne's groin. He fell to the ground, clutching his genitals as pain crawled up into his belly. He curled up into a fetal position, trying desperately to draw a breath.

Stacy stood, looking down at Wayne's pain-wracked body. He'd be a much easier target now. The old man had gotten in the way at the last second, but now nothing stood between her and offing this scumbag.

Then, it hit her. She'd just killed an old man, someone who had nothing to do with this game. She'd just aimed, pulled the trigger, and blew someone's candle out. A human being who would never again draw breath, or laugh, cry, love, fuck, anything. She'd ended someone else's life.

Tears began to flow, and she couldn't stop them, no matter how hard she tried. She wanted to steel herself to continue the game, but she lost it. She fell back onto her ass and brayed out her sobs. "I didn't mean to shoot him. I'm sorry. God, I'm so sorry."

The pain slowly diminished as Wayne listened to her cry. When he could move, he sat up, and she instantly scuttled away from him in a crab walk.

"Please don't kill me. I didn't mean to shoot your friend." Her eyes shifted around, looking for the gun.

Wayne tried to speak, but he croaked instead. He cleared his throat, and this time he sounded more comprehensible: "I'm not going to."

Stacy paused, sniffling. "Why not?"

"I need help from people in the same boat as me. I want to take down the rich fucks behind all of this."

~

Coppergate laughed. "There's one every year."

~

"What about your friend?" Stacy asked.

Wayne inhaled deeply, trying to hold back any anger that might rise in his throat. Part of him wanted to kill Stacy for what she'd done, but he needed her. He needed help badly. "He was dying anyway. He probably preferred it quick, like you gave him, instead of long and drawn out, like the cancer would have done. I know that's how I feel about myself." The words didn't feel right in his own mouth, but he knew they'd have to *be* right.

Stacy thought about the billion dollars again. "What if I tell you to go fuck yourself?"

Wayne saw the gun within arm's reach, behind a pile of garbage. He leaned over and scooped it up, hoping he looked tough enough to deliver his line. "I guess I'll have to kill you, then."

"You wouldn't. You need me, like you said."

Fuck. He couldn't ever let her be too sure of that. She looked too snaky to know everything. "There's five others who can help."

Stacy nodded. "Okay, then. What's in it for me?"

"The satisfaction of doing something right?" Wayne asked.

"Can't buy anything with that."

"Then maybe you can steal a bunch of their shit. Besides, I'm sure they have a billion dollars, ready to be paid to the winner, the transfer all set up. Maybe we can make them give it to you."

Stacy thought it sounded like a good idea to team up with Wayne. Not only that, but there was the old saying about how two heads were better than one, especially when it came to finding people. If the others didn't want to join up, they'd probably have to kill them. If, on the other hand, they all teamed up, and if things didn't look like they'd work out in their favor, Stacy would be able to kill them all at once. She did, after all, still have two clips left.

She thought about how Old Shit's head had shot blood out from the hole she'd put in it, and she wondered if she could do something like that again. She remembered how sick she'd felt mere minutes ago over having killed someone. Maybe it wouldn't be so bad the next time.

Could she kill Wayne? Probably. Why not team up with him? What better way to keep an eye on him?

She shrugged, hoping she looked indifferent. "I guess you can count on me, then. Now that we're a team, what do we do?"

"We need to get the others on board with us."

"Sounds like a plan."

Wayne could hear sirens in the distance, and they were getting closer. He turned the gun around and handed it to Stacy butt first. "Grab your clip and let's go."

As Stacy bent down to pick up the full clip, Wayne took one last look at Old Shit's body. He felt his eyes sting as he watched the remainder of the old man's blood pour out of his broken head. "Goodbye, friend."

"They're coming!" Stacy said. "We have to go!"

They both walked away quickly, leaving the scared fuckslingers to howl for help in competition with the sirens.

"Walk faster!" Stacy grabbed his arm and pulled him along with her.

By the time the police came to a stop by Old Shit's body, Wayne and Stacy were nowhere to be seen.

CHAPTER 6

1

Unlike Stacy and Wayne, when Skank woke up, she remembered everything with stark clarity. Her eyes zipped open, and hatred burned its way through her heart immediately, and she didn't have to think things through. She knew right away what she needed to do.

She pulled herself to her feet and rubbed her temples. Out of the corner of her eye, she saw the Nutmobile. A classic car from about a hundred years ago, it had been made to drive its own path on whatever road it wanted to. Maybe fifty years ago, some previous owner had converted it to be compatible with the road tracks that now dominated America's landscape. That had not stopped Nutsack from making it his own car. Etched onto every inch of its paint job were either penises of various shapes or lyrics from his favorite punk bands.

Behind her stood the Mudhole, where she'd been just before being kidnapped by Coppergate's henchmen. She remembered the show, one of the best she'd seen in a long time. The Two-Fisted Nunfuckers had come to town, and they'd torn the shit out of everybody. The lead singer had fucked the bass player on stage, wiped his dick with the American flag and had slapped his patriotic cum rag on a lucky member of the audience. The drummer cut off his own dick during a guitar solo and stapled it to his chest. A classic. By next show, he'd have a new one, maybe with two heads like he'd had on the tour from five years ago. Skank remembered sucking Nutsack's dick while they waited in line to shoot up in the bathroom. Nutsack had popped some T after, and his dick got sucked up into his body, transforming into a temporary vagina, which Skank fingered the fuck out of with all six fingers on her right hand.

And then she remembered what came after. Nutsack, his momentary cunt unfolding back into a cock, had walked outside to drive her home for the night. Someone had been waiting for them, and they'd shot—

Skank edged around the Nutmobile, knowing exactly what she'd see, hoping more than ever to be wrong.

Nutsack. Dead. A hole in his head, a halo of blood around him. He stared at the sky, and flies crawled all over his viscous bits. Their fellow punks had not been kind to his body; they'd painted his face up to look like a clown's. His shirt had been ripped open, and his pierced nipples had been pulled out. His pants were down to his ankles, and his penis had been forked and spread open. Someone had written on his lower belly, "I have a small dick."

Skank wondered if she'd have done the same thing, if she'd found a body in the parking lot after a show. Would she have laughed about it with . . .?

"Oh God, Nutsack." Her voice trembled. Nutsack had been shot when his seed had still been drying on Skank's face.

She touched herself where Nutsack had last laid his fingers, and tears poured out of her eyes in body-shaking sobs. She knelt next to him and grabbed his hand. It wouldn't yield to her attempt at bringing it up to her lips; his death-hardened skin wouldn't let her.

Despite the ghoulish feeling that crept beneath her skin much like the insects in Nutsack's bullet hole, she couldn't let go of him. Black tears carved their way down her cheeks, easing over her chin line and down her throat.

"God, Nutsack. I'm so sorry. I love you so much."

She eased her head down to his hand and pressed her lips against his rigor mortis flesh. She felt every hardened blood vessel like cords with her kiss.

"I'm going to make those pigfuckers pay," she whispered. "I'm gonna' track them all down and kill their stupid asses."

She glanced over her shoulder to the Nutmobile. "Fuck, I'm sorry. But I'm going to need your car. Please forgive me."

Skank always carried a knife, and she slid it out of her pocket know. The Nutmobile was an old model, so she needed Nutsack's hand to open the car and start the ignition, but as the blade hovered over his wrist, she knew she couldn't do it. She gritted her teeth and tried to push the metal through his flesh, but something in her kept her from doing it. She roared and stabbed the knife back into her pocket. Instead, she dragged the corpse over to the driver's side and put his thumbprint on the plate. As soon as the door opened on its automatic hinge, she pulled Nutsack up with all of her might, pushing him into the front seat and then over the console. Finally, when she'd gotten him all the way over, she climbed in after him.

She pressed his thumb into the ignition, and the car juddered to life. The radio blared with the Two-Fisted Nunfuckers:

Leave me alone!
Gay sex with my clone!

Throw him a bone as soon as he's grown!
Sit in my throne!
Getting blown!
By my clone!

She turned them down almost all the way. Then, she tore out of the parking lot with her first destination in mind: the nearest grocery store.

2

Skank didn't have much money left in her account, so she knew she'd have to be sneaky. As she walked past rows of aspirin bottles, boxes of Alka Seltzer and gauze bandages, she found what she needed: an eye patch. Without thinking twice, she opened the box and stuffed the eye patch down the front of her pants.

Then, she headed over to swim wear, and among the snorkels, goggles and suntan lotion, she found a package of ear plugs. She ripped one open and took a single ear plug, putting it into her panties with the eye patch.

Now she needed to find one thing in this place that she could afford to buy. She only had five bucks left to her name, and finding something that cheap didn't come easy. Personally, she didn't believe anyone would prosecute over the things she intended to shoplift, but one could never be too careful.

She found a candy bar and put it down on the checkout belt. A robot picked it up and scanned it for her. "Will this complete your purchase?" it asked.

"Yep." Skank hadn't locked the door to the Nutmobile, in case she needed to run, just to be on the safe side.

"One-oh-five."

Skank ran her left hand over the scanner, and one minute later, she sat back in the Nutmobile. Since social media relied on a user's right eye for video and right ear for audio, she put her ill-gotten gains to their proper use. Just before she put the eye patch on, she gave herself the middle finger, knowing who would see it.

~

"Huh," Edward said. "That's actually pretty clever. I wish I'd have thought of that."

"Please," Charles said. "There's one every year. It stifles the entertainment. It's not clever, it's annoying."

~

Skank peeled out, aiming the Nutmobile for her next destination.

3

Cars lined the sidewalk. A good sign. From above her, Skank could hear music pounding at closed windows. It sounded like Spotty Pope's version of Ledbelly's "Yellow Gal."

She parked a block away before walking back down to the flat where Necro Cock lived. Necro Cock was a close friend of Nutsack's, and he was also the drummer for FUCK, a band in which each member named themselves after a letter in their name. Necro Cock called himself K on stage, while the singer got F, the guitarist U and the bassist C. Every time a big punk band came to town, Necro Cock threw a party afterward.

Skank hoped there would be a lot of people there. She would need all of them.

Once in the foyer, Skank looked at the various door bells. She found Necro Cock's real name, Orville Anguson, and pressed the button next to it.

"This better be fucking good," the speaker said. She could hear Spotty Pope behind the voice.

"Open up, Necro. It's me, Skank."

She heard a click, followed by a buzz. Skank opened the door and walked up the flight of stairs to Necro Cock's second floor flat. Necro waited for her at the door, stick thin with bulging blue eyes and sharp cheekbones. His red hair stood out in all directions except for the white stripe down the middle. Tattoos and piercings covered his body, barely concealed by torn jeans and a fishnet shirt. A tattoo of a headbanging Grim Reaper showed through on his chest, moving to the beat of Spotty Pope in the room behind him. His pants bulged with all three of his cocks and their respective piercings..

"Holy shit, Skank. I was wondering where you guys were. Where's Nutsack? And what's with the eye patch?"

"I need to talk to you," she said. "In private."

"Sure. Nutsack didn't dump you, did he?"

"I'll explain everything."

In Necro Cock's bedroom, Skank told him her story, from Nutsack getting shot to her being kidnapped, to the contest and to why she now wore an eye patch. She also explained her plan.

As soon as she finished Necro Cock whistled. "Damn, that's heavy. A lot of us are going to get killed, you know."

"I know," she said, "but we need to do it for Nutsack. For all of us."

"You know I'm in. Nutsack was my best friend, man. Hell, he was my bro. But these others?" He hooked his thumb at the door. "These others, they're not like us. They're mostly punks because they think it's cool. They only like violence when it's directed toward someone else. They'd probably chicken out at the thought of getting killed, themselves."

"Are you kidding? They think they're invincible. The thought of getting killed probably hasn't even entered their own thoughts, except for when they're publicly mulling over their phony suicides."

Necro laughed. "Well, there is that, I suppose." He paused. "You think they'll go for it?"

"They'd better. Just you and me doing this wouldn't be impressive."

"All right. I'll make some calls, get some more people down here, and we'll see what we can manage. I have a few favors I can pull in for this one."

"Fuckin' awesome. Thanks, Necro."

"It's my pleasure."

4

When they were at maximum capacity, Necro Cock turned off the music. He heard a few groans and threats throughout the room, but Skank shushed them all with a hiss. Now, only two people made sounds, and they couldn't help it. The two had dosed on O and were still experiencing the throes of their chemically induced orgasms. Their moans of pleasure served as the backbeat to Necro Cock as he began. He explained everything that Skank had told him earlier, emphasizing her plan.

When he finished, everyone looked up at him, their faces blank, as if they hadn't understood a word of it. Finally, C—the bassist from FUCK—said, "That's fucking crazy. More than crazy, it's fuckin' stupid. Do all that shit for Nutsack? No offense, but I couldn't stand the little dick-licker."

"Cocksucker!" Skank howled. She leapt at C, her hands outstretched like eagle's talons, her lips curled up into a hideous, pierced snarl.

Necro grabbed her around the waist. "Wait!"

"Son of a fuck! Son of a fucking fuck!"

C backed up slightly, although Skank could never reach him.

"Skank, hold on," Necro said.

She turned on him. "You want me to stop?! Didn't you hear what he said?!"

"Yes, I did."

Skank stopped and looked into Necro Cock's eyes. There, she saw that he wanted her to cut C's fucking nuts off, but she also saw they needed C. They needed them all. Skank nodded and looked away from everyone else.

Necro Cock turned back to C. "This is about more than Nutsack. This is about those rich fucks and what they do to people like us. We'd be doing the world a service."

"Fuck the world," C said. "Anarchy, remember?"

"Do you even know what that means?" Necro Cock asked. When he didn't get an answer, he said, "If you don't want in, then get out, okay? We don't want anyone here with a smooth spot where a giant set of balls should be."

C looked down at his feet, but he didn't move.

"So come on, guys," Necro Cock said. "Are you cool with this? You wanna' tear some shit up?"

"YES!" everyone cried out.

He looked at Skank and grinned as everyone around him screamed their assent.

"Looks like we're in business, then," he said. "Everyone, go home and find some weapons. We'll meet up here in an hour. Then, it's time to fuck some shit up."

CHAPTER 7

1

"Hey."

The voice sounded familiar, but he couldn't place it. Moreover, he didn't care to. He just wanted to go on, sleeping.

"Wake up, Randall."

"Fugoff," he muttered.

"Goddammit, Randall. Get your faggot ass off the sidewalk."

When he heard the slur, his eyes opened, and he felt ready to kick someone's ass. When he saw a pair of stilettos and the giant feet they encased, he knew offense hadn't been meant. His eyes continued up the stout legs, the fake tits, the adam's apple and the make-up until he saw Susie, peering down at him through shaded glasses. The thick lenses made his eyes look larger, lashes and all.

"Sorry, man," Randall said. He forced himself up to his feet. "Didn't know it was you."

"That's okay, hon," Susie said. "Have a little too much to drink?"

Randall rubbed the back of his aching neck, and when he felt a barely perceptible lump there, he remembered everything. Fury suddenly shot through his veins, and he brought his fist down on the building next to him. "Goddammit!"

Susie flinched, and he automatically touched his throat. "What? What'd I do?"

Randall looked at his knuckles, at the blood oozing from them. He felt no pain. He sighed. "Sorry. It's not you. It's my fucking father."

Susie relaxed a little, although he still breathed a little too hard. "I've never seen you so pissed before. What's up with your father?"

Randall mentally debated telling Susie about everything, in particular his father, but he knew he had to handle this alone. Susie would not only get in the way, he might also get hurt. Randall wouldn't be able to live with himself if he got Susie killed. "Nothing. Nothing's up."

"Bullshit. You should have heard yourself yell."

"Yeah, well, I'm pretty pissed off right now. But I don't want to talk about it."

"You should. You'll feel better."

He shook his head, pulling himself up to his feet. "I doubt it. Besides, I have some shit I have to do."

Susie nodded. "My door is always open."

"See you around."

"Ta." Susie sashayed down the block, where he lived in a studio apartment.

Randall walked to his own apartment two blocks away. He made quite a bit more money on the streets than Susie did, so he had a much better place. Bedroom, bathroom, kitchen and living room, all pretty spacious. As soon as he walked in, he stripped out of his clothes and placed them in a hamper. He could still smell his last client on him, from before he'd been kidnapped, so he got into the shower and washed him away.

Just the thought of his last customer added a dash of rage to what he already felt. The guy had been a soft businessman who didn't want anyone thinking he was gay. He had no problem sticking his dick in Randall's ass, but after he'd blown his load, he changed his tune. Called Randall a faggot. Had even pushed Randall down. Randall, who had been at this game a long time, let him. Just so long as he'd been paid—and he always demanded cash up front—he could live with a little degradation. Just so long as he lived with as little physical damage as possible.

He resisted the urge to punch the tiles of his shower. His hand hurt enough from hitting the brick wall earlier. Water made it sting, but he no longer bled.

After he dried off, he dressed in looser, more comfortable clothes and went to the shoebox he kept under his bed. From it, he pulled out an old .44 revolver. He'd bought it after being on the receiving end of a nasty beating. One of his johns had followed him home and had beaten him with a baseball bat. More self-loathing from a man who couldn't accept that he loved cock.

Randall had sworn that would never happen again. He'd never fired a handgun before, and for the longest time, he hoped he'd never have to. He'd chosen a .44 not because of the damage it could do, but because it looked like a scary motherfucker. Now, though, he couldn't wait to use it.

He cracked open the cylinder and saw six copper shell-backs returning his gaze. Good.

There had been a time he actually liked his father, and there were still times he wished his father had been a more accepting man. His childhood had been remarkably fun. He'd really enjoyed hunting with his old man, using rifles to track down not the usual targets, like deer or squirrels, but dangerous animals like bears and wild cats. He'd been well on his way to becoming Samuel with just one exception. Randall thought it should have been inconsequential to his father, but the good old days were gone. Forever.

Before tonight, he thought he might have enjoyed being in the warm embrace of his father, but that would never happen now. The last time had been in junior high, when Samuel had hugged his son for beating the shit out of a bully. Randall thought about that moment many times over the years. Now, it made him sick to think that he wanted anything more to do with his father.

Randall closed the gun and donned his leather jacket. The .44 went in his pocket, where it weighed down that side of his jacket. If only he had a car, he could easily take care of business.

He thought about calling a cab, but then he remembered how the kidnappers had gotten him in the first place. They'd paid him for a night of sex, and they'd paid top dollar. He had a lot of money in his account. Why not hire a limo for the night? It would only be fitting, considering what he had planned.

He rolled his eyes up and saw that while he didn't have complete access to his apps, he could at least use a search engine. He found a limo company and accessed his mobile account. He heard the ring in his ear, and he waited for them to pick up.

2

Forty-five minutes later, the limo pulled up in front of his apartment building, and the driver honked twice. Randall rushed down, and when he saw the driver, he couldn't help but think, *Yum.* He wore a nice suit, and he stood at five-seven, all of him pure muscle. He wore a bad pencil-line mustache that had to go, but otherwise, very cute.

"Mr. Marsh? I'm Roberto. I'll be your driver tonight. How are you?"

"Hello, Roberto. Thanks for coming out."

"No problem." Roberto opened the door for him. "Where to, sir?"

Randall got in. "Find me a cheap liquor store that's still open."

"That's going to be a bit difficult. Most close around midnight."

"Not on the Sleaze Strip. They're open all night."

"Yes sir." He closed the door and went around to the front. Through the divider, Randall could see Roberto using the dash computer to plot their course. He could tell the driver didn't want to go to the Sleaze Strip this late, but he'd do it anyway. Randall thought it might be the average client's favorite place to stop. Randall couldn't count the number of times he'd been solicited by men—and the occasional woman—in limos.

Randall saw liquor in the back and considered taking a drink. But no, he'd need his wits about him for what lay ahead. He would have to enjoy his first self-financed limo trip without a pleasant buzz. Too bad.

3

Henry's Likkker stood at the very end of the Sleaze Strip, where no cop in the city dared to tread. Only the most extravagantly desperate human beings walked—or more likely, crawled—here. Anyone who didn't meet this criterion tended to be shot on principle, even if the person in question wore a uniform. Most ordinary corpses were left where they lay, but everyone knew if a dead cop were to be found here, there would be hell to pay. So dead cops tended to go missing. More often than not, they wound up being fed to the homeless who lived on the streets here.

Not even Randall had ever seen this area. He couldn't believe how many people lay on the sidewalks with needles in their arms and smoking pipes clutched in their bony white hands. The fuckslingers didn't even look appetizing. They held cardboard signs that advertised prices which no self-respecting human would accept. One woman, covered in warts and filth, had a sign that said she'd blow anyone for a sandwich. Sex cost a bottle of rotgut.

All the store fronts had a crumbled look about them, as if they were on their last legs. Dirt smeared all the windows, many of which sported cracks and taped-over bullet holes. He wondered if anyone really operated businesses out here. Upon closer examination, he saw a number of pawn shops and taverns had neon OPEN signs in their filthy windows.

"Jesus. Do you go down here often?"

"Only when I'm told to," Roberto said. He let the limo park itself and went around to open Randall's door. "Be very careful, sir. If someone conscious and sober enough comes along, they will mug you. I'm not kidding."

"I'll be fine." Randall patted the gun in his pocket.

Roberto leaned against the side of the car, smoking as he watched after his customer.

Randall headed for the liquor store. Laying near the doorway was what he initially took to be a passed-out junkie. As he got closer, he saw the puddle of blood circling the corpse's cracked-open head, making him look like a bizarro saint.

He looked away as he focused on the liquor store's dirty glass door. Upon entering, he noticed an enormous man behind the counter. His shaved head gleamed in the overhead light, and tattoos of swastikas and KKK symbols covered his body. A smear of red marked the floor where a customer buying booze might stand.

"There's a body in front of your store," Randall said.

"I know," the clerk said. He produced a lead pipe from behind the counter. One end had been taped up, and the other shone red with blood. "I put him there."

Oh fuck. "Uh, what did he do?"

"Tried to hold me up."

Randall thought it might be best to not ask any more questions. Under a handlebar mustache, the clerk's mouth curled up in a snarl, and his muscles bristled like an angry cat's fur. He still held the lead pipe, and he looked eager to use it again.

"That's cool." Randall turned away from him to look at the selection. There were no big name products here, but he didn't want that, anyway. He needed cheap slop with a high proof – higher than was legal. He didn't have to search long before he found some moonshine at 196 proof. *Perfect*. He started gathering bottles into his arms.

The clerk cleared his throat. "You ain't planning on holding me up, too, are you?"

"Nope."

"Then why're you grabbing all that booze?"

"I'm going to a party," Randall said. "I want to make sure everyone has their own bottle."

"That's a lot of money you're talking right there, man. You're already holding fifty bucks worth."

Randall looked down at the four bottles he held so far. He restrained the urge to laugh, as he figured that might get him a lead pipe head adjustment. "I've got the money to back up my grip."

Something changed on the clerk's face. "You a faggot?"

Henry's Likkker was not the kind of place to get up on a soapbox about prejudiced assholes, so Randall yet again restrained himself. "Nope."

"I don't like the way you talk."

Randall thought about answering with a witty quip, but again, he didn't want to get his ass kicked, or maybe even killed. Instead, he came up to the counter with about twenty bottles of rotgut. The clerk scanned them and said, "Including Uncle Sam's cut, that'll be two-seventy."

Randall held his hand over the chip reader and transferred the money. As soon as the reader dinged with a green light, the clerk put the bottles into a box. Randall carried it out to the limo, and Roberto took it from him and loaded it into the trunk.

"Where to next?" he asked Randall.

"102 Bingham."

Roberto laughed. "That's in the rich neighborhood."

"That's right. That's where I want to go."

Randall got in the back, and Roberto closed the door for him. As soon as he knew his client wouldn't be able to hear him, Roberto muttered, "Talk about variety."

4

Roberto opened the door. "102 Bingham, sir."

Randall got out and asked him to please fetch the box of booze from the trunk. While the driver went to do this, Randall went to the gate, to the intercom. He pressed the buzzer and waited.

"Yes?"

Huh. That voice sounded familiar. "Johnson? Is that you?"

"Yes. Whom may I ask is there?"

Wow. Johnson had been old back when Randall still lived here. He couldn't imagine him still doing butler work. "It's me, Junior."

"Mr. Barnabas! We haven't heard from you in quite some time, sir."

"Is my father there?"

"I'm afraid he's out at the moment. May I be of service?"

"Hm. Could you let me in?"

"I'm afraid Mr. Barnabas—your father, I mean—issued strict orders not to admit you, Mr. Barnabas."

Shit. He hadn't counted on that, but he did have one thing in his back pocket. Suddenly, he felt grateful that Johnson still worked here. "Need I remind you that you owe me?"

A pause. Then: "Of course not, sir. I'll buzz you in."

Randall smiled as the buzzer went off, and the gates opened. He turned to Roberto and said, "You wait here, okay? I'll get back to you shortly."

"Sure." Roberto handed over the box. Then, as soon as Randall was out of sight, he started up the Waiting Ritual. He lit up a cigarette, discreetly hid himself in the shadows thrown by towering bushes and relaxed.

Randall walked down the drive until he reached the sprawling Barnabas manor, where Johnson waited for him on the doorstep. Johnson, who stood stiffly as his crisp suit. He'd been with the family since Randall had been a boy and longer, yet he still looked strong and firm.

"It's been a long time, sir."

"Good to see you, Johnson."

"May I take your box, sir?"

"No, I'll carry it. However, you can take the rest of the night off." He balanced the box against the door frame and held out his left hand for transfer.

Johnson looked at it momentarily before shifting his gaze to Randall's eyes. "Might I be so bold as to ask why?"

"Just take it and go."

Johnson held his left hand against Randall's and accepted a three hundred dollar transfer. "Thank you, sir."

"Is there anyone else here?" Randall asked.

"Just the maid."

"Take her out with you. Have a night on the town."

"Most respectable places are closed for the night."

Randall grinned. "Then take her to an unrespectable place. Get the old long and gnarly wet."

"I detest that remark, sir. You know I prefer the stable boy."

Randall laughed and clapped Johnson on the back. "Just get out of here, all right? And don't look back."

Johnson nodded. "Certainly, sir."

Randall entered the house he hadn't so much as seen for the past three years. Everything looked the same. Art everywhere, outnumbered only by stuffed animal heads. He set the box down and waited in the foyer until Johnson returned with the maid and exited. He noticed they both carried suitcases, as if they knew exactly what he had in mind. He also wondered if they'd taken some of his father's valuables to go with their clothes. He hoped they did, especially since they no longer had jobs.

He walked through the mansion, taking a last look around, remembering the good times, when he didn't have to sell himself to get by. The playroom still contained his favorite toys, as if waiting for their master to return to them. The game room, a favorite hang-out for himself and his friends in high school, still had the pool table where he'd spent many evenings scamming people out of their money. Though his father never knew it, he'd fucked Tommy Sanders on it after they'd played a game with their assholes as the stakes.

He found his bedroom and marveled at how it looked the exact same as it had before, if a bit dusty, as if Samuel had sealed it after finding him fucking his boyfriend in the back seat of his car.

Randall stopped in his father's study, filled with old, crumbling books Samuel had never read. A monstrously large oak desk stood at the heart of the room, everything meticulously cleaned and organized. All around the study were stuffed animals, all of which had been killed by Samuel except the panda. When Samuel had heard the last panda had died, he bought its corpse for a hefty donation to the zoo. The most impressive of his trophies, however, was a lion and grizzly bear couple. They'd been stuffed and positioned so it looked like they were battling with each other.

He thought about that bear and remembered his first hunting trip. Both father and son had taken the bear down, and even though Randall had merely been ten years old at the time, Samuel had given him his first beer so they could celebrate together. It had been one of his happiest moments.

A glass case ran the length of one of the walls, filled with Samuel's most prized possessions. A signed manuscript of Ernest Hemingway's *The Old Man and the Sea*, a signed first edition of Robert Ruark's *Use Enough Gun* and many other things, mostly Civil War antiques, a six-shooter reputed to have been used by Wyatt Earp and a tri-cornered hat that supposedly had belonged to George Washington.

A gun case took up the wall opposite, which Randall found empty, much to his surprise. Every rifle, shotgun and handgun was gone.

Then, he noticed that even the blackjack was gone. He remembered the only time he'd ever seen his father use it, which stood out in Randall's mind as his absolute favorite memory of his father, even though a lot of terrible shit had led up to it.

When he'd been eight years old, Randall had been a Boy Scout. He'd been out with Samuel on the annual father/son camping trip. While Samuel had been taking the other boys on a hike, the scout master stayed behind with Randall, who had been stricken with a charley horse and couldn't walk very comfortably.

The scout master had taken it upon himself to make Randall very comfortable in one of the bigger tents. He'd stripped down to his undershirt and shorts, and as the scout master surrounded him with pillows, his hand accidentally brushed the young boy's crotch.

"I'm sorry," the scout master had said. When Randall shrugged it off, the scout master thought the boy wouldn't mind. He slipped his hand into the front of Randall's shorts and began to massage softly. "Do you feel better now?"

"What the fuck are you doing?" Randall had shouted. He punched the scout master as hard as he could in the face, but he just didn't have the power an adult would have had. He couldn't stop the scout master from overpowering him. His charley horse howled, crippling him as the scout master flipped him over and pulled his shorts down. The scout master jabbed himself into Randall's ass, twisting and gouging until blood flowed freely.

Randall didn't know which hurt more, the rape or the charley horse. His mind went crazy trying to find some way to rescue himself.

When the scout master finished, he pulled up his pants and cleaned the boy off. "Don't tell anyone about this, or I'll kill you. I'll kill you and feed you to my dog. My dog loves to eat little boys."

Randall couldn't say anything through the tears he cried into a pillow.

He didn't intend to tell his father, but when Samuel saw blood in the boy's underwear, he demanded to know what had happened. He demanded an explanation, and Randall, more afraid of his father than the scout master, told all about it. Samuel took the blackjack from his pack and marched toward the scout master's tent, Randall following behind.

Without a word, Samuel grabbed the scout master and whipped him in the face with the blackjack. His nose exploded in a geyser of blood, and Samuel struck him again, this time in the mouth. The scout master fell, spitting out jagged teeth and even more blood. He drew in a breath to scream, but Samuel booted him in the head, knocking him face down.

"You like fucking little boys, huh? I hope you like this, then." He yanked the scout master's pants down and beat his ass. Literally. The blackjack came down so hard and often that it tore the flesh from the scout master's body. By the time he'd finished, his ass had been reduced to pulped meat with a bit of tail bone sticking through.

When Samuel's arm got tired, he stopped and turned the scout master over. The scout master's eyes were wide, and his throat tendons stuck out like bars. "Peeshe," he managed to say. "Nuh mr."

Samuel stomped on the scout master's bare genitals and ground his heel. The scout master's breath whooshed from him, and he made some rather pathetic noises as he tried to regain his lungs.

"You're the biggest piece of shit I've ever seen," Samuel said. He put all of his weight on the one foot. "I'd kill you, but I'd rather have you suffer for the rest of your life."

He lifted his foot and brought the blackjack down on the scout master's dick over and over until it resembled a broken, bloated and split sausage. The scout master couldn't even scream anymore. Empty eyes dripped tears as he fell away into a world of shock.

Samuel pointed the gory blackjack at the scout master. "Feel free to tell everyone who did this to you." Then, with one last blow to the face, Samuel walked out of the tent, wiping blood from his blackjack.

Randall had been so proud of his father in that moment. He knew that no matter what might happen to him, his father would be there to make things right.

"God, I loved you so much," Randall muttered to the stuffed animals.

He thought once again of the night when his father had caught him in the backseat with his boyfriend, the star quarterback, but he shook it out of his head. Why dwell on the point now?

He went back to the foyer and looked down at the box of booze. He wished he could have gotten actual explosives, but this would have to do. He picked up two bottles and went back to the study, where he broke the seal on each and splashed their contents on everything. The desk, the animals, the glass case. He only stopped long enough to go through Samuel's papers. An old fashioned guy, he was the only one he knew who actually kept a physical address book instead of just using an app. He found the book and tucked it away in his pocket.

The next two bottles doused everything in his father's bedroom. He went back and forth between the foyer and each room in the house, pouring rotgut whiskey all over everything he could find. He did this so often that he couldn't even smell the acrid stink of it.

The last bottle he used to run a trail from the closest room—the parlor—to the front door. He carelessly tossed the empty behind him, where it shattered on the floor. Satisfied, he reached into his pocket and pulled out a book of matches. He plucked one and held it above the strip on the back, pausing to reflect on this moment.

"Fuck you, Dad." He struck the match and dropped it into the booze. It ignited immediately, and he watched it burn down the hallway into the parlor, which practically exploded into flames. It soon stretched into the next room and the next and the next.

Randall exited the house and walked down toward the gate. The blaze behind him blew out the windows and licked at the night sky so brightly he could see his own shadow stretch out in front of him in the dark of the night.

~

Edward laughed harder than he ever had in his entire life. After a moment of hilarity, he began coughing . . . and then broke out into laughter again.

"Are you all right?" Elizabeth asked.

"Samuel . . . he's . . ." Edward gave up trying to speak and lapsed back into laughter.

"Samuel's going to be pissed," William said.

"To hell with Samuel," Coppergate said. His teeth shone from between his withered lips. "His son is more like himself than anyone could have ever imagined."

~

When Randall got back to the limo, he saw Roberto sitting inside, listening to the radio. He saw his client and jumped out, opening the back door. "I think we should be going, sir."

"Why's that?"

"I just heard on the radio. There's a riot going on about a mile from here. There's a bunch of people cutting their way through the rich neighborhood, and they're on their way here."

Randall laughed. "Then I beat 'em to the punch." He got into the back.

Roberto glanced at the house and saw the conflagration. "Oh." His client had just made him an accessory to arson, but what the hell? Roberto never really liked the rich, anyway. They usually tipped badly.

"Who's rioting?"

"A bunch of punks."

"Like, the Two-Fisted Nunfuckers type of punks? Or just layabouts?"

"No, real punks. Spiked hair, piercings, moving tattoos, mutilations and all."

Randall thought about one of the other contestants. Skank, wasn't it? She had been just as opposed to the game as he was. Could it be . . . ? "Drive in closer to the riot."

Roberto forgot himself. "Are you nuts? Get *closer* to the riot?" He didn't even think about his job at this point.

"Yeah. I think I might know someone in that neighborhood." He thought Skank had maybe decided on a scorched earth policy when it came to fighting back against the rich fucks, as evidenced by her tearing the east side to pieces. Of course, Randall would make things much easier with the help of his father's address book.

"This sounds bad," Roberto said.

Randall flicked his eyes over and saw he still had an extra two hundred from the kidnappers. "I'll pay you two hundred right now if you'll do it."

"Right now? Up front?"

"Up front." Randall held up his left hand.

Roberto thought about it for maybe two seconds before he raised his own left hand. As soon as he saw the money in his account, he ran around to the driver's door and got in. He hovered over the dash computer and said, "Where to? Specifically?"

"Just wander around. I'll know where we're going when I see it."

Roberto cursed under his breath as he waited for the road track to engage and take them away from the burning Barnabas mansion. Soon, he manually piloted the limo as they headed closer to the sound of screams, gunfire and explosions.

CHAPTER 8

1

When Steve opened his eyes, he saw a shingle hanging over his head. He blinked some fuzziness away from his eyes, and when he could see clearly, he recognized it as the sign for Lenny's. He pulled himself up into a sitting position and saw an empty street. Only a couple of illegal cars remained with tickets under their windshield wipers.

With a groan, he stood and peered into the window of Lenny's. Closed. The Budweiser clock said it was four in the morning.

"Damn." He tried to remember how much time had passed since he'd been in here, drinking with his old buddy, Bob—and then he remembered everything. It all struck him as absurd, like the old kidney thief urban legend. A bunch of rich people getting together to kidnap those who were less fortunate, only to throw them into a game where the winner gets a billion dollars and the losers get paupers graves?

Steve wouldn't believe it if not for the tiny bump on the back of his neck.

His head cleared immediately. The thought of actually playing the game never occurred to him. He only wanted to expose these rich sons of bitches—and in one case, just plain bitch—as the pieces of shit they really were.

Details. He tried to access his social media so he could play back his LiveStream. Some of his apps weren't working, but he could access his memory and watched it again. The other contestants came through clearly, but when it came to the rich spectators, their words were bleeped out, and their faces were clouded over. Shit. He remembered the old man in the wheelchair. How could he forget? He also remembered the woman, but only because of her sex. He tried remembering the others, but he came up with nothing.

Wait! The homeless guy with the Red Death had called one of them by name, hadn't he? Eddie, maybe? Ring-Piece Eddie! He'd also mentioned his real name, too. Edward something. Rivers? No. Close. Bridges! Edward Bridges!

It wasn't much, but he could start with this. He accessed his mobile account and as soon as he heard the dial tone in his ear, he called 911.

A feminine voice came on the line: "This number is no longer in service. Please check your number and try your call again."

No fucking way. Unless . . . right. The rich fucks didn't want him calling the police. Well, too bad. He thought he might still have some connections at the seventh precinct, where he used to work. Not everybody hated him, at least, he hoped not.

He went over the information again in his head as he started walking.

2

About an hour later, as Steve walked up the steps to the seventh precinct, he felt like he'd moved back in time. He hadn't been near this building since he'd been kicked off the force, and he never expected to be back. It suddenly occurred to him that his old friends would see him like this, a messy and desperate man. Though he couldn't smell himself, he suspected he still reeked of booze. The idea disgusted him, but he knew he had to do this.

As he pushed through the double doors, it felt like the old days, like he'd just arrived for another day on the Job. The cold air greeted him like a friend. They always kept the lobby heavily air conditioned, even in the winter. It made people waiting there uncomfortable, and uncomfortable people tended to make mistakes. Just another trick from your friendly neighborhood police officer.

The same familiar scent wafted over his nostrils. He could never identify what it was, exactly. Paper and ink were a part of it, even though records had gone completely to digital two hundred years ago, and coffee reared its strong head, too, yet he could detect something else in there, and he just couldn't put his finger on it.

He walked up to the main desk, where a woman sat looking at something on an ancient computer. The station rarely got financial help from city hall, so it would probably be another twenty years before they got any equipment that would be considered good by today's standards. Some things never changed.

He didn't recognize the woman, and he felt relieved by this. The woman who used to sit in the lobby had been an ex-lover. He'd been going out with Cindy for nearly a year, and they were talking about maybe one day getting married. Then came the day he got kicked off the force, and because she came from a cop family, and many relatives had badgered her about him, she dumped him.

"Can I help you?" The woman didn't look up from her work.

"Is Travis Wyndorf in?" Steve asked.

"Hold on." She moved a few things around on her screen and scrolled down through something. "He should be in. Up in vice."

Vice? His old friend had moved up in the world. Last Steve had known him, Travis worked the streets, just like him. "I know the way. Thanks."

"Wait. I have to ring you up. What's your name?" He gave it to her, and instead of using her own phone, like everyone else, she used the wall mounted antique. Which made sense. Why use your own plan when you can use the city's? "Detective Wyndorf? Hi, this is Tammy. There's a guy named Steve McNeil here to see you. Huh? Okay." She hung up. "Go on up."

"Thanks."

A flight of stairs later, Steve took a deep breath to let out some of his tension. He knew how badly he looked, and he didn't want Travis to see him like this, but again, he forced himself to forget about it and do what had to be done. He stepped into the vice office and saw a lot of empty desks. It made sense, this time of night. Most of the guys were probably out on calls. Only two detectives sat up here, a stranger and Travis Wyndorf. Upon seeing his old friend, Steve couldn't help but be surprised. He remembered Travis as a skinny kid with a crewcut. Now he had a beer gut, and his hair had grown out to his shoulders, almost as greasy as his own.

"Steve Mc-fucking-Neil. How the fuck are you? What the hell're you doing here?"

"I'm in a bit of trouble," Steve said. "I—"

"Damn right, you're in trouble. If the captain caught you here, he'd pitch a fit. Luckily, he's home for the night."

"I'm in more trouble than the captain can throw at me. I—"

"What're we talking here? Drugs? Or maybe your horse didn't come in. That it? Or is it the cards?"

Heat flushed Steve's cheeks. What the hell? Travis should have known better. He'd only known Steve for years. "Shit, I'm not a fucking junkie, and you know it. And I don't gamble either. I've got something big I have to tell you about. Would you just listen?"

Travis flicked his eyes, and Steve knew his old friend had just checked the time. That fucker.

"Fine. Have a seat and tell me your woes. Only make it quick. I got a bunch of shit I gotta' do."

Steve looked over at the other detective and waited. Travis sighed. "Hey Dave. Take a break for a few minutes, would you?"

Dave looked up from his computer, eyebrows raised.

"Just a few minutes," Travis said. "Get a coffee or something."

Dave shrugged and got up. As soon as he'd left, Steve sat down at the chair across from Travis's desk and told his story. Travis listened to the part about Lenny's and Bob Whiteman. Yet when Steve got to the part about the rich people and their game, in particular the old guy in the wheelchair, Travis held up his hands. "Whoa, Steve-o. Hold up right there."

"What? You know the guy"

Travis licked his lips. "Maybe. Hold on a second." He picked up the phone and punched in three numbers.

"What are you doing?" Steve asked.

Travis held up a finger. "Tammy? Are Dick and Mark around? Send 'em up, would you? Thanks." He hung up the phone.

"Who're Dick and Mark?"

"I'll tell you when they get here. We got us a bit of a problem, though. You're talking about a very rich, very powerful man."

"So you do know him," Steve said. "Who is he?"

"I can't tell you that. You're right about being in trouble, buddy, but I can't help you. Orders, you know."

Something cold slipped down Steve's spine and chilled his belly. He understood what this meant, but he just couldn't believe it to be true. "What are you talking about? This old guy and his friends are—"

"I know what they're up to," Travis said. "They do this every year, and every year, there's someone who thinks they can come to us for help. I'm just sorry it had to be you."

Steve grimaced. He could understand these rich fucks getting to a lot of cops, but to a guy like Travis? He'd always been a good guy. Honest. He'd even believed in Steve when he'd told the truth about what had happened with the mayor's son. How could he have turned into this dirty slob he now saw before him?

Dick and Mark, two very large guys in uniform, came in, holding their nightsticks in their hands. Not threateningly, but they made sure everyone saw the weapons.

"Sorry, man," Travis said. "I'm under orders to ignore you. I like you and everything, but I like my kids better. These rich guys, they're going to pay for them to go through college. My son wants to be a doctor, and my daughter wants to be a lawyer. That ain't cheap, Steve-o. You understand." He looked to Dick and Mark. "Throw this guy out, would you? Don't be assholes about it, but make sure he doesn't come back."

The gorillas grabbed Steve under each arm and pulled him up out of the chair. "Don't do this, man. Don't turn your back on me."

"Sorry, Steve-o." Travis returned to his work.

Dick and Mark dragged Steve to the door. "Didn't all of those years on the street mean anything? You're letting the bad guys win!"

Travis shook his head, and then Steve saw the closing door. He shook his arms. "Let me go. I'll walk."

Dick and Mark exchanged a glance before releasing Steve. Sure enough, he walked on his own. As soon as he headed out the double doors of the precinct building, he looked back to see Dick and Mark standing with the doors between them, their arms crossed. Not that Steve wanted to go back in, anyway.

Back to square one. No allies, no plan. What could he do without the police?

Well, who do people go to when the police can't help them? He remembered Jimmy Monaghan from back in the day, a reporter who had always taken his side, even after he'd fallen from grace. Maybe he'd be able to help out.

He checked the time. The Trib building had to be closed, but he knew Jimmy liked to burn the midnight oil. Maybe, just maybe . . .

He started walking, hoping with all his might.

3

Jimmy Monaghan thought they might drop Steve off back at Lenny's, but after waiting for a couple of hours, he knew he'd been wrong. He thought about going home and maybe getting some sleep, but he felt consciousness humming through his entire body. Instead, he went back to the office. The building closed down at midnight, except for the night guy, who cruised the news feeds in case something interesting happened overnight. Jimmy had special privileges, being a popular columnist. His thumbprint could get him into the building at any hour.

He tried to work for a while on an opinions column for next week, but he couldn't focus on it. Besides, he already had three in the can and ready to go. After he checked the 'net for any breaking stories from the AP, he figured he'd go home. He needed a cigarette anyway, and maybe Jack had tried to contact him.

Jimmy stepped out into the street and lit up. Just as he started down the block for his car, he saw someone walking swiftly toward him. He couldn't see through the shadows, but he knew well enough to be ready for anything. He reached into his pocket for an extending club he kept for such instances. He readied himself to flick it out and bring the club to its full extent, but then he saw a familiar face on the approaching figure. The blue circle confirmed his identification.

He put the club back. "Steve McNeil? What are you doing here?"

"Looking for you," Steve said. "Listen, I need—"

"I know all about it. Come with me. Now." He grabbed Steve's elbow and led him down the street to his car.

"Hold on, Jimmy. I got something real important to tell you."

"I know. The game. We need to talk, just not here, okay?"

"How do you—"

"Get in." Jimmy opened the passenger side door for him before going around to the other side. As soon as he got in, he programmed the car for home and swiveled in his seat. "Tell me everything."

4

Steve hadn't finished by the time they got to Jimmy's place, so they took a break until they were up in his apartment. Then, over a bottle of bourbon, Steve finished his tale.

"Now," he said, "what about you? How do you know about the game?"

Jimmy lit a fresh cigarette and blew SyntheSmoke up at the ceiling. "I don't know everything. About five years ago, I caught wind of a rumor. I couldn't substantiate anything, but I kept my ears open. Then, a John Doe came through the sixth precinct. No one seemed to know much about the dead guy, but after a day's worth of investigating, the department dropped it. The corpse vanished. I had detectives refusing to admit that it had ever been there.

"Turned out to be one of the contestants," he continued. "I kept my ear to the ground, and over the next few years, I learned a lot about it. Tons of money goes into this thing every year, and it's always run by the same guy. Richard Coppergate."

"Uh, as in Coppergate Tower?" Steve asked.

"That's the guy. You'd know him if you saw him. Old guy in a wheelchair. Nasty looking. Blank eyes—"

"And those sharp, metallic teeth," Steve said.

"Just like in your story. I also know Edward Bridges because he came out of nowhere about a year ago. New rich. He just rode into town with a billion dollars, and suddenly, after some very thrifty investments, he became a big name. I *suspected* he might have been a winner from last year's game, but now that you told me your story, I *know* it."

"Do you know anyone else who's involved?"

Jimmy nodded. "The woman you mentioned is Elizabeth Drake. There's also one other person I know for sure is involved. Did you see a guy with silver hair there?"

Steve thought about it for a moment. "Maybe."

"That's Charles Wingate. As for the others, I have no idea. I also have no proof, which is why I haven't been able to write the story yet. But with you here, I finally have something to go on."

Steve uttered a nervous laugh. "I'm glad to hear you say that. The cops are being paid off by these guys. They can't help us. It's up to us to expose these motherfuckers—"

"There's a slight problem with that," Jimmy said.

"Oh no. Not you, too."

"It's not like that. When have I ever backed down from powerful people? I'm just telling you that you need to take a look at the masthead on the Trib sometime. If you did, you'd see that it's owned by Coppergate."

Steve sat for a moment, his mouth hanging open, eyes staring into nothingness. It hadn't struck him until now how hopeless things were in the world. And then, another thought occurred to him. "We can go to the competition."

Jimmy shook his head. "Wingate owns the Times."

This time, Steve couldn't help but laugh. No humor came through his voice. "Wow."

"Yeah, I know. All it means is we can't write about those fucks, at least not now. Maybe someday, but someday doesn't help us."

"Then what can we do?" Steve asked.

"Well, I *do* have an idea."

5

Down in Jimmy's car, Steve couldn't stand the suspense anymore. "Where the hell are we going?"

Jimmy programmed the dash computer, and the car pulled out into the street, racing along its track through the pre-dawn, empty city. "To meet an associate of mine."

"Looks like we're headed out of the city."

"We are."

Steve gave up trying to get information out of Jimmy and just relaxed in the passenger seat, watching the city flow before his eyes. About a half an hour later, they rode out past the suburbs, and an hour after that, they were in the middle of nowhere. The sky turned pink, and the sun threatened to rise over the eastern horizon.

The car stopped, and Jimmy had to disengage from the track. Wheels came down, and they rolled down a dirt path. Once again, Steve felt tempted to ask questions, but he knew he'd get no answers.

Jimmy stopped the car next to a sign that said TRESPASSERS WILL BE DESTROYED. "From here on out, we have to walk. Follow me, and step where I step. Look out for bear traps."

"Bear traps?" Steve looked at the sign, an eyebrow raised. "What the hell?"

Jimmy didn't answer. Instead, they got out of the car, and Steve followed him into a wooded area. The sun now peeked its head up, and its light filtered through the trees, allowing Steve to get a good look at his surroundings. Sure enough, there were plenty of bear traps out here. He spotted a few ambushes. Spikes sticking out of a log held up by a chain. A soft spot in the ground that showed through to a pit. A boulder suspended by a thick tree. Whoever lived out here didn't fuck around.

Soon, they saw a cabin up ahead. Around it stood several burnt crosses. Spray-painted on the walls of the cabin were horribly spelled racist comments. GOE HOME DARK BASERD on one wall. FUCK U NIGER on the door. Steve thought the cabin might have been set on fire at some point, judging from the dark marks on the roof.

"Who the fuck lives here?" Steve asked.

"STOP RIGHT THERE, MOTHERFUCKERS!" The voice came from on high, and it sounded strong enough to buttfuck a bull.

Steve looked up to see a very tall, very muscular man standing at a window on the upper floor of the cabin. He aimed a shotgun down at them.

"Jack! It's me, Jimmy! I have a friend with me!"

Jack didn't lower the shotgun. "I know that! Who the fuck is *he*?!"

"Steve McNeil. He's the guy I told you about last night."

Jack disappeared from the window. Steve turned to Jimmy, wondering about the comment about last night. He figured he'd ask about it later.

Jack reappeared at the door, the shotgun slung over his shoulder. He approached Jimmy and shook his head. "Good to see you."

"You, too. We finally have some information on these rich fuckers. Can we come in?"

Jack raised an eyebrow. "Pardon me?"

"I said—"

"I know what you said."

Jimmy rolled his eyes. "All right, fine. *May* we come in?"

"That's better. Come on." He turned to Steve. "I'm Jack LeCroix."

"Nice to meet you." Steve nodded to the burnt crosses. "Visitors?"

"Ah, just some kids. I think I hit one of them with some buckshot."

"Aren't you going to do anything with the crosses?"

"What am I worried about, my property value? Fuck that. Besides, maybe it will remind those cum rags of getting shot at last time, and they'll think twice about coming back."

Jimmy laughed. "Catch any lately?"

"No, but I know a couple of them stepped into my traps. I found them sprung and covered with blood. Too bad they got away."

"What would you do if you ever caught one?"

"Kill it, stuff it and put it on my mantle."

They entered the cabin and followed Jack through to the kitchen. Steve had never seen such an old fashioned room, at least not in real life. In school, he'd seen pictures of a place where you needed to actually flick light switches on, and where appliances had to be touched in order to make them work. The walls seemed to be made of plaster instead of the phony stuff they used today, and the flowery wallpaper looked atrocious. There were actually spider webs in the corners of the room.

Then, Jack pulled on the sink's faucet, and a portion of the floor popped up. He pulled the panel to one side, revealing a set of stairs leading down.

"After you," he said to Jimmy.

Jimmy went first, and then Steve, with Jack at the rear. He pulled the panel closed after he made it through. He heard a whirring sound and knew the carpet had moved forward to cover up the trap door.

Once at the bottom of the steps, Steve whistled. Computers filled the entire room. Top of the line, not like the shit the PD had to use. All of them busily chattered information in a steady hum.

"Goddam, Jack," he said. "It's like the fucking Batcave down here."

Jack ignored the comment. He indicated the table with a few chairs around it. "Have a seat. Tell me what's going on."

Jimmy took out a pack of smokes and handed Jack and Steve cigarettes. Once they lit up, Steve began his story for the third time since he'd woken up outside of Lenny's.

CHAPTER 9

1

"It's good to see you're alive, Barry."

Barry opened his eyes and saw a grand, vaulted ceiling. It reminded him of church, but he didn't recall ever going into one. He moved around and realized he lay in bed, dressed in silk pajamas and topped off with an old fashioned sleeping cap, tassels tickling his cheek. He hadn't experienced such opulence in a long time. Not since . . . not since the download.

He didn't like thinking about it. In the depths of his twisted and overstuffed mind, he knew what had happened. He remembered being a smart kid in school, obsessed with knowing everything he possibly could. Everyone warned him, even the websites he accessed to pull it off, but he just couldn't help himself. Besides, the human mind had more storage space than any computer in existence. It should have been able to contain all knowledge.

He hacked around the legal safety protocols and managed to download the entire 'net into his head. At first, it had felt like an orgasm, if he'd been old enough to know what that was like at the time. Except excitement didn't flow out of him; it went in. He knew the entire history of humanity, and it broke his mind. He overloaded quickly and could no longer function as a regular person.

His parents tried to reverse the process. They went to the best minds their money could buy, but no one could figure out a way to wipe his mind without losing the boy he'd once been. He rambled and raved paranoid screeds even at the age of ten. His dad tried to keep him home, tranquilized, but very soon it became apparent that something like that couldn't work.

By the age of thirteen, they had him committed quietly, where the doctors didn't care about him, the nurses barely treated him and the orderlies mocked him and, on occasion, raped him.

One day, a man calling himself John F. Kennedy befriended him in the institute. Without John, Barry wouldn't have been able to make it through. A kindred spirit, John comforted him by telling him about how everyone, from his most powerful enemies to his most trusted friends, was out to get him. He could only trust his brother. That sounded very familiar to Barry, who couldn't even trust his own father. How could a man condemn his only son to suffer in this hell hole?

But that didn't matter anymore. The hospital turned him loose on the streets, and he'd been surviving by wit and John's help. Even when those strangers had come up to him and kidnapped him, John had tried to tell him to run. Run and not look back. If only he'd listened to the former president. Things would have been different.

He dimly remembered the rich fucks behind the unbreakable glass. He remembered seeing his father back there. He remembered the game, but it didn't concern him very much. He knew only that he had to get the fuck out of the city, or his father would kill him for sure.

But how did he get here, in this bed? He rubbed his eyes, wondering if maybe he'd suffered another flashback in time. On occasion, a piece of history would engulf him and push him back into another era, where he would see famous events. He'd seen the Civil War first hand. The same for the crucifixion and the invention of penicillin and countless others.

This didn't feel right, though. He looked around again, and this time, he saw who had woken him up. He grinned. "Hot damn, Bobby! I'm glad to see you!"

"Yes, and let me assure you that John is very proud of the control you maintain while under pressure. I share his sentiment."

"You're my friends. I'd do anything for you."

"John would be honored to once more be in your presence, to personally thank you for your discretion in certain matters. We know you've been through a very trying ordeal, but he is eager to see you. Are you prepared for such a meeting?"

"Shit yes."

"Excellent. You'll find the appropriate attire in the closet. I'll wait for you outside the door."

Barry hopped off the bed like a kid eager to watch cartoons. When Bobby left, Barry threw open the closet door to find a set of ceremonial robes. Would he be receiving an award?

He couldn't wait to see his old friend. John had been laying low because of a lot of government spooks looking to put a bullet in his head. Now, the two of them would finally be reunited.

After he dressed up, he went out and walked with Bobby down a long, echoing hallway. They reached a giant set of double doors, so tall that Barry couldn't see the top. They just kept going until they disappeared into the clouds.

Bobby pushed one door open and waved his hand over the threshold. "After you, Barry."

Barry stepped into a room as colossal as the double doors. It was so long and wide he couldn't see any walls, aside from the one behind him. In the middle stood a throne with an American flag at the top, and it struck Barry as a bit gaudy for someone as important as John.

People stood around, talking with each other, and Barry could recognize quite a few of them. Important figures, one and all. In their midst sat John, silent, nibbling on a thumbnail, staring down at the floor, lost in thought.

"John!" Barry called out.

John looked over the heads of his many advisors and saw Barry standing beyond them, nearly panting with excitement. "Barry! What a pleasant surprise! I feared you would prefer the comforts of your bed until your wounds ceased to be troublesome. I'm grateful for your presence."

"What's all this?" Barry asked.

"We're discussing politics. To be honest, it was starting to get rather dreary."

A fat middle-aged man with giant muttonchops and a lazy sneer on his face stepped forward. "Who's this guy?" A Southern accent as lazy as his sneer, yet as flamboyant as his sparkling jumpsuit.

"Everyone, this is Barry Taylor. As I'm sure you are all aware, Barry has saved my life many times over, and my debt to him is more than I can possibly explain."

A skinny, longhaired kid with a giant beard and a swastika carved in his forehead rocked on his heels. "Then we're sure glad to know you, Barry."

A blonde-haired beauty in a white dress that kept trying to blow up from her legs pooched her lips and blew Barry a kiss. Others nodded their agreement, and Barry started recognizing a lot more of them. Some were iconic actors and musicians, others great scientists and even more famous politicians. He saw the guy who bombed the White House in 2045, a World War III general and even the guy who found a way to implant the 'net into everyone's heads.

"Glad to know you all," Barry said.

John looked to his advisors. "I need to speak with Barry alone for a moment. We'll finish our discussion later."

After they left, John turned to Barry. "Before we continue any farther, I feel it is incumbent upon me to inform you that what you are experiencing is nothing more than a dream."

Barry cast his gaze around. "You mean, this is all fake?"

"No, these proceedings are not false. What I have to tell you is quite real and very important. I cannot stress how vital it is for you to pay me heed. However, this realm is not physical. We are now on a mental plane of existence. Your corporeal self is presently resting on a sidewalk just outside the park where you usually sleep."

Part of what John said made sense, but there were too many mental blocks in Barry's head to fully understand it. His brain overload had fried a lot of connecting points. "Okay," he said.

John must have seen the confusion on Barry's face. "You have saved me many times over, and now it is my turn to save you. Do you understand that?"

Barry nodded.

"Your present tribulation is the most precarious event of your life. If you don't do as I say, you will die. This is not speculation. I purvey truth. Once you awaken, I will not be able to provide you with assistance, so you'd do well to hark my words now, when I say the very first thing you need to procure is a firearm."

"A gun? What for? How?"

"By any means necessary," John said. "If you don't, this man will terminate you." He held out his hand, palm up, and a picture materialized out of nowhere. A middle-aged man stared back at Barry. He had short hair, but it looked like it had grown out from a crewcut. A handlebar mustache took up much of his rock hard face. His flinty blue eyes showed no emotion, just a hint of cruelty. "You've already encountered this iniquitous cad. His name is Samuel Maxwell Barnabas, III, and he is hunting you. And, not to distress you, but you're running out of time. We'll have to expedite these matters."

Barry waited, still barely comprehending anything John had told him.

"As soon as you have procured a firearm, you must find an adequate refuge, at which point you must prepare for the arrival of Samuel Barnabas. I cannot stress this point enough: you must terminate him upon first sighting. To neglect his immediate murder would be to invite your own."

"What about those other rich folk?" Barry asked. "What about Daddy?"

"The other contestants are busy saving their own lives. They are not out to kill you. As for your father, I . . ." John trailed off, and his eyes grew distant, as if something had grabbed his attention.

"What?" Barry asked.

A panicked look poured over John's face. "FUCK! We're out of time! There's one last thing I need to do! Are you ready?"

"I—"

John didn't give him enough time to think. He leapt off the throne and shoved his hand into Barry's head. He could feel the president moving things around, gathering as much of it as he could. Just as he pulled back, Barry blacked out.

2

Barry's eyes opened, and he squinted into a streetlight overhead. He sat up, pain throbbing dully at the back of his head. Looking around, he didn't recognize anything about the neighborhood. He tried to remember anything at all, and then he remembered his plan. He wanted to download all human knowledge into his head. Had he started that process yet? He didn't think he felt any smarter.

He ran a tongue over his teeth, and his stomach nearly fell out of him. So many of them were missing, but he didn't remember that happening. He remembered playing basketball with one of his friends last week, but there hadn't been any injury. He touched the gaping holes in his mouth and shuddered. He didn't even want to see himself in the mirror.

And then he felt a scraggly beard on his face. It couldn't be. How could an eight year old kid have a beard?

Don't forget me.

Who had said that? He looked around, wondering, but he didn't see anyone else on the street. But then again, it had seemed to come from inside his head, hadn't it? He could still hear the familiar, Boston accent . . .

"Oh God, this isn't happening," Barry said. His eyes filled with tears, and he cried out into the night. "Daddy! Please help me! Where are you?!"

~

"Something's wrong," Martin said. He stood and went to the control panel. "Which one is Barry's sound feed?"

Coppergate nodded to his assistant, who handled the task for them. It turned on just in time to hear Barry's cry for help.

"Why is he shouting like that?" Martin said. "It's almost like . . .he's . . ."

Edward felt a flush of impatience hammer at his heart like a dwarf with a pick. "He's what? Spit it out, already."

"Oh Jesus," Martin said. "He's a kid again. He doesn't have that shit in his head anymore. He's cured. He's . . . no! That bastard's going to kill my son!"

"Please," Coppergate said. "Shouting is not necessary."

The image on the screen flashed back and forth, and although everything blurred together, Martin could see Samuel in the midst of it all. The hunter drew closer. "No! We can't let him! We have to stop him!"

William stood by his side and grabbed his arm. "Don't."

Martin yanked his arm away. “Don’t you dare touch me!”

William grabbed his arm again. “Stop! Pull yourself together! What are you, some kind of animal? There’s nothing to be done, old boy.”

Martin’s eyes widened, and tears streamed down his cheeks. His knees gave out, and William grabbed his other arm to hold him up.

When Martin spoke, he sounded as if his soul had been cored out. “He’s going to kill my son. My only son. We can’t have any more kids. Barry would have been my heir.” He drew in his breath and let it out in a moan. “Oh God. It’s not him. It’s *me*. *I* killed my son. Me.”

“No, you didn’t,” William said. “Just sit down.”

Martin sat down, but he couldn’t look at the screen. He buried his eyes into the palms of his hands. Elizabeth patted him on the back, but he didn’t notice.

~

“Barry Taylor?”

Barry looked to his left to see a middle-aged man with a handlebar mustache. He looked very familiar, like maybe he’d seen the guy recently. Nothing certain clicked, though.

But he saw the weapons, and he couldn’t help but feel fear clench down on his asshole. The stranger held a shotgun in his hands. There were holsters under his arms for handguns, and strapped to his waist were more guns. A large Bowie knife hung from his belt, along with a blackjack. A quiver full of rifles rested slung across his back.

Not him, Barry. Run.

Maybe this guy was a police officer. Only cops could have that many guns. Maybe he could help.

“That’s my name, sir. I’m lost, and I’m wondering if—“

Samuel paused, confused. “You’re lost?”

“I’m looking for my daddy. Could you help me?”

No, he can’t. He’s going to kill you.

“Help you?” Samuel’s brow furrowed. He flicked his eyes up and double checked the dossier Wingate’s people had given him. He lined up the picture next to the man who stood before him. All points of recognition matched. But this didn’t make sense. He checked his LiveStream feed and selected Barry’s. Sure enough, he could see himself through Barry’s eyes.

“You’re a police officer, right?” Barry asked.

Of course he isn’t. You have to leave. Now.

Samuel shook his head. “What the fuck is wrong with you, boy?”

Barry didn't think cops could use profanity. Worry wormed its way into the back of his neck. He thought maybe he should listen to the voice in his head.

For God's sake, Barry! Run! Now!

Barry suddenly wanted to pee very badly. He swallowed, hoping his nervousness would dissipate.

"Ah fuck it," Samuel said. He aimed the shotgun at Barry's face, and before the man could so much as flinch, he squeezed the trigger. Barry's head vanished in a hail of buckshot and a spray of blood. His jaw remained attached at the ragged stump of his throat, clinging like a barnacle.

~

"NO! GOD NO!"

~

The corpse fell to the ground and shuddered. Samuel fired into the chest, and all movement ceased.

"Fucking schizo," Samuel muttered. He reloaded the shotgun and slipped it into the quiver on his back. Pleased with himself for fulfilling his promise to Martin, he ambled into the night toward his next kill.

CHAPTER 10

1

Martin remained quiet when Edward started laughing about Randall burning Samuel's mansion to the ground. He didn't utter a word when William and Charles started betting over who would die next. He didn't open his mouth when the riot started. Since Barry died, Martin only stared at a blank wall, motionless except for the rise and fall of his chest.

Edward drank deeply from a fresh glass of whiskey. "You know, this has been a blast so far. People dead, a riot, some kind of underground movement. I like it. It's much more fun on this side of the game."

Coppergate smiled, mercifully not showing his teeth. "A gladiator who escaped death in the Coliseum, just so he could view the other gladiators in their tireless struggle with death." He laughed, but it sounded more like a hawk being choked.

Edward turned to George. "How do you like it?"

George cleared his throat as he removed his glasses to polish them with a handkerchief. "I . . . well, it seems kind of . . . you know. Cruel." He replaced his glasses upon his greasy nose, just above a bulbous, ripe pimple.

William's brow furrowed. "You don't like this?"

"Well, I didn't say that." George's glasses had already slid down, so he propped them back up with a finger. "I know it's wrong, but I kind of like it. It excites me. Weird."

"I think I understand," William said. "I remember the first time I saw someone die. I was much older than you at the time, of course. There is that guilty feeling at first, but there's a particular exhilaration that comes with watching a person breathe their last breath, especially if you just won money because of it."

"You're making it sound like a sexual experience." Elizabeth. She looked at William with a cold smile on her dead fish face.

William's well-mannered countenance flared up, and he looked at his shoes in exact imitation of his son's nervous tick. It was the only time father and son completely resembled one another. "I'm not ashamed to say that it turned me on. If it didn't, I wouldn't be here."

"I understand." The smile became more playful, and she licked her lips theatrically.

Edward and William glanced at her, as if they thought their sidelong eyefuls could escape Elizabeth's detection. George, on the other hand, watched her with eyes wide and pants bulging.

"That was rather gratuitous," Coppergate said. A gentle smile played at the corners of his mouth, almost making him look human. A kindly grandfather admonishing a little girl.

George finally looked away, and Elizabeth settled back into her chair. Edward felt the front of his own pants tighten a bit, and he thought it might be time for another line. "I'll be right back," he said.

No one noticed. He walked past Martin, who still stared into space, as if he'd fallen asleep and his body didn't know it yet.

Edward stepped out into the hallway and toward the bathroom. Once he'd locked the door, he withdrew the vial from his pocket and tapped out a rough line out next to the sink, which he then painstakingly perfected with the edge of his business card. He snorted quickly, twice, and he lost all sensation in his nose. His heart raced for just a moment and then settled to a light rush. He licked the counter and the card.

He looked down to see the lump at the front of his pants. It had wilted slightly, just enough to not jerk off. He thought he'd be all right now that the coke had taken his thoughts away from Elizabeth.

He washed his hands, and just as he toweled them dry, he heard a light rap at the door. When he opened it, he found himself face to face with Elizabeth.

"Huh?" he said.

She pushed past him into the bathroom, shutting the door. "Give me some. I'll be nice if you do."

Edward grunted. "Nice? I was hoping for something more substantial."

Elizabeth stood a little closer to him. "Let's get something straight between us."

"Yes. Let's." Edward grinned so hard his lips hurt.

She ignored his stupid comment. "Look, I can't have my guy deliver here. Wingate would flip out, and Richard would mark it down in my permanent record. Just give me a couple of bumps."

"How much do you like me?"

"That doesn't matter. What matters is how much I *could* like you." She reached to his crotch and kneaded the lump she found there. Instantly, he went rigid again, and she pulled his zipper down. She yanked him out and held him in her palm, running her fingers over his glans. Petting a kitten.

"Wow." The word felt lame in his mouth, but he couldn't find the time to hate himself for saying it. He could only marvel as she stroked him gently. How long had he wanted her like this? How many times had he been with a fuckslinger, pretending it was Elizabeth? He didn't think they made numbers that high.

His cock had only been in her hands for a half a minute before he lost it. Ropey strings of satisfaction pulsed out of him and all over her hands, up to her elbows.

"That was quick," Elizabeth said. She dropped his dick and went to the sink.

"You took me by surprise." He wiped his slick penis down with toilet paper. "I'll be better next time around."

"Next time? You just came on me. You owe me some coke."

Edward's jaw dropped, and his eyes burned. "But you hardly touched it!"

She shrugged. "Not my fault you have a hair trigger."

"You fucking—"

"You owe me, Bridges." Cold. No more kind and tender from her.

Someone knocked on the door. Gentle. Unobtrusive.

Edward and Elizabeth glared at each other. "Who's there?" he asked.

"Martin. You almost done?"

Elizabeth folded her hands into fists, and she looked down at his limp cock. She drew back, ready to strike his exposed member.

Fuck. He held out a vial to Elizabeth. "In a moment," he said to Martin.

She lined up two fat rails and sucked them back into her nasal cavity. She did this while Edward washed off his dick and hands before putting himself away. Finally, they composed themselves and opened the door.

"It's all you," Edward said. He walked past Martin, who didn't say a word. He didn't even acknowledge Elizabeth as she followed Edward out. Martin just shuffled into the bathroom and closed the door behind him.

When they got back to the observation room, they ordered more drinks from the butler. Coppergate spoke, and at first it seemed like he was talking to himself. Then, they realized he had accessed his mobile account.

"What's he doing?" Edward asked.

"Something quite interesting," Charles said. "I can't say that a contestant has tried this before."

"What?"

"It would seem that Samuel's son found the punk girl. They've teamed up, and they're tearing the east side apart. Richard is calling in some favors to get guards on our houses. The mob, I think."

"No shit?"

Charles's eyes gleamed with violent excitement. "He's asking for their best killers."

"Damn."

2

When Martin didn't return after a half an hour, Edward started to wonder. "Where the hell is he? He's been in the bathroom for a long time."

Elizabeth looked into his eyes, and he knew she thought the same thing he did. "Maybe he's sick," she said. But she didn't sound convinced.

"Maybe we should check it out."

Coppergate turned his wheelchair so he could look at Edward. "Do you think something is amiss?" His flat tone revealed none of his thoughts, but Edward knew Coppergate had the brains to come to the same conclusion.

"Yeah," Edward said.

"His son's death was rather unfortunate."

"No," Elizabeth said. "He didn't have any qualms about us using Barry in the game. He didn't feel a damned thing until Barry died. He's just being a hypocrite."

"It may be more complex than that," Coppergate said. "If you'll notice, Barry reverted to a sane perspective right at the very end. Martin wanted his schizophrenic son killed like a horse with a broken leg. But with his son cured? That's unfortunate. But it's also of his own making."

Edward couldn't take this babble anymore. He stood. "I'm going to check on him."

"We'll come with," Charles said.

3

Edward knocked on the bathroom door and received no answer. He looked around to his companions, all of whom had followed him, and none of them seemed very surprised. Just to make a show of it, he knocked again.

This time, when no one responded, Coppergate gave him a nod. Edward tried the knob, but it wouldn't move. "Key, Charles?"

"Hold on." They watched as Charles flicked his eyes back and forth, accessing his home security account, and the door clicked, opening slightly.

None of them entered the room, but they all leaned forward, hoping to get the best glimpse they could. Many people died over the course of the years during the game, but all of them had been contestants. One of their own dying? Unthinkable.

Martin lay sprawled on the floor, blood coagulating around him. The knife he'd used to slash his wrists and forearms rested on the rim of the sink, a solitary strand of red slithering down to the drain.

Charles moaned. "What a mess."

"Poor fool," Coppergate said.

Edward couldn't speak. Even though he knew what he'd see in here, he couldn't help but be surprised to actually see it.

"Clark!" Charles said. "Clean this up, please."

The butler eyed the mess, his nose wrinkled slightly. "And what of Mr. Taylor?"

Coppergate cut in. "Dispose of him. But discreetly. Try not to be too undignified with him. He may be colored, but he was still one of us."

"Certainly, sir."

"What about his wife?" William asked. "Should we notify her?"

"God no," Charles said. "I think it's not out of the question that Martin was overtaken by rioters tonight and tortured to death. It's far less scandalous than suicide. More dignified, I should think."

They went back to the observation room, letting Clark get to work. In his time working for the Wingate family, he'd cleaned up his share of corpses. Maybe not on a regular basis, but it happened enough so he didn't feel shocked or disgusted by this task. He doubted this would be his last body disposal, either.

CHAPTER 11

1

Wayne couldn't remember the last time he had felt this good. Clean water coursed down his body not from a fountain, nor from a fetid creek, but from an actual shower. He could even control the temperature. And soap! He'd forgotten about that luxury. He hadn't used it in years, and he marveled at how clean his own body smelled.

While he bathed, Stacy offered to clean his clothes. Part of him felt reluctant to let himself get into this situation, since he didn't fully trust her yet. It would be very easy for her to sneak up on him in the shower and stab him in the back. Then again, he realized that maybe it didn't matter. While he wanted to do good by taking on the rich fucks, he also knew that death stood around the corner, waiting for him to catch up.

She'd also given him a disposable razor, which he'd used to scrape his natty beard away. Now, as he stepped out of the shower and toweled himself dry, he saw the fogged-over mirror and wiped at it with his hand. For the first time in a while, he didn't mind looking at himself. The lesions stood out against his pale skin, sure, but he didn't bleed, and his clean and smooth face looked almost youthful. The skin where his beard had been looked as soft as baby flesh, and it almost gleamed, free from any lesions or marks. Flawless. The air felt a bit cooler on his face, but he felt so fresh and reinvigorated that he didn't care.

He wrapped the towel around his bony waist and stepped out of the bathroom into the front room. Stacy sat there, watching TV. She'd flipped through stations, bored out of her mind. The news kept talking about some kind of serial killer and a stupid riot, so she changed it to a late night sitcom called *Daddy Needs Love,* which turned her stomach. Finally, she found an *Eightball Gabe* marathon. Just then, she noticed Wayne.

She gave him a once over, fondling her chin. "You clean up pretty well. I'm sure without the, uh . . . you know. You'd look pretty hot."

"Bullshit," Wayne said. "But thanks. And thanks for not killing me in the shower."

She laughed. "No problem." Although she had given it some thought. It wouldn't have been all that difficult, and besides, how badly did she really need him? Sure, two heads were better than one, but she would only end up killing him later. Why bother waiting? But then she thought about all the dangers they might encounter. It would be a good idea to have an ally by her side, at least for the time being.

She nodded to his clothes, folded on a nearby table. He took them, shocked to see how nice they looked. They still had stains, including a really bad brown one that took up the entire seat of his pants, but they smelled good and felt crisp.

He jimmied his pants up under the towel, and when he'd buttoned and zipped up, he let the towel fall. Soon, he felt the cleanest and coziest he'd been in a while, fresh from the shower in clothes that no longer smelled like shit. He felt comfortable enough to sit on the couch next to Stacy. She turned the volume down and switched it to a news station, so she wouldn't be distracted.

"Now that we're all freshened up," she said, "what's our plan?"

"We have to find the others and convince them to join us," he said. "On our own, we don't stand a chance, but maybe if we can get them all on our side, we can do something to really hurt those rich bastards."

She felt uncomfortable with the idea, considering how she felt about the billion dollars. She had no doubt that the others probably thought along the same lines as her. They couldn't trust anyone else, even if they agreed to join them. But at the same time, she knew Wayne wouldn't like that thought. Instead, she tried the passive route. "What if they don't want to join us? What if . . . you know."

Wayne grimaced. "I thought of that, too. Maybe some of them would want to kill us. But I'm sure that most of them would want to join us. We're all in the same boat. We're being fucked with because the rich fucks think we're worthless to society and no one would miss us. They're using us. No one likes to be used."

"We should get weapons, just in case. Besides, even if they do join us, if we're going up against rich people, they're going to have guards. We'll probably need to fight our way through them first."

Wayne hadn't thought of that. He knew they'd maybe have a night watchman or something, but armed guards? "We'll have to worry about that later. For now, we need to find the others."

"How do we do that?"

"When I was out on the Sleaze Strip, I was looking for you and the other fuckslinger. We could probably find him here. Maybe that homeless guy and the punk chick, too. I don't know about the others, but it's a start."

She shook her head. "After what just happened down there? No, cops will be looking for us."

"Yeah, but who are we?"

She took his point, but it didn't matter much to her. "There were a lot of witnesses. They might not know you, but they sure know me. Besides, the sun's coming up. No one's going to be down there."

Wayne sighed, rubbing the bridge of his nose. "Well, you got any bright ideas?"

She turned away from him, tired already of trying to figure out what to do. The TV showed more footage of the riot, and she got ready to change the channel again when she saw . . . "Actually, I do."

"I'd love to hear it."

She grinned, pointing to the screen.

Wayne followed the path of her finger until he saw the riot. At first, he didn't get it. A bunch of punks tearing shit up on the east side. Then, he saw her, the punk girl, and she wore an eye patch. She bled from her nose, and she shouted something while beating a cop in riot gear with a baseball bat.

Behind her stood another familiar person: Randall. Two for one.

"Well, I'm pretty sure this is good evidence that they'd be on our side," Wayne said. "Let's go down there, have a chat with them."

She wanted to say no. If they waited long enough, maybe the riot would kill Skank and Randall, thus lightening their load to finding a mere three people. Still, they could make for valuable allies, just in case the others turned out to be shitty. She decided to stick with Wayne a while longer, but going into a riot? That sounded dangerous. "I don't have a car," she said.

"Shit." He rubbed his eyes. "We have to get down there. Do you know how to hotwire a car?"

"Afraid not."

"How about money for a cab?"

She did have that, but she didn't want to admit it. She had to pay her rent next week, and she barely had enough to cover that. Then again, she remembered she might not need to pay rent. Either she'd be dead by tomorrow, or she'd have a billion dollars. Fuck the rent, she could get a house. Outside the city.

"Yeah. I guess I do."

"Then call us a cab and let's go."

"Will a cab take us there? Remember, we want to go to a riot."

"We've got to try, and the longer we wait, the more likely that Skank and Randall will die."

"What if *we* die?" Stacy asked.

"Then it won't matter," Wayne said. "We're as good as dead, anyway."

Fuck. She wished he hadn't said that. They sat for a while, watching the news on mute, the awkward silence growing.

Finally, she sighed. "Fine. I'll call a cab. But remember: If anything goes wrong, it's your fault."

That sounded a bit too grim for Wayne, but he nodded his head in fatalistic acceptance.

She looked at him. No, this wouldn't do. She had to figure out a way to kill Wayne's idea, or to at least embarrass him enough to get him to back down. Then, she realized they had one more thing holding them back. "We're going to have to cover those blotches on your face. No cab's going to want to take you anywhere with those lesions. I'll have to use some makeup—"

"Wait, makeup? No fucking way."

"You want this to work, right?"

Wayne had never worn makeup in his life, and this close to death, he wouldn't start now. He'd had a few girlfriends who'd wanted to paint his face and make him look pretty, but he'd turned them all down. "Not on your fucking life."

2

A half-hour later, Stacy stepped back and admired her work. She'd effectively covered any sign of Wayne's illness. Not a single lesion managed to get through the layers she'd applied to his face. Yet . . . it just did not look natural. Anyone would look at him and know something was wrong.

She explained this and said, "Maybe you should go drag. With your face like that, you could pull it off. That might take attention away from the makeup."

"Fuck no. I let you do this to me. I'm drawing the line at cross-dressing."

"What, you afraid someone will think you're a faggot?"

That was exactly what Wayne feared. Not that he had anything against gays—at least not these days, post-David Nelson.

She saw the resignation on his face and sighed. "Fine. You're right, anyway. We'd have to wax your body hair, and that will take too much time."

"Just call the cab, all right?"

3

While Stacy looked up the number, Wayne looked at himself in the mirror. If a younger version of himself had seen the present version, he would have beaten the shit out of himself. His father had always told him to live by the Gregg Richards Rules of Life: Don't trust anyone with skin darker than yours; if a guy's sexuality is questionable, you should beat some sense into him; football comes before all other things; and don't be a fucking girl.

After everything Wayne had been through, he knew the first two rules were bullshit. He didn't know about the third one, but he still felt that a man should be a man.

Stacy caught him looking at his reflection. "You don't look so bad. Too bad I couldn't get you in a dress. You'd fucking dominate the Sleaze Strip."

"Let's just get the fuck out of here, all right?"

Stacy suppressed a laugh. "Cab's on the way. It should be here in ten minutes."

Wayne looked at himself again and wanted to scrub his face clean. He hoped they could get this shit over with as soon as possible so he could.

4

They got in the cab and saw the driver was an old woman, fat with a slight cinnamon scent to her. She almost looked like a grandmother. “Where to, sugar?”

Neither of them thought it would be a good idea to tell her to drive into the middle of a riot, so Stacy told her to take them to the corner of Bingham and East. Technically, it wasn’t the east side, but it would be close enough to the riot to suit their needs.

“That’s quite a ways,” the cabbie said. “No offense, but it don’t look like the two of you can pay me.”

“Oh yeah?” Stacy offered her left hand, ready for a scan to prove she did, indeed, have money in her account.

The cabbie looked at it for a moment, as if Stacy had offered her a rotten fish instead. She then looked to Wayne and lingered on his face, make-up and all. Somehow she seemed to find that even more distasteful.

“Fine. I’ll take you.” She punched in a few directions into her dash computer. The cab engaged with the track and eased down the street.

Wayne and Stacy relaxed in their seats. The cracked leather didn’t do much to support either of their bodies, but neither of them minded. It didn’t need to be luxurious, just so long as it got them where they needed to go.

“How much time do you think we have left?” Stacy asked.

Ahead of them, the sun slowly rose over the skyscrapers from the tourist part of the city. Stacy looked at the countdown and saw they had little more than eighteen hours to go.

They glided down the Sleaze Strip and saw no one on the street. The fuckslingers had left, and everything was calm before the stores would open their gated doors for business. Daylight had scoured away the iniquities of the night, and soon they would be replaced by dubious people wearing respectable masks. Just until sunset.

Wayne saw the cabbie kept looking into the rearview mirror at him, a look on her face like she needed to take a shit, but she had to hold it. He felt so self-conscious about the make-up that he wanted to rub his coat sleeve across his face.

When the cab reached the street it should have turned down, it continued going straight. They headed down the Sleaze Strip to the end, where not even the strongest sunbeams could dispel the unsavory life.

Wayne leaned forward. “You missed the turn off.”

"Yeah, I know. There's another way down here. Quicker."

Quicker? Wayne hadn't been down this way often, but he didn't think there was a shortcut back here. In fact, he thought they might be headed for a dead end.

The cabbie pulled over in front of an all night booze store. Henry's Likkker.

"What's going on?" Wayne asked.

The old woman turned around, and Wayne found himself looking down the twin barrels of a shotgun. "That's funny. I was thinking about asking you the same question, faggot."

Stacy spoke without thinking. "What the fuck, lady?"

The cabbie turned to Stacy. "You poor girl. What did this degenerate cum-sack do to you?"

"Degenerate?!" Wayne said.

The cabbie cocked both hammers, and Wayne instantly shut up. "A man who wears that much make up has got to be a faggot."

"I'm not a—"

The woman jabbed the shotgun against his chest, and he flew back into his seat. "Shut up, faggot." She turned back to Stacy. "Well? Did he rape you?"

Stacy thought it wouldn't be prudent to mention that gay men weren't very likely to rape women, but something else occurred to her. If the cabbie killed Wayne, it would make things easier. She could probably find Randall and Skank pretty well and off them in the midst of the riot. But she thought she might not be smart enough to find the others.

"No," she said. "That's ridiculous. He's my friend."

The old woman's eyes clouded. "Poor girl. Brainwashed her, huh? What kind of deviant sex shit did you make her do, huh?"

Wayne didn't dare speak.

The cabbie honked the horn quickly, keeping her eyes and shotgun on Wayne. Soon, a large, bald man with tattoos and a wife-beater stepped out of the store. It took a moment for Wayne to recognize the tattoos, and he suddenly knew why there were three K's in Henry's Likkker.

"What's going on, Ma?" Henry asked.

"Look at this sorry sackashit I got. This faggot did all kinds of sex shit to this poor girl."

"That so?" Henry leaned into the window, taking a close look at Wayne, his jaws flexing as if he were chewing gum. "What'd you do, faggot?"

"Nothing," Wayne said. "I've done nothing."

"How about it, honey?" Henry touched Stacy's chin, and she violently drew her head back from him.

"She won't talk," the cabbie said. "Brainwashed."

Henry grunted. "Thought so. Just like the rest of the world, right Ma? They ain't gonna' live to take our rights and Christmas away. Heh." He spat on the ground. "You know what we do to monsters like you?"

Wayne didn't answer.

This time, Henry shouted. "I said, do you know what we do to faggots around here?!"

Wayne cringed. "No."

"Well, you're gonna' find out." He turned to the cabbie. "Let's get 'em into the store, Ma."

"You heard my son. Out of the cab." She motioned with the shotgun.

5

Henry led them to the back room of the liquor store, where he made Wayne strip down before being tied to a chair. Ma took Stacy aside, but she didn't point the shotgun at her. Still, Stacy felt the implied threat and didn't make any sudden moves.

"Be right back," Henry said. He headed for the bathroom, which was where he'd been going when his mother honked the horn. He unbuckled his pants and pushed them down to his knees, revealing a small nub of a dick without a glans. Carefully, he pinched it between his thumb and forefinger and leaned forward so he could aim. The stream that came out sprayed all over the bowl. He groaned as he leaned over more, shortening the length from his disfigured member to the toilet.

According to his mother, the rabbi who had circumcised him accidentally cut off too much. It made sense to him that a fucking Jew would cut most of his cock off. He thought about all the attempts over the course of history to wipe them off the face of the earth, and he wished they'd succeeded. If they had, he wouldn't have this mess to deal with.

His father killed the rabbi, and he got sent to prison for life because of it. That didn't last long, though. His mother told him a nigger had knifed his father in the joint. A hero! Getting killed in prison by a goddammed spear-chucker! Henry didn't know what this world was coming to, but he knew what to do about it.

He tore away some toilet paper and dabbed the end of his stub before he pulled up his pants and went out to check on his prisoner. The woman would have to go to some meetings with the rest of his chapter of the KKK in order to return her mind to the right way of thinking, but the fag? Henry knew what to do with their sort.

He stood in front of Wayne. "You know what comes next?"

Wayne couldn't speak. Fear vibrated in his guts so badly that he couldn't force any words out. He could only shake his head, trembling. Being naked didn't help, either. He wanted to fold in on himself to protect his most tender bits.

Henry produced a pocket knife and opened it. "I'm going to make you a woman, just like you want."

Wayne's eyes went to the blade like magnets. He felt himself shrivel slightly, and he struggled against his bonds, trying to break free.

Henry knelt down before Wayne's legs, gazing at what used to be an impressive cock. Seven inches hung down over the edge of the chair's seat, but lesions dotted the shaft. One on the end of his penis bled slightly.

Henry grimaced. "What the fuck is this shit?"

Wayne felt something rumble deep in his gut. Suddenly, he saw a way out of this, and he felt relief flood his brain. "I have the Red Death. If you get my blood on you, you'll get it, too. You'll be just like me." An exaggeration, of course, but one ignorant assholes could easily buy.

Gurgling in his guts. Something burned inside of him, and he knew for sure what would happen next.

"Ma, you hear of this shit? He telling the truth?"

"Yeah, I heard of it," she said.

Wayne felt himself loosening up. Any second now, and he wouldn't be able to control himself.

Henry sighed. "I guess that's out." He put his hands on his knees, on the verge of straightening out, when Wayne let go with everything he had. He heard a loud ripping and sputtering sound, and Henry's face turned brown and red in an instant. Shit dripped down Wayne's legs and pooled on the chair around his ass. It also caked Henry's face and eyes and his open mouth.

"Fuck!" Henry rubbed at his eyes, spitting and gagging. "What the fuck?!"

Wayne stared at the blood-stained shit that covered Henry from his bald head to his belt and couldn't believe he'd just done that.

Stacy didn't have time to be sick. Instead, she saw her chance. She pulled the gun from the band of her jeans and pistol-whipped the cabbie. "Get down, bitch!"

The old woman saw it coming at the last second, and although she tried to duck the blow, it still caught her on the shoulder. She didn't go down, but she spun slightly. It took her a moment to right herself, and she brought the shotgun up with every intention of blasting Stacy to pieces.

Stacy quickly recovered and fired twice, sending both bullets into the cabbie's chest, one of them directly into her heart. Blood oozed from her chest as she fell back into a file cabinet, knocking it over. Still, she stood on her feet with a dazed look on her face.

Stacy fired a third time, and the cabbie hacked up blood before she fell to the floor, the shotgun clattering away from her grip. It had been Stacy's second kill, and she thought back to the old guy, Wayne's friend. She remembered how she'd felt when she realized she'd snuffed someone's life out, but this time? She didn't feel any remorse at all.

"Ma!" Henry shouted. His eyes squinted shut against the shit on his face, and he lashed out with his knife, trying desperately to find Stacy.

She took careful aim at Henry's face and fired twice. The skinhead hit the floor without so much as a grunt.

Wayne stared at her with wide eyes, unbelieving. Again, the thought occurred to him that she could kill him without any compunction, and he wondered again if he should be teamed up with her. "Jesus Christ. You're too good at this kind of thing."

"They had it coming," Stacy said. "By the way, that was the most disgusting thing I have ever seen. Couldn't you think of anything better than shitting on him?"

"I wasn't thinking. It just happened. Sorry, all right?" But he didn't feel very sorry. He wanted to hurt her in some way, and being disgusted seemed to do it. He thought about Old Shit and reminded himself that he needed her around. Besides, hadn't she just saved his life? "I wish we didn't have to kill them, though."

She rolled her eyes. "Please. That guy wanted to cut your dick off. They would have killed you. Us. But instead, I killed them. They were assholes. End of story." She took Henry's knife and cut Wayne's bonds. She put the blade in her pocket, since they could use all the weapons they could find. "At least we have their shit now. You know how to program a cab?"

Wayne rubbed his wrists. "Yeah. Well, I used to. I'm sure nothing's changed over the last few years."

As he got dressed, Stacy took the old woman's shotgun and checked to see if it was loaded. Satisfied, she looked for more ammo in the cabbie's purse, and then her pockets. Nothing. She only had one bullet left in the pistol and an extra clip, so it would have been nice to have more ammo for the shotgun.

Wayne went to the bathroom to wash himself off in the sink. He didn't have much to go on, but even more than the shit clinging to the inside of his thighs, he wanted to get rid of the make up. If he hadn't been wearing it, they wouldn't have gotten into this mess.

When they both were ready, they checked on the cab. Locked. "Fuck," Wayne said.

Stacy looked at the thumb plate that would open the car. "I'll be right back."

"Where—" But Wayne stopped himself. He knew the answer, but he didn't want to hear it.

Stacy came back with the cabbie's severed thumb. She pressed it against the plate, and the door opened up. She slid inside, but Wayne stared down at her.

"Well?" she said. "Coming?"

He nodded his head and got in the back. He wanted to say more, but he couldn't bring himself to get into another argument.

Stacy pressed the thumb against the plate by the dash computer, and the cab roared to life. "Now what do I do?"

Wayne told her how to use the touch-screen to program their destination, but when she entered it in, the system wailed. An alert appeared. "What's it say?" he asked.

"It's about the riot. It's warning us not to drive there."

"There's got to be a bypass."

"Uh . . ." She stared at the screen for a moment, then pushed her finger down on it. The warning disappeared, and she tapped the screen again. The cab moved down the street with purpose.

"Thank Christ," Wayne said. "I don't know how to rewire this thing. That was lucky."

She shrugged, still not happy with driving into a riot. Still, she felt better about having extra firepower with her. By the time they reached the end of the block, she'd completely forgotten about killing Henry and his ma.

CHAPTER 12

1

Skank and Necro Cock spent the hour drinking beer and listening to Shakespeare on Acid's mellow, half-hour song, "Dead Friends," in honor of Nutsack. They remained silent, Skank lost in her memories and Necro trying to come up with a plan. When the song ended, Skank wordlessly pressed the reverse button, and the song began again.

Necro stood and went to a blank wall, one he'd been saving for a punk mural he wanted to buy. Taking up a marker, he began to draw some kind of design. Skank watched without questioning him, and soon she recognized it as a map of the rich neighborhood on the east side.

Just before "Dead Friends" ended again, their fellow soldiers filtered back in. Most arrived with baseball bats and chains, some had knives, and a couple even had handguns. C arrived with a lighter and fluid.

"What the hell's that going to accomplish?" Necro asked.

"I'll fill my mouth with fluid," C said, "light up, and I'll be able to spit flames."

"You . . . you're just going to burn your face off. Besides, that's not a very quick weapon. You have to take the time to fill your mouth first, and by then, someone will probably plug you in the guts with a bullet. It sounds dangerous and stupid."

"Nah, I saw it in a movie. It'll be cool."

Necro Cock rolled his eyes, disgusted. Then, he went to his room and came back with a baseball bat for Skank and a shotgun for himself.

When everyone arrived, Necro and Skank looked over the crowd, marveling at how many had showed up. There had to be a hundred people packed into his loft, elbow to asshole, raring for a fight. They had themselves a regular army.

"All right, everyone, listen up!" Necro shouted. When the room quieted down, he continued. "I hope you all have means of transportation. My car can only fit four, maybe five guys in it." They all laughed, and even Necro Cock had to crack a smile. "All joking aside, we do have a long ride ahead of us. Those of you who don't have a ride need to team up with someone who does."

"What's the plan?" This from a forty-year-old punk named Pisser.

Necro pointed at his map. "This is the east side. Where all the rich people live, right?" Everyone made a sound of agreement, or disgust. A few people spat. "By now, you all know what these rich fucks did to Skank and Nutsack. We don't know who, specifically, but goddammit, we're going to find out. We're going to scour the entire east side until we find the right fucks."

"That could take forever," F, from FUCK, said. "There's a lot of us, sure, but not enough. The riot pigs'll toast us within a half an hour."

"I know. That's why we're going to split into two teams. My team will start in the northeast side while Skank's team will start in the southeast side. That way, the swine will have to spread themselves thinner, and we'll last longer. We'll also cover more ground."

"I don't know, man," C said. "This sounds like a suicide mission. I'm not down for that."

"No, this is about revenge for one of our fallen."

"Then how are we going to get out of this one? All the pigs gotta' do is wait for us to come together in the middle and surround us. Then we'll be fucked."

"First of all, the pigs can't stand by and let us torch the neighborhood until we're in a vulnerable position," Necro said. "Secondly, you're assuming we'll even make it to the middle. I'm sure we'll find the right fucks before then."

"And how will we find them?" F asked. "Knock on every door? 'Hello? Are you the Bad Rich People? No? Oh, thank you. Goodnight.'" A few others laughed, but most kept their peace.

"Of course not," Necro said. "We're going to crash every mansion. Skank already described what we're looking for, so when we find it, we'll know. But we have to be quick about it."

"I don't know," F said. "This sounds fucked."

"It's the best plan we have. If you want out, then get the fuck out."

F didn't say anything more after that.

Necro Cock motioned to the left side of the room. "All of you are on my team. The rest of you are on Skank's. My team will take our cars and drive up to the north here." He indicated the location on the map. "There's a parking lot up there, from which we can walk the two blocks to the rich neighborhood—"

"In case you haven't noticed," C said, "it'll be dawn soon. Don't you think we'll look a little strange? A bunch of heavily armed punks walking toward the rich neighborhood?"

Necro grimaced at that. He didn't like it anymore than C did, but they had no choice. "It's the best we can do."

C shrugged. "Just asking."

Necro Cock nodded and turned back to the map. He indicated the bottom. "Skank's team will drive to the parking lot of the old theater here. They will then walk the block north to the rich neighborhood. From that point—"

"Hold on, Necro." From Kelly, a young man who dressed without the pretense of the rest of the punks. He wore a t-shirt and jeans, both without a single tear or rip. At first, the rest of the group, aside from Necro Cock, had despised him, taking him for a square slumming it. But over the years, they discovered Kelly had a nasty bend to him. Sometimes, without provocation, he would beat the shit out of someone or something. He never warned anyone, and this habit endeared him to the others.

"What is it?" Necro Cock asked.

"That's a gated community there. They got guards. Armed guards. It'd be a bitch getting in there. If those guards saw us, and I'll bet they would, they'd be on the radio to the real cops, and then they'll start shooting."

"There's only townhouses in there," Skank said. "The place I was in was a fucking mansion."

"Okay, then," Necro said. "Forget the gated community. Just go for the mansions."

"Wait, how'd she know she was in a mansion?" F asked. "She only told us about the two rooms."

"Townhouses aren't that big," Skank said. "They wouldn't be able to build a place like that in a townhouse."

"What about the fences around the mansions?" C asked. "And what if they have dogs?"

"You've got weapons," Necro said. "As for the fences, are you telling me that you people can't climb a fucking fence if it came to it?"

"Well, they could be electrified," C said. He didn't look at Necro when he said it.

Necro said, "Will someone please hit him?"

"What? It's a reasonable fear."

Pisser advanced on C, his fist pulled back, but Necro Cock held up a hand. "No, don't. We can't afford to fight each other right now. There won't be any electric fucking fences, okay?"

C didn't respond.

Necro Cock continued. "We'll split our two groups into a bunch of groups of five or ten, whatever it takes. Each of those groups will take a different street. Everyone clear?"

"Will that be enough?" Kelly asked.

"It's going to have to be. We'll go down our assigned streets, and we'll storm every mansion we find until we get the rich fucks who started this. Any questions?"

"Yeah," C said. "When this is all done, or if the bacon gets to be too hot, how do we escape?"

"Any way you can. I don't know about the rest of you, but Nutsack was my best friend. My fucking brother. I've known him since we were still shitting our pants. I'm going all the way. Either I get the bastards that killed my brother, or I die. I hope you're all with me."

"Fuck yeah!" Skank yelled.

When the crowd shouted their assent, Necro Cock smiled. "Then let's fucking go!"

2

The Midas Theater had been standing at the corner of Clinton and East since it had been built in 1930. In its glory days, it had been a palace of a theater, complete with sweeping, gold-embroidered velvet curtains, bright plush chairs and an orchestra pit. They played all the classics when they were first run, from *Dracula* to *East of Eden*. Then, in 1956, the theater caught fire because a drunk patron dropped a cigarette, and while the firefighters managed to save most of the building, the ceiling collapsed, and eighty-four people died that night. So did the theater's relationship with what most considered decent movies.

They rebuilt the Midas in 1957, based on the original blueprints, but the owners nearly went bankrupt in the process. They sold the place in 1960 to a young man who started showing monster movies instead. The theater's original clientele stopped attending out of disgust, but a new crop of customers came pouring in, eager for the next schlock fest. The Midas did well until the first years of the 21st Century, when everyone turned to the 'net for their cult classics. The cost of keeping up the utilities suddenly wasn't worth staying open, and the bright young man of 1960 shot himself in the projectionist booth while watching one of his favorite movies.

After that, the city boarded the Midas up. Every once in a while, the council talked about razing the building, or maybe turning it into a historic site, but nothing ever came of it. Before long, it lay fallow and forgotten by all except the teens who liked to hang out there, smoking, drinking and fucking.

Skank had many fond memories of the place, most involving Nutsack. She tried to hold back her tears as she parked the Nutmobile in the spot they usually took in the old days. She didn't want anyone else riding with her, since she still had Nutsack in the car. He'd gone stiff and started to smell, but she wanted to be in his presence, at least for a little while longer.

She watched as the others parked around her. Gently, she reached over to the passenger seat and kissed Nutsack's cheek. "We've almost got the bastards."

She got out, and the other punks gathered around her. Pisser stood next to her, holding a lead pipe taped up on one end. The others held their weapons at the ready, and many of them popped Berserker pills. Usually, they reserved them for the mosh pit, but now, they waited for it to puff out their muscles and add more mass to their bodies. Others who had swapped some of their body parts in the name of body modification, strapped on cybernetic limbs to replace what they'd lost. Some of them bore blades in them, others had projectiles. One of them had a flamethrower built into his arm. They all bristled for action.

"You all ready?" she asked them.

"Yeah!" they all shouted.

"Let's fuckin' do this," Pisser said. He grinned through his scraggly beard.

"All right," Skank said. "We'll split into teams here." She went down the rows of them, giving them each a number, as if they were back in high school gym, trying to figure out who would be on which team. In the end, there were six teams of ten and one team of seven, which included Pisser, C and herself.

"As we walk down East Street, I'll point each team to a block. Those on the east, follow your streets down to the lake, crashing houses as you go. Head north on Lake Street, crashing more houses until you meet some of Necro's boys, then all of you head back west.

"Those on the west," she continued, "follow your streets to Maple, and then head north. When you see Necro's boys, head back east. We'll all meet up on East and Greenspan and figure things out from there. Got it?"

The crowd agreed.

"Let's go."

3

Get in the zone!
Grunt and moan!
Butt-fuck my clone!

Skank turned up Nutsack's favorite song and put it on repeat. It seemed only right.

She and her team walked calmly down East Street. As they went, Skank pointed the way for the sub-teams. Soon, the sounds of panic and violence filled the air around her. Screams and gunshots prevailed, and soon, she turned and saw flames behind her.

Down to the last three sub-teams. They could now hear sirens approaching from the west. "Things are in full swing," she told the others. "Be careful."

When she'd sent the last sub-team off, Skank turned to her remaining friends. "We're going down this way. Starting with this place."

They headed for the enormous mansion on the corner of East and Jobs, eager to bust down the gates. They hammered at the lock for a while, but it only tired them out.

"Fuck it," Skank said. "We'll climb over. Gimme a lift."

Pisser, despite his age, had the stoutest, strongest body of the bunch. He helped everyone over before jumping up and pulling himself to the top. The spikes that crowned the gate in an iron diadem cut his hands and ripped his jeans, but it didn't seem to bother him.

No one stopped their rush toward the mansion. Upon arrival, C and a little smelly guy everyone called Windy Winston beat the door down. The entire team rushed down the corridors, howling and destroying as they went, but it soon became evident that they were in the wrong place. C wanted to stay behind and smash the place Just Because, and Skank had to drag him out so they could move on to the next mansion.

Outside, Pisser helped everyone over once again, and just as he dropped down to the other side, they saw flashing red and blue lights. Cruisers off the track squealed down the street, and cops jumped out of the cars, guns aimed and ready to kick ass.

"It's about fuckin' time!" C shouted. He filled his mouth with fluid, and produced his lighter, ready to rock and roll.

The officers shouted their usual litany of "Freeze!" and "Drop it!" They stood behind their open car doors, guns pointing out.

C lit up and spit with all his might through the flame. A bright burst of fire sprayed forward, causing the cops to cringe despite the fact that C didn't have the distance. One of the cruisers caught fire, and one of the officers slapped at it with his jacket.

C, on the other hand, screamed when his hand blazed to life. He waved it around, trying to put it out, but the flames quickly moved to his spiky hair.

"Help!" he shrieked.

The cops stood and stared in awe, and one of them smiled, holding back a laugh.

Skank saw that smile and rage billowed out of her head in a smoky cloud. She rushed forward and beat the cop's face in with the baseball bat. He yelped and fell to the ground, holding his flattened nose, blood streaming between his fingers. He gagged, rolling around, completely forgetting about his surroundings.

Skank hit him again and again. Pisser slipped in and picked up the cop's gun. Before the others could do anything, he'd shot one of them.

And so began what would eventually be known as the East End Riot of 2200.

4

Skank noticed the limo and the news helicopter at the same time. It had been a half an hour since the riot started, maybe more, and since news traveled fast, the battle had grown. Not only had the riot police shown up, but many thrifty entrepreneurs had also arrived, eager to join in the fighting and looting. These new looters brought better weapons with them, which had really spiced things up.

Sadly, by then the original punks had been whittled down a bit. Skank and her team had left C behind, a smoldering crisp where his head should be.

Skank saw the limo and wondered who the hell would drive into a riot in such style. She thought about it too long; she didn't even see the cop approaching. He slugged her in the face with his gloved fist. Pain lanced through her cheek as she fell, scraping her elbows on the pavement. The cop followed up with a kick to the ribs, knocking her wind out with his jackboots.

"Like that, bitch?" the cop said. He drew his weapon, but he didn't get the chance to use it. A loud *crack!* sounded, and the cop felt a very brief stabbing in his throat. He didn't feel much after that. The bullet had blown his neck out so badly that his head rolled back, no longer attached at the spine. His body quivered before dropping to its knees and falling next to Skank.

Randall looked down at the man he'd just shot. Never in his life had he had to kill anyone, and it had happened so quickly. It couldn't be real. This had to be some kind of dream. Shock set in, and he suddenly didn't want to play the game anymore.

Then, he saw a cop about a block away, stomping a punk's head over and over again, blood sticking to his boot like paste.

No. He had to be heartless. He had to kill his father, and he wouldn't be able to do that if he pussied out now. He stepped toward the person he'd just saved and offered his hand to her. "Hello, Skank. Fancy meeting you here."

She blinked her vision clear, and when she saw Randall, she felt anger flare in her heart once again. Now she'd never get to avenge Nutsack's death. She could only hope that her friends succeeded in getting back at everyone else.

And then she realized that Randall didn't point a gun at her. Instead, his hand was empty, waiting to help her.

She grabbed his hand, and he whisked her to her feet. Then, she touched her cheek to see how bad it hurt. It throbbed at her touch, but nothing felt broken. "What are you doing here?"

"Looking for you, actually," Randall said. "Nice riot you have going here. How'd you get this crowd together?"

"They're friends," Skank said, "and they'll kick your ass if you kill me."

Randall held both hands up, the gun now stowed in his pocket. "No worries here, Skank. If I were going to kill you, I'd have let the cop do it for me. I'm here to help you."

Skank offered him a lopsided grin. "Would you excuse me for a moment?"

Randall nodded.

Skank picked up her bat and started pounding on the headless body of the cop with all her might, a stream of expletives pouring Biblically from her mouth like blood from her target's ragged neck wound.

"Looks like we're being watched," Randall said. He pointed up to the news helicopter. "If Mom was still alive, I'd wave."

Skank's arms grew tired, so she stopped beating the dead cop. She took a second to gather her wits—and breath—before she looked up at the chopper. "I guess you know what I'm doing, then."

"Yeah. Attacking the rich neighborhood in the hopes that you'll find the right mansion. Kind of a silly plan."

"Why?" Skank's voice took on a sharp tone.

"Because that's like killing everyone in an apartment complex because a pedophile might live there. Besides, the cards are stacked against you. If I hadn't come along, you would have eventually lost to the riot police."

"And what the fuck makes you so special?"

"This." He pulled his father's address book out of his pocket.

"What is it?"

Randall then realized that Skank had probably never seen a physical book before. "This contains all of Dad's friends and business associates. I've narrowed the possibilities down to a few places. We can take care of this much easier my way. Quicker, too."

"Possibilities?" Skank asked.

"My father's place is out. I burned it down."

"Fuckin' awesome."

Randall laughed. "Yeah. Anyway, there are still a bunch more to choose from. Edward Bridges, Richard Coppergate, Elizabeth Drake, William O'Neill, Martin Taylor, and Charles Wingate. Those names have stars next to them in the book. Shall we gather your group and try them alphabetically?"

"Too late. There's too many of us for that, and we're all over the place. We'll need—"

"Look out." Randall stepped around her and calmly shot an approaching officer. The cop had his nightstick out, ready to give Skank a wood shampoo. Holy shit, he couldn't believe he'd done that. Like something out of the movies. Part of him thought he should be horrified with himself, but at the same time, he also hoped he looked kind of cool while doing it.

"Thanks," Skank said.

"No problem. I've got my limo here. Let's see how many people we can gather in there. I probably have room for six, maybe seven."

"Including us?"

"Unfortunately. Tell me about your set up."

Skank briefly told Randall their plan, and after, he flipped through the address book. "That narrows it down a bit. Bridges lives south of here, so your first sub-team probably trashed his place already."

~

"What the fuck did he just say?" Edward asked.

Coppergate offered one of his weird smiles. "I believe he said that your mansion has been, to use the parlance, 'trashed.'"

"Goddammit, Richard. I heard what he said."

Coppergate fingered one of his teeth. "Temper, young Edward."

The blood fell from Edward's face as he realized that not only had he cursed, he'd also taken the name of the Lord in vain.

He turned away from Coppergate and accessed his mobile account. He dialed 911, hoping to get someone down to save his home.

~

"Also, your friend Necro Cock must have gotten O'Neill's place. He's way north of here, the first mansion."

~

William grew pale, and he accessed his own mobile account. He wondered if he should call the authorities first, or home, to see if his wife had made it out.

George couldn't breathe from the shock. Whoever had trashed their place probably found the stash of dirty pictures he'd drawn of the girl in his

English class. They might have even read his diary, where he wrote about some of his darkest sexual fantasies. They might have even found his hidden porn files in the closet. His face turned red at the thought.

~

"That leaves Coppergate, Drake, Taylor and Wingate," Randall said. "Drake's place is the closest, then Taylor's, then Wingate's. Shall we?"

"Fuck yeah."

"Okay, then we'll pick up some of your guys and then drive around to the others to tell them their new destinations. We'll take one for ourselves. Which one do you want?"

"I like the sound of Coppergate," Skank said. "It sounds really rich. Like that building downtown."

"That one's out of our way. Necro Cock's got a better shot at it. I think we should try something closer. Tell you what, since we're the only one with a car, let's give Drake and Taylor to the rest of these guys. We'll take the farthest that's still on the southeast side. Wingate's place."

~

"Thank Christ your guards showed up," Wingate said. "They're the best, right?"

"Aside from the ones I have guarding my own home," Coppergate said.

"That will definitely suit me."

Coppergate steepled his decrepit fingers together. "I think things are about to become very interesting."

~

"Wingate." Skank tasted the word, rubbing it against the roof of her mouth. "I like that, too. It sounds English."

She took a gun from the fallen, headless officer, and Randall laid down some cover fire for the surviving members of her team to make it to the limo. All that remained were four bashed and bloody punks, one of whom was Pisser. Blood stained his beard, running from his mouth, dotted with bits of his chipped teeth.

"I'm all right," he said. Slobber drooled down his chin. "They were dentures, anyway."

CHAPTER 13

1

Steve finished his story, and Jack leaned back in his chair, thinking. Finally, he said, "I have an idea. It might take a while, but I think I can get into your head and access your original LiveStream."

"Uh, okay. That sounds kind of dangerous."

"It's not. Just don't fight me, and you should be good."

Steve didn't like the sound of that. Still, Jimmy trusted this guy, and they didn't have many options. They had to go ahead with this.

"You want a trank?" Jack asked. "It'll just put you out for an hour, and I'll be able to pick through your mind a lot quicker."

That sounded like an excellent idea, but Steve knew he couldn't risk being sedated. It would be better to suffer through it and still be conscious. "I'll be all right."

"Okay." Jack sifted through a drawer until he came out with a pill bottle. He popped one and sat down next to Steve.

"What was that?"

"It's going to help me leave my body and enter my wifi connection," Jack said. "From there, I'll be able to get into your head and take a look at things. I'm pretty sure I can clean up the images from your LiveStream, and if I can do that, we'll at least know what we're dealing with."

Steve blinked, unable to understand what Jack had just told him. He'd been on the force for many years, and he knew all sorts of fucked up things people could do on drugs, but this one? He couldn't get his head around it.

Jack must have seen his confusion. "Look, just don't think about it. You'll probably feel me rooting around in there, and your natural instinct will be to push me out. I'm just asking that you don't fight me once I'm in, okay?"

"I don't think I'd know how to fight you," Steve said.

"You will. Like I said, instinct."

Steve cleared his throat. "Okay, then. I'll do my best."

"Just relax. Don't think about anything, if you can help it."

"No problem." Except as soon as Jack had said not to think of anything, Steve couldn't help but think about everything. Clearing his mind became impossible, especially when he thought of a stranger rummaging around in his head. He didn't like the idea of someone having access to his most intimate memories. He also felt repulsed by the idea that Jack might stumble upon memories of him jerking off or picking his nose and wiping his findings under the car seat.

Jack closed his eyes and settled back into his chair. The drug took hold of him, and he could feel himself rising from his dissolving body, and he suddenly became aware of all the energy flowing around him. Information streams zipped by him as he felt himself getting sucked into his wifi connection. Then, he had to force himself to take direction. He didn't want to go to the virtual city, so he pushed himself toward Steve, hoping to be caught up in the web of Steve's 'net access.

2

Steve watched Jack, expecting some kind of rush to overcome himself. Nothing happened. He glanced over to Jimmy. "What now?"

Jimmy shrugged. "We wait."

"I'm not feeling anything. Are you sure this is going to work?"

"Jack's the best. Of course it will work." Jimmy leaned back and lit up a cigarette, blowing SyntheSmoke up at the ceiling, where the vents sucked it away to be recycled somewhere into energy for Jack's generator. Jimmy could never figure out how it worked, but it sure seemed to.

"I don't know about you, but I could sure use a drink," Steve said. "Jack have any here?"

"Sure. I'm sure he won't mind." Jimmy stood and started looking for Jack's whiskey.

Steve felt slightly more relieved, knowing that booze would help him ease into his situation. He felt out of place in Jack's basement. Nothing would make him happier than relaxing at Lenny's, worrying only about his own money problems, not this crazy game. He—

Something tickled at his frontal lobe, but when he touched his forehead to soothe it, he couldn't reach it. It irritated him, like whenever he got an itch behind his kneecap. He wanted nothing more than to eradicate the sensation when he remembered what probably caused it. He forced himself to stay calm and let Jack do his work.

3

As soon as Jack's consciousness came close enough to Steve's system, he felt himself tugged in, kind of like being too close to a black hole. A rush of memories vied for his attention, but he pushed them away because he didn't want what the brain had to offer. He needed the artificial wiring instead.

A wall of flame erupted from Steve's mind, almost too hot to bear. Jack felt the heat push him back, and he flinched. He cursed to himself and forced a message out to Steve: *Stop fighting me. Let me do my work.*

The flames drew back instantly and snuffed out. Though telepathy at this point remained impossible, Jack felt certain that the power of suggestion could hold sway over a target. Maybe someday, he could actually plant instructions in someone's head—and what a glorious day that would be!—but for now, that day was far off.

He accessed Steve's social media and found most of it locked off. Whoever had done this knew what the fuck they were doing. Then again, these rich fucks could certainly afford the best. Jack gritted with no teeth and tried to force his way through the locks.

It took a lot of effort, but Jack also knew what the fuck he was doing. Instead of trying to go through the barriers, he sought out the backdoor and hacked his way through that. Once in, he started filtering through Steve's social media, looking for the LiveStream. It didn't take him long to find the part he needed: the observation room.

A lot had been cut out of the stream, or obscured, but Jack could fix the edits with no problem. He'd had a lot of experience repairing redacted government files, and finding the missing pieces wasn't a problem.

Jack cleaned up the faces behind the glass, and he recognized a lot of them. Jimmy had been right about most of them. There they were: Richard Coppergate, Charles Wingate, Elizabeth Drake and Edward Bridges. He worked on the other faces and discovered that William O'Neill and his son George were also there. Odd. Kids weren't usually involved. Unless this was Bring Your Kid to Murder Day.

Coppergate's assistant proved to be a bit more difficult to figure out, but after a while, Jack found her. Cynthia Baker. Not a big name. No record. No connections. No military background. Just a person.

Then, Samuel Maxwell Barnabas, III, came through clearly. Jack should have known. He'd seen Barnabas on the news a lot, and he'd made quite a character out of himself. An intense hunter like that? Why *wouldn't* he be involved?

The one that surprised him most, however, was Martin Taylor. As far as Jack knew, Taylor had a ton of money, but he kept to himself. No showboating like Barnabas. No cutthroat dealings like Coppergate. No society gatherings like O'Neill. No extravagant philanthropy like Wingate. No rags-to-riches story like Bridges. Hell, he didn't even have sex appeal, like Drake. How could someone so bland be involved in this game?

Okay, now he had to find out everything he could on the contestants. He used the info Steve had given him on what he could remember first, knocking the easy ones out of the park. It took him a moment to work through the others, and when he finished, he just couldn't believe it. These savages hadn't just picked anyone this year; two of them had thrown their own sons into the mix. Randall Marsh was really Samuel Maxwell Barnabas, IV, and then there was poor, insane Barry Taylor.

Jack noted with some amusement that Martin still thought Barry was institutionalized. He'd definitely been paying the bills, but Barry had been out on the streets for quite some time. Some loony bins just didn't have scruples.

The toughest one to find out about was Toby James Munger. He got a date of birth, a brief description, some insignificant details about his early life and not much else. The guy didn't even have much of a social media network. Sure, he had the same implants everyone else did, but he didn't seem to use them. In this day and age, everyone absolutely had to share every waking moment of their lives with anyone who might be watching them. The idea pervaded society so much that people just didn't pay attention to their own LiveStreams; they just let them go. Toby never even turned his on. That implied a couple of things: either he had no interest in sharing himself with the world, or he had something to hide.

Given the choice between the two, Jack always suspected the latter.

Now that he knew the players, he needed to know the location. He used his own connection to access public records, looking for blueprints for each of these people's mansions. Then, taking measure of the rooms he could see in Steve's LiveStream, he compared it to all the blueprints. Automatically, it canceled out everyone except for Coppergate and Wingate. Getting down to the details, he managed to determine they were at Wingate's mansion.

Perfect. Now he needed just a little more information. Still using his own connection, he accessed satellite footage and centered it down on

Wingate's address. Sure enough, there were guards. Lots of them. From the street view, he looked around and saw they had machine guns.

Not good. Still, he thought he had a good idea as to how to work their way around this. He drifted out of Steve's mind and back toward his own body, waiting to reconnect with himself.

4

Jack's eyes popped open. "I hope you motherfuckers like my whiskey."

"Sure," Jimmy said. "Even poured you one." He pointed to a glass with three fingers of booze in it.

"Well thanks, Jimmy. Thank you for giving me my own whiskey." He downed it all in one go.

Steve ignored both of them. "What did you find out?"

Jack gave them a quick rundown of what he'd discovered, and he used the nearest computer to show them first hand. He introduced them to each of the contestants involved before he moved on to the rich people. He pulled up files on each of them and transferred them into Steve and Jimmy's respective minds.

"There is one guy you should know more about, though," Jack said to Steve. "Just so you know what, exactly, we're up against."

He pulled up a picture of a young man with a full head of dark hair slicked back, complete with baby blue eyes that could have made a woman's panties drip down her legs. He had a narrow nose, and his lips stretched out in a roguish grin. The teeth behind them were straight and angel white. A well-manicured hand held a cigarette loosely between the index and middle fingers. "Handsome" just didn't cover the power of his attractiveness. He could have been a movie star.

"Do you know this guy?" Jack asked.

Steve shook his head. The guy looked somewhat familiar to Jimmy, but he couldn't place it.

"This picture was taken in the year 2000," Jack said, "when this guy was thirty years old. You'll probably recognize him more here."

He flicked the image away, and another one replaced it. A decrepit old man in a wheelchair with milky white eyes and metallic piranha teeth. They couldn't mistake this one.

"No way that's the same guy," Jimmy said.

"That's impossible," Steve said. "He'd have to be 230 years old. I'm not sure of the world record, but it's not even close to that."

"Actually, the record belongs to a guy from China," Jack said. "Dude lived to be 186, but he's been dead for fifty years. Coppergate has done his best to hide his background from everyone. He has some of the best computer guys in the world handling it for him. Not as good as me, of course."

"I don't believe that," Jimmy said. "Even if he's got guys hiding his past, the fact remains that no one can live to be 230 years old."

"Given the right amount of knowledge and an astronomical bank account, a man could probably live forever," Jack said. "You're right, I find it hard to believe, myself. But I've researched this motherfucker for most of my life. All avenues lead back to the same information."

"I've been after him for a few years myself," Jimmy said. "How come I never found this?"

"Because you're not as slick as me. I can show you my homework later, if you want, but if we're going after this guy for real, we should know what made him the way he is, just so you know how ruthless he can be."

Jimmy turned on his mental recorder and prepared himself to take notes for what might one day be a profile piece. His paper would never upload such a story, but it would be nice just to have this information.

"Coppergate was born into wealth. His father came from a long line of steel barons. His grandfather made the family money during World War II, although he got his start-up cash from bootlegging during the Great Depression. However, when Coppergate was a kid, his father made a lot of lousy investments. He lost a lot of money and wound up being investigated by the SEC. He went to jail for a long time, leaving his kid to fend for himself, since his mom was a lush."

~

"Oh, come on, Richard," William said. "Be a sport and turn the volume back up on McNeil's feed."

"No," Coppergate said. He didn't look at anyone else, and his tone reverberated throughout the room.

Edward wondered about what the black guy had said. Could Richard Coppergate actually be that old? It didn't make any sense. He remembered from his childhood, when his parents made him read the Bible, that a lot of people back when time began lived a super-long time, almost a thousand years, but he knew it was probably symbolism. No, Coppergate couldn't have lived for more than two centuries. That kind of thing just didn't happen.

He wished he could hear more about Coppergate's history, though.

"Are they going to reveal secrets?" William asked. "I don't care about secrets. I just want to know what they're saying."

Coppergate whirled on him, his fangs bared. "I do not wish to hear what they have to say."

William started, eyes wide. He quickly looked away from Coppergate, his mouth pursed shut.

Coppergate turned back to the screens, and for the first time in centuries, he felt his eyes start to burn. If he had tear ducts, he thought he might have cried. Through the conflicting waves of emotion in his guts, he still felt a cold objectivity showing through. He thought it an odd sensation, but he didn't dare face the others. Not now.

~

"Coppergate and his mother lived in a tiny flat near what would eventually be called the Sleaze Strip," Jack continued. "This infuriated the kid. He thought the Coppergates should be throwing extravagant parties, not eking out a shoddy living on the shitty side of town. When his father committed suicide in prison, Coppergate swore to himself that such a thing would never happen to him. He turned to a life of crime, just like his grandfather before him. When he had enough money, he went into the security business. Perfect timing, since 9/11 had just happened. Money poured into his firm, and he soon found himself on the forefront of the war on terror. He lucked out even more. About 2030, he invested in a company that eventually found a way to implant the 'net into people's heads. By 2035, he was the richest man in the world.

"But also by then, he was starting to age. Technology had advanced enough so that implants were a routine matter. He started by replacing his hair and teeth. When his organs started going bad on him, he had them easily replaced. By then, 3D printing had advanced so far that getting replacements was pretty easy. Shit, according to the medical records I found, he even had his dick replaced with a porn star's."

Steve barked with laughter. "You can't be serious."

"He's serious," Jimmy said. "Imagine if you had all the money in the world, and your dick shriveled on you. Tell me you wouldn't get a new dick."

"Why not have it 3D printed, though?" Steve asked.

"The problem is, 3D printing, when it comes to biological items, is it's only good for making copies," Jack said. "He's like any of our fellow Americans. He wants bigger and better."

"That's . . ." Steve couldn't continue.

"He doesn't use a porn star's dick anymore, now that stem cell tech has been combined with foreign DNA. He's literally got a dick farm now."

Jimmy glanced at Steve, unable to say a single word.

"Anyway," Jack said, "when he realized he just couldn't beat the aging process, at least not without replacing his entire skin, which still isn't possible, he decided to accept his role as a monster. That's when he had the eye implants. That's when he got the metal fangs. That's when he let himself go a little. But he still kept the important shit up and running. The dude's heart isn't even his own."

"Jesus," Steve said. "If he keeps this up, he'll never die."

"He'll die, all right. That's what we're all here for. I've wanted to put this spooky fuck in the ground for a long time, and I think I'm finally going to succeed now."

Steve looked to Jimmy. When he didn't see any moral objection on his friend's face, he felt like he had to say something. "Do we have to kill him? We could probably find a way to—"

"Don't bother," Jack said. "I know where you're headed with this, and there's no fucking way. He'd only buy his way out of prison."

Steve sighed. "Fine. I guess. I was just, you know, hoping."

"Don't. He's not worth your hope."

They sat in silence for a moment. Steve wanted to say more. He knew the value of killing someone who needed killing, but at the same time, his Catholic upbringing tried to pull him back from that idea. Did he really want to risk his soul for something like this?

Jimmy broke the silence. "What can we do, then?"

"First thing we have to do is cut off their connection with Steve," Jack said. "They can also probably hack into us, if they needed to. They've got the money for something like that. I don't use my LiveStream. In fact, I have a device implanted in my head so that any video footage of my face will be scrambled. I suggest you shut your social media off, Jimmy."

With a flick of his eyes, Jimmy did just that.

"What about me?" Steve asked.

"You can't shut yours down. Whoever worked on you made sure that you would constantly broadcast back to them. It's pretty simple for you. Hold on."

Jack stood and went to the back room. Steve and Jimmy heard something rattling back there, and then something fell and clattered all over the place. Jack cursed loudly, but when he came back, he handed two things to Steve: an eye patch and a set of ear plugs for people who liked to practice shoot.

"The LiveStream works through implants in the right eye," Jack said. "Cover it up, and you'll cut off their visual. Audio comes through the right ear, so plug it, and you'll cut them off entirely. But don't plug the other one. You'll need to hear."

Steve nodded and followed instructions.

~

"Aw," Edward said. "Not another one."

William grunted and glanced at Coppergate. "It's not like we could have enjoyed that feed, anyway."

~

It took Steve a moment to get used to 2D vision and not being able to hear out of one side of his head, and he really didn't think he'd ever get fully used to it, but he felt like he could handle it.

"Now what we really need to do is find the other competitors," Jack said. "If we can get them together on our team, we'll have the numbers to take on Wingate's mansion."

"And how do we do that, exactly?" Jimmy asked.

"I can track them," Jack said. "Which reminds me, we're going to have to remove Steve's credit chip."

"Uh . . . why?" Steve asked.

"Because they can track you through it. If they know where we're going, they'll know our plan."

"Well . . . what about your chip?"

"I don't have one," Jack said. "I'm off the grid. I can launder any transactions I might need."

"Oh, come on," Steve said. "You don't need—"

Jack produced a knife and flicked his lighter beneath it. "You don't seem to understand. Those rich fucks might call this a game, but it's not. Your life is at stake. That chip has got to go. Don't worry, I have drugs. You won't feel a thing."

Steve felt the color drip from his face. "Put the knife down, Jack."

"Jimmy, go in my drawer and fetch me the syringe and the topical anesthetic. Steve, I wish I could knock you out for this, but we need you awake and alert. A topical will have to do."

"Goddammit, Jack. I need that chip."

"You'll get it back when we're done with Coppergate and his cronies."

"No, and that's final!"

5

Samuel steered his motorcycle around the car parked on the dirt path. As he cruised his way down through the woods, he marveled at some of the traps he saw. Whoever lived back here didn't fuck around. These traps weren't here to scare anyone; they were here to kill. How did the cop know someone like this?

Then, he saw the house ahead. He turned off the motor and got off the bike. He thought it might be a good idea to bring the jet pack for this one, in case he had to make a hasty retreat, so he strapped it to his back, dropping the quiver of guns next to the motorcycle. He selected the shotgun from the pack and made his way to the house.

As he came closer, he noticed the racial epithets, and he wondered about the kind of man who would not just live back here, but who would also leave such graffiti up. He had to be dangerous, no doubt about it. His blood moved a little faster through his veins, and he looked forward to meeting the guy.

CHAPTER 14

1

By the time Wayne and Stacy made it to the east side, the cops had blocked off the neighborhood. Over the barricade, they could see the chaos of punks, riot police, fire and violence. Neither of them had seen anything like it before. They could hear screams and smell death wafting on the air, acrid and dull.

"How do we get through that?" Wayne asked.

Stacy didn't need to think about it. "Put the shotgun under the seat. Let me take care of this."

Wayne followed orders, and Stacy looked at the dash computer. The display showed that the riot area had been blocked off, and no cars were allowed in. She thought that maybe if they got close enough, the car would lock on the tracks, and she couldn't have that. She switched to manual and felt the wheels pull away from the track. She stayed on it, though, just for appearances.

She pulled the cab up next to the guard and rolled down the window, giving him a clear view of her.

"You can't come through here," he said. "You'll have to turn around."

"But I have to get through here, officer," Stacy said. She used the best cute-little-girl voice she could muster, the one that her daughter-issues clients liked so much. To sell it, she pouted her lips out a bit.

The cop didn't look impressed. "Out of the question, ma'am."

Stacy moaned in mock disappointment. She pushed her chest out and pretended to scratch her belly, but what she really did was use that hand to pull her shirt down a bit, revealing a perfect cleavage shot. "It's an emergency."

This time, the cop's eyes darted down to admire the view of her gorgeous valley, but he didn't do more than furtively glance, as if he thought himself to be a master of stealth. "I'm afraid I can't let you through, ma'am." But now, his voice had softened a little.

"Why not?" The neck of her shirt stretched just a little bit more, showing off the inside curve of her right breast completely. If that didn't get him hard, and stupid, she thought, then he probably liked to suck cock.

The cop breathed through his mouth. "Uh . . ." He forced his eyes away from her. "There's kind of a riot, uh, going on down there." He nodded down the road. "I wouldn't want you to, you know, get killed or anything."

Stacy wondered if maybe she would need to grab this guy's dick to get through the barricade.

The cop looked into the back seat and saw Wayne. "You need to be down there?"

"Yes," Wayne said.

"You don't look like the type of guy who needs to be in that neighborhood. What's wrong with your face?"

"My doctor lives here," Wayne said. "I need to see him. Now."

The cop turned back to Stacy. "Sorry. I can't let you through. Turn around."

This time, Stacy pulled sharply on her shirt, and one of her breasts popped out. The cop's jaw dropped, and though he tried to act casual, his tongue just wouldn't stay behind his lips.

She reached out and touched the growing lump at the front of his pants. Four inches. Nothing much, but she could definitely work with it. She massaged him, cupping her palm so that it fit around as much of his dick as it could. Smiling, she looked up at his shocked face and saw his nostrils flaring almost enough to make his nose hairs shiver. Bulging fish eyes stared down at her hand.

"I love a man in uniform," she said.

He moved his mouth, but nothing came out. He licked his lips and reached down his head, as if to kiss Stacy. Just as he caressed her breast, pinching her nipple between his middle and ring fingers, another cop approached. "Yo, Nick! What's with the fucking cab? Get rid of it, pronto!"

Nick drew back right away and looked over the roof of the car to his partner. "I'm—" But Stacy chose that moment to dig deeper and cup his balls. She wiggled her fingers in the damp, sweaty mess of Nick's taint.

His partner's eyes narrowed. "Jesus, Nicky. There's a fucking riot going on."

"I . . ." Nick trailed off, incapable of finding the right words. This was his second day on the Job, and already he'd scored his first handy from a blonde knockout. He'd read a lot of porn stories that ended up like this, but he never thought they could be true, and that they could happen to him.

His partner, Groboski, walked around the cab and slapped Stacy's hand away. "Listen, lady. We've got a riot on, and we don't have time for this touchy-feely shit. Get this fucking cab turned around, or I'll book you on obstruction, *comprende*?"

"No need to be hard on her," Nick said. His cheeks flared up when he realized he'd just said "hard on," and he clasped his hands together over his crotch to hide his excitement.

"Goddammit, Nick. Get your hands off your cock. And yes, I need to be rough on her. This is a fucking riot!"

While Groboski ranted at his partner, Wayne leaned in close to Stacy's ear. "Gun it," he whispered.

Stacy didn't question him. She stomped on the gas just as Groboski turned back, a finger pointed at her, ready to reprimand her more.

"All right, lady—" And then the cab lurched forward. Its back tire rolled over his right foot, flattening it and shattering his bones. At first, he didn't feel pain, he just knew something had happened to his foot. When he understood, he clenched his jaws, waiting for the pain to set in. When it registered, he howled, falling to the pavement, holding his ankle, afraid to grab himself any lower.

Nick's hard-on vanished magically as he knelt down next to his partner. "You all right, Charlie? Huh? Did she get your foot?"

Groboski didn't want to look at his foot, and he guessed he wouldn't be able to until a doctor cut his boot off. He didn't want to respond to Nick's stupid question, either. He only wanted to be in bed, dreaming all of this.

Neither of them looked up to watch the cab as it sped away.

2

"Shit, did I get his foot?" Stacy asked. She looked up into the rearview mirror, watching the one cop on the ground, screaming.

"I think you did." Wayne peered out the back window. "Yeah, I don't think he's on the ground because he likes it there."

"Didn't mean to do that. But, he did slap my hand."

Wayne grunted. "Nice rationalization."

"Shut up and get that shotgun out from under the seat. Keep an eye out for fuckers."

3

Roberto sat in the driver's seat of the limo, accompanied by two punks they'd picked up along the way. They were F and U, still unaware of their bassist's death. In the back, Randall and Skank sat surrounded by four other punks with Pisser on the floor. They felt packed in and claustrophobic, and they all fidgeted, fighting with limbs that were starting to fall asleep.

They'd already driven around to reassign some groups to take on Drake and Taylor's houses, so now they were on their way to the Wingate mansion. No one said a word, as if they were paratroopers in a plane waiting for the Jump.

Outside, the world went crazy with screams, gunfire and just plain old fire. The riot police stalked the neighborhood, trying to contain the violence while firefighters did their best to snuff out the ever-growing blaze that had started somewhere on the southeast side. Every once in a while, something struck the limo. Nothing big or dangerous, but it never failed to make its occupants jump just a little. Randall reassured himself that the limo had bulletproof glass and the chassis was reinforced to protect high profile customers.

In the front, Roberto had to steer the limo manually. A while ago, the cops locked down the tracks, so he had to disengage to get the job done. As he tried desperately to not run anyone over, he kept reminding himself of the money Randall had given him. He took comfort in the fact that it would buy a metric shit-ton of weed for him to relax with after his shift.

But then, he noticed the man standing in the middle of the road. The guy held a Molotov cocktail.

"Rich fuckers!" the man yelled. He lit the cocktail and reared back.

"Isn't that Kelly?" U asked.

No one had the time to answer. The cocktail arced toward them in a fiery blaze.

"FUCK!" Roberto screamed. He tried to swerve out of the way, but he just didn't have enough time. The Molotov cocktail struck the hood of the car and exploded. Fire zipped up the front of the limo and completely obscured Roberto's line of vision. He tried to keep control, but the limo wasn't built for maneuverability. As soon as he'd turned the wheel, they went into a skid, and then gravity took over.

The divider was up, so no one in the back knew what had hit them. They remained quiet as the limo jerked first to the right and then started drifting across the road.

Pisser slumped forward, hitting his head on the door. "What the fuck? Keep this fucker straight, asshole!"

Everyone else felt their guts slop around in their bellies as the limo toppled over and rolled onto its roof. They screamed as the limo flipped over and over again. None of them wore seat belts, so they all tangled up with everyone else as they banged their heads against the ceiling and windows.

Finally, the side of the limo hit a tree and came to a halt. Silence, except for a soft ticking sound as the engine cooled off.

Randall groaned as he shook his head. Blood trickled down from his nose, but otherwise, he felt fine. Skank, on the other hand, had fallen across his lap, unconscious. He could feel her blood soaking through his jeans.

"Oh shit," he said. He pulled Skank up to see her forehead had been split open, most likely from the ceiling light. A large cut now bisected her FUCK YOU tattoo, showing the bone of her forehead. She still breathed, though, so he shook her gently. "Wake up. Come on Skank. Wake up."

"What the fuck?" Pisser. He moaned as he sat up. His flattened nose looked right at home on his fight-ravaged face. One of his legs, however, had been twisted at an unnatural angle. He didn't seem to notice either injury, though.

The punk who had been sitting by Skank's side had gone halfway through the window, his battered body broken and twisted, his head split open and filled with glass. The three on the other side of the limo weren't so bad off, except the one nearest the smashed side. His body had been pierced by glass, metal and wood, and his face looked more like sloppy joes instead of something belonging to a human being. Still, he breathed.

Skank shuddered and her eye popped open. She rubbed at the other one under the patch and sat up. "What the fuck just happened?"

"I don't know," Randall said. He could smell fire, though, so he had a pretty good idea. "Let's get out of here. Fast."

Pisser screamed when he saw his leg. The bone poked out, but for some reason, Pisser's mind refused to recognize it. He thought something unusual must be stuck in him, so he reached down to pluck it out. When the shard didn't move, and pain shot through his body again, he realized the truth.

Randall tried to open the unscathed door, but it didn't budge. "Goddammit! Open, fucker!" He kicked at it with all his might.

Skank moved over, and they timed their kicks together. Once. Twice. And third time, lucky. The door fell off its hinges, and the hot scent of fire wafted in at them.

"Go," Randall said to Skank. As soon as she got out, he ducked down to grab Pisser under his arms.

Pisser pushed his hands away. His pale face jiggled and sweat dripped down and diluted the blood on his shirt. "Get me to a hospital. They can fix me."

"Yeah, in a minute," Randall said. "We gotta' get you out of here now, or the limo's going to blow. You ready? Because this is going to hurt."

"Just do it quick." Pisser's jaw tightened, and his gums ground against each other.

Randall snaked his hand under one of Pisser's arms, feeling the sweaty cheese of his body odor coat his palm, and he reached around Pisser's back with his arm. He gave one quick heave, and Pisser came up on his good foot. Still, his twisted leg moved, and Pisser screamed again.

"Almost there," Randall said. "Stick with me, man."

He moved backward, doing his best to support Pisser. Just before he got the aging punk out of the limo, Pisser went down on his bad foot, and the screaming intensified. Randall could smell Pisser's fishy breath, and it took all of his power to not just leave him there.

Finally, Randall fell backward, and the punk rolled over him. He staggered to his feet and did his best to drag Pisser to a safe distance.

Skank peered through the flames into the front seat. She saw the charred, skeletal remains of Roberto, F and U.

"Are they . . . ?" Randall asked.

"Dead."

"Help me get the others, then."

Randall stepped forward, but before he could go any further, the car exploded, driving them both back, as if they'd been punched by an invisible giant.

Dazed, Randall sat up and saw flames crawling up his shirt. "Fuck!" He battered at the fire with his bare hands, snuffing it almost right away. It hadn't spread far, but it had eaten through the fabric and had melted the hair on his chest.

"Skank, you okay?" he asked.

Before Skank could answer, bullets from the guns that had been left in the car started going off. Randall fell backward, holding Skank down, looking for anywhere they could use for cover.

Pisser didn't notice. He kept screaming, holding his ruined leg until two bullets found him. One of them got him in the ass, and it probably wouldn't have been very life threatening if the other hadn't nailed him squarely in the head. His brains spat from his head in a gruel on the pavement.

Randall pulled Skank behind a fire hydrant. It wouldn't be enough to cover them well, but it lessened the chances of catching a stray bullet. Finally, after a few more seconds, the volley died down to nothing.

Randall stood, offering Skank a hand. "You okay?"

She took his hand and allowed him to help her to her feet. "I think so. What the hell happened?"

"I don't know," Randall said.

"Holy shit! Skank, is that you?"

Randall and Skank both looked toward the sound of the voice. They saw Kelly running toward them.

"Shit, I didn't know you were in there," he said. "I'm so fucking sorry. I didn't fucking know."

"What did you do?" Skank yelled.

"It was a Molotov," Kelly said. "I thought it was a bunch of rich people. What were you doing in a limo?"

Randall glanced over and saw Pisser's remains. He thought about the other punks who had died in the back of the limo. He didn't even know these people, but he felt sorry for them, nonetheless. Just a few poor souls who wound up sucked into this horrible mess.

"They're all dead!" Spittle flew from Skank's lips. "You fucking killed them all!"

"I didn't mean to!"

Skank roared as she jumped on him, her fingernails tearing into Kelly's face in a mad frenzy. He screamed, but he didn't do anything to stop her, as if he knew he'd done wrong and had to atone for it.

Randall realized he had to stop her from killing Kelly, but he truly didn't want to. Kelly had just killed a carload of people—and almost Randall, himself—so he fully deserved Skank's wrath. Also, she attacked him like a woman possessed. Randall honestly didn't think he could stop her.

Still, he had to try. "Stop, Skank. We need him." He pulled at her arm.

"Fucking asshole!" Skank screamed. She raked her nails across Kelly's face, splitting his lower lip down the center in two flaps.

"Come on!" Randall yelled. "We need him!"

He pulled her away, even as she still tried to get at Kelly. Neither of them noticed the riot cops approaching. They moved in quietly, like ninja, training their rifles on the arguing punks. "Freeze!" one of them shouted.

Randall turned immediately to face them. He thought about his gun, which he'd left in the limo, and he didn't know if he wished to have it or not. It might help him defend himself, but on the other hand, if they saw a weapon, the cops would definitely fire on him. He raised both hands.

Skank didn't notice. Instead, she rushed from Randall's side and jumped on Kelly again. She screamed, beating at his face.

"Stop that!" another cop shouted. "Get away from that man right now!"

"Skank," Randall said. "They're pointing guns at us."

She dropped her knee on Kelly's balls, and while he rolled on the pavement, trying to draw a breath, she continued ripping his face to shreds.

"You've got till the count of three!" the cop yelled. "One . . . two . . ."

4

Stacy and Wayne had driven up and down the grid of streets in their search for Skank and Randall. The southeast side blazed too badly, so they avoided that part of the neighborhood, but they scoured everywhere else they could think of. Twice, the police tried to stop them, but when they sped away, the authorities realized they had bigger fish to fry. Once the rioters tried to pull them over, but they weren't fast enough. Even so, someone threw a brick at them. It dented the trunk but didn't do significant damage.

A half an hour had gone by, and they worried that they were working at in impossible task. And then, at that very moment, they saw the flaming limo, and the altercation taking place nearby.

"There she is," Wayne said. He pointed.

Stacy stopped the cab and followed the path of Wayne's finger. She also saw Randall and mentioned it. The riot cops had surrounded them, and they all watched as Skank mutilated some poor bastard on the ground.

The cops shouted at Skank, who ignored them, and it looked like they were about to fire on her. "Shit," Wayne said. "We have to hurry."

Stacy knew she had only one bullet left in her clip, so she got the other one ready for a quick change. Then, they got out of the car just in time to hear the countdown begin. "One . . . two . . ."

5

Skank stopped attacking Kelly and pushed herself deftly to her feet. She whirled around, her face twisted by the anger that burned in her heart. "What the fuck do you want? You want some, too? Huh?"

"Calm down, Skank," Randall said. "They've got—"

"I'm tired of seeing people die!" she yelled. "First Nutsack, now all my friends!" She turned her face to the sky and howled, an odd mixture of rage and sorrow, a sound that sent chills down Randall's spine. It sounded like a mixture between a war cry and a death song.

Skank dipped down and plucked a knife from Kelly's belt. She gnashed her teeth, brandishing it at the police.

"Drop the knife!" one of the cops yelled.

The image of Nutsack with a hole in his head seared its way from the folds of her brain so harshly she could almost see it whenever she closed her eyes. "Fuck you, pig!" She drew her arm back, ready to throw the blade.

One of the cops drew a bead on her chest and fired, sending a rubber bullet in her direction. But then, she leaned forward to give the knife its best momentum, and her head dipped down. Instead of nailing her just above her heart, the bullet popped out her left eyeball and entered her skull, mashing up her brain, ending all thoughts of Nutsack.

"Skank!" Randall cried. "No!"

6

"Oh fuck," Stacy said.

"Let's move," Wayne said. "Hurry!"

7

Randall fell to his knees beside Skank, his fingers scrambling at her neck, hoping to find a pulse. No matter how much of her flesh he touched, he came up with nothing. The bat tattoo that fluttered around her skin drew close to her heart and folded in on itself, dying mere seconds after she did.

"Oh God, no. Not you, Skank. Don't be dead."

~

Another screen went to static, and Charles cried out in victory, pumping his fist in the air. "Thank you thank you thank you! You're all too kind!" He held out a hand to William, who sighed.

"I don't think that should count," William said. "She wasn't killed by one of the contestants. Or Samuel."

"She died next, that's all that counts. Right, George?" Charles grinned.

William gave Charles a look that could have withered kudzu. George didn't utter a word, not knowing what to say.

"Pay up, Willie, old boy."

William sighed again. This time, he held out his hand and transferred the funds.

"It's just not your night," Charles continued. "I hope you don't mind me pushing for another wager?"

William merely looked at him. "I think my sporting blood is running out."

"Don't be like that. This is supposed to be fun."

"In that case, I'll take the fuckslinger. Stacy."

Charles laughed. "Excellent choice! I think she's tougher than you give her credit for, though. I'm going to have to go with the guy with the Red Death."

"He *is* kind of a nancy," William said.

"Shall we say a million this time?"

William thought his luck had to hold at some point. Why not now? "Sure."

~

A loud pop rang out, followed by a deafening roar, and Randall cringed, hoping death wouldn't be too painful. Perhaps it would even be nice to finally get answers about the afterlife.

When he didn't feel anything tear into his flesh, and when he realized he could still open his eyes on this mortal world, he turned toward the sounds and saw that of the four cops, two were on the ground, one dead with a hole in his chest the size of an open hand, the other dying and coughing up blood. The two still standing now ran for cover. Behind all the action, Stacy and Wayne stood by a cab. Stacy reloaded her weapon, and Wayne held a double barreled shotgun, but he must have been out of ammo for it, since it hung by his side, smoking.

Stacy took a couple of quick shots at the retreating cops, and she nailed one of them in the back of the leg. He fell down, and his partner came back for him, trying to help him up. She aimed carefully at the good Samaritan, but Wayne gently touched her arm. "Let them go. They're not going to hurt us."

Stacy wanted to plug them, just in case. But she also knew she only had four shots left, so she lowered the gun. "Nice shooting, by the way. You sure you've never killed anyone before?"

Wayne tried to remember if he'd ever told her that he hadn't killed someone before. He couldn't recall. But he knew he'd never admit to David Nelson. No, not at all. He looked down the street to the cop he'd nailed with the shotgun. Even from this distance, he could see the corpse's innards through the gigantic hole in his chest. To see a man unraveled like that made him feel a bit sick, but not nearly as bad as he thought he'd feel. Maybe killing David Nelson had inoculated him in some way, allowing him to kill more easily in the future.

The thought frightened him.

Stacy saw some kind of conflict in Wayne's eyes, but she didn't want to push him. Instead, she said, "Let's check on them. See if Skank's okay."

He followed her down the street, to where Randall knelt next to Skank. "She dead?" Stacy asked.

Randall stood, wiping at his eyes. "Yeah. Fucking cops."

Stacy nodded.

"I really hope you're not here to kill me," Randall said. "That would be the perfect end to my day." He eyed them both, hoping for yet another reprieve.

"Nope," Stacy said. "Wayne and I teamed up, and we came looking for you guys, hoping you'd join us."

"We're going to take down the rich fucks who did this to us," Wayne said. "We're trying to get as many of us together to do it. You in?"

Randall uttered a humorless laugh, looking down at the rubber bullet that still jutted from Skank's eye socket. "The more the merrier."

"Then we need to find a place to hole up," Wayne said. "The heat's getting to be a bit too much out here. The place is crawling with cops." He glanced over his shoulder and saw a cop car speed by, lights swirling.

"We had a plan," Randall said. "We were headed—"

"Later," Stacy said. "I'm almost out of bullets, and Wayne's shotgun is empty. We need to go."

"Where can we go?" Randall asked. "I'm sure the cops've got the east side tied off from the rest of the city. And besides, we can't leave Skank out here." He looked down at her body and still couldn't believe that mere minutes ago, she'd been alive and screaming.

"I know it's a horrible thing," Stacy said, "but we have to leave her. She's dead, and we're not. We have to look out for ourselves."

"And that guy?" Randall pointed to Kelly. They could see that he still breathed, even though he was clearly unconscious.

"Grab him," Stacy said. "We might need him."

Randall looked down yet again at Skank and felt his eyes moisten. "Sorry, Skank. I'll make them pay for you. For us."

Wayne helped him pull Kelly to his feet. The punk moaned, and blood ran down his face in streams. He still didn't come to.

"You know anyplace we can hide out?" Stacy asked.

Wayne shrugged. "I don't know. Maybe one of these mansions is vaca—"

"Not a fucking chance."

"Then we've got to get out of this neighborhood. And fast." He looked down the street, where another group of riot cops approached.

"I might know a place," Randall said. "That your cab?"

"Yeah," Stacy said. "Tell us on the way. Let's go."

Randall helped Wayne put Kelly in the back seat before they got in. He took one last look at Skank. "I'll make them pay," he said again. "Goodbye."

CHAPTER 15

1

Jack wrapped a bandage around Steve's left hand. The operation had taken a half an hour. Taking the chip out only took five minutes, but the rest of the time had been taken up by carefully sewing up the wound. Jack knew how to do it, mostly from closing up his own injuries over the years, but performing on another person threw him off a bit.

He knotted up the end of the bandage. "There, you pussy. See? Didn't feel a thing, did you?"

Steve had, but it hadn't been pain. He still felt Jack tinkering around under his skin, though. Uncomfortable, but it didn't hurt.

Jack poured him more whiskey and put a pill next to the glass. "This pill won't knock you out, but it'll dull the pain when it kicks in. The booze will take some of the remaining edge off. Okay?"

Steve nodded and downed the pill. Ordinarily, he wouldn't take a stranger's medical advice, but he trusted Jack. After all, the man had been in his brain, hadn't he?

"Now that that's settled," Jack said, "I think it's time we got some guns." He touched the screen of one of his computers, and a panel in the wall slid open, revealing an overstuffed cache of weapons.

Jimmy whistled. "Holy fucking shit, Jack. Planning on supplying an army?"

"Shut up, Monaghan, and grab something. Grab lots of somethings."

Jimmy selected a .38 and a .44 and took holsters to go with each. The former clipped on to his belt at the small of his back, and the latter went under his shoulder and weighed his left side down considerably.

Steve stepped up. Remembering his crack from earlier, he said, "Got a batarang?"

Jack only glared at him.

Steve took a couple of .45's, just like he'd had back on the Job. One of each went under his arms.

Jack loaded down with a couple of shotguns, handguns and other hand-to-hand weapons.

"Got enough?" Jimmy asked.

"Not yet." Jack went and got a duffle bag and loaded more guns into it.

"Isn't that excessive?" Steve asked.

"Not if we find out the other competitors want to be on our side. They'll probably need guns, too."

Steve knew how much each of those weapons weighed, and he thought an average man wouldn't be able to heft such a bag. Jack had giant muscles, though, and he shouldered them with ease. "You guys ready?"

They nodded.

"Up we go."

Jack led the way, and he opened the ceiling panel. Once up top, he put the guns down and waited for the others to come up. "You guys get a head start. I'm going to lock up the trap door. It takes a second because of the broken latch."

"Sure." Steve walked through the kitchen and into the living room, Jimmy following behind. He walked to the door and opened it up. Outside, the burnt hulks of crosses rested in the distance, looking like dead creatures from a forgotten time. They tried to hide behind the tall grass, as if they thought they were being sneaky. Despite what they stood for, they almost looked beautiful, in a dirty kind of way.

Jack cursed at the broken latch, and Jimmy turned to give him a little crap. Behind him, Steve stepped outside the door.

Then, Jimmy heard an explosion from outside, and he whirled around to take a look.

2

Samuel pressed his back up against the side of the house to the right of the front door and aimed the shotgun to his left, waiting patiently for the first person to step out. He supposed he could have stormed the house like a SWAT team, but judging from the booby traps he'd found on his way here, he had no doubt the house had a few inside, as well.

A half an hour passed, and he spent the time accessing the intranet on which the contestants broadcast their experiences. He saw the cop in a super high-tech room with a nigger and some other guy. He zeroed in on the stranger, captured his face, and ran it against a database until he came back with Jimmy Monaghan's name. The nigger, on the other hand, had no records. Interesting.

Samuel checked the countdown. They had about sixteen hours before everyone's head exploded. Still plenty of time.

He dropped his aim and wiped sweat from his brow. As the sun climbed up into the sky, he knew it would turn into a hot day. Suddenly, his patience wore thin, and he wondered if he should maybe just blow up the cabin.

No, that would be too easy. He wanted to hunt, not just blow shit up.

He forced himself to calm down and shoved a power bar into his mouth. The jet pack weighed him down a bit too much, so he sat down and scanned the other LiveStreams. He felt a bit irritated when he saw another stream had blacked out. It took him a moment to figure out it belonged to Skank. He'd looked forward to putting that cunt down. He switched over to the others and saw that the fuckslinger and the homeless guy had teamed up with . . . that piece of shit who called himself Randall Marsh. That only left Toby Munger. Toby's stream showed him sitting at the same dive bar, nursing that same glass of whiskey. How long could he sit there doing nothing? Fucking creep. Still, Samuel knew he had to be careful with that one. He struck him as a sneaky bastard, and such prey always had a proclivity for fighting back in interesting ways. He would probably be the most fun, so Samuel decided to save him for last.

He switched back to Steve's LiveStream and saw them still talking. Boring. He felt tempted to do something else while he waited for them to come out, but he knew he had to concentrate. It wouldn't do to get sloppy this early in the game.

3

A half an hour later, Samuel saw them move from the tech room at last. They seemed to be in some kind of hidden basement, and they now carried what looked like a complete arsenal of weapons.

Interesting. The nigger was full of surprises.

Samuel watched as they climbed through the floor of the kitchen and started toward the front door. He stood and aimed the shotgun once again, only this time, he fished something out of one of his pouches. He held the gun over one forearm while he put his finger through the loop of a hand grenade and waited.

The door opened, and Steve McNeil stepped out without so much as a glance to his right. Samuel lifted the shotgun higher until it pointed at Steve's head. Steve took another step, gazing off into the distance.

Samuel's finger tightened around the twin triggers, but at the last second, he decided not to fire. He couldn't just gun a guy down without warning. There wasn't much sport in something like that.

He puckered his lips and blew out a quick whistle.

Steve's head jerked to the right, and his eyes settled on both barrels of the shotgun. Samuel gave him a moment for reality to settle in, for him to realize the proximity of death.

And then he pulled both triggers.

4

At first, Jimmy thought some kids might have been playing with firecrackers in the woods, but when he saw the door had been blown back nearly off its hinges, he knew something else had happened.

And then he saw the chunks of meat stuck to the door, saturated with crimson. He knew instantly what they were, and bile burned in the back of his throat.

Steve's headless body slumped to the ground, halfway out the door, and blood poured out of his neck stump, puddling in the foyer. Jimmy tried to scream, but instead he vomited all over himself.

Just then, a gray rock rolled into the room, coming to rest almost between Jimmy's legs. It took him a moment to recognize it as a hand grenade, and he froze, unable to move.

In that moment, he knew all of those years spent drinking and writing and ignoring personal relationships led up to this ignoble death, and he felt his nuts shrivel into his body.

Then, Jack grabbed him and yanked him back into the kitchen, throwing him to the ground. He whirled, hoping he could close the kitchen door in time.

~

All faces in the room stared at Steve's screen, shocked by the sudden static. Finally, Charles broke the silence. "I never thought Samuel would get the best of a cop."

"Me, neither," Edward said. He'd always thought cops were hardcase lunatics who rarely ever lost because they had the law on their side. Yet Steve's wits had been knocked out of his head with a shotgun. No law to back him up now.

"So much for that wager," Charles said. "Shall we retain our choices for next round?"

"Of course," William said. "Nothing's changed. This was just a bit of a surprise, that's all."

5

As soon as Steve's body dropped, Samuel pulled the pin on the grenade and casually flipped it through the door. With that done, he slapped the switch on the back of his jet pack and found himself instantly airborne. He couldn't fly very high or for very long, since the metal plates that protected his lower body would melt under the intense flames, but he felt himself boosted away from the impending explosion rather quickly.

He turned and hovered, watching until he heard the eruption and saw the boarded windows blow out. The front of the house collapsed on itself and covered Steve's corpse nicely.

Then, he lowered himself to the ground and turned off the jet pack. He reloaded the shotgun and waited to see if the others would come out. When they didn't, he assumed he'd gotten the both of them, as well.

It had been too easy. Maybe he should have given them more of a chance.

He shrugged and checked the LiveStreams again, this time focusing on Stacy. He saw that they'd found refuge in a mansion. He examined the footage carefully until he saw a Goya nude on the wall. Only then did he recognize it as Elizabeth Drake's place. He laughed at the idea. He knew Drake's mansion very well, having fucked her in many of the rooms. He could easily take out Stacy, Wayne and Fuckface with one fell swoop. Then, only Toby would remain.

He should be back home in time for a quick nap before dinner.

Samuel grinned as he walked back down the path to where his motorcycle awaited him.

6

Just as Jack pushed the kitchen door closed, the explosion rocked the house. The force of it blew through the door and knocked him back, where he landed on top of Jimmy before he blacked out.

Jimmy, his senses rattled, couldn't seem to get it straight in his mind. He felt like he was in a war zone, and the smoke coming from the ruined living room didn't help. He gagged as he tried to stand up.

The house rumbled, and dust snowed down from the ceiling. In the other room, he could hear absolute chaos as he watched the upper rooms collapse down into the living room. He threw up a hand over his face, just in case of debris.

Then, the thought occurred to him that the ceiling might collapse in here, too. He stooped to drag Jack away, but the large man wouldn't budge. "Come on, Jack. Wake up. We gotta' get out of here."

Nothing.

Jimmy heaved with all of his strength, and Jack finally slid across the floor. He dragged Jack's unconscious body toward the back door at the rear of the kitchen, but he knew that he'd never make it in time.

Finally, his strength sapped, he dropped down next to Jack, hoping the house wouldn't fall down on top of them.

7

It didn't. As soon as Jimmy felt strong enough, maybe fifteen minutes later, he tried pulling Jack out of the house again. This time he succeeded, and as soon as fresh air filled Jack's lungs, his eyes opened, and he hacked out brownish saliva.

"What the fuck happened?" he asked between coughs.

Jimmy started to explain, but when he got to the part about the hand grenade, Jack roared out with rage. He ran around to the front of his house and saw the devastating damage.

"FUCK!" he yelled. "Motherfucking cuntlapping bitch fuck!" He turned to Jimmy. "Did you get the guns?"

Jimmy shrugged. He hadn't even thought of them.

Jack went back into the kitchen and retrieved the duffel bag. Outside, he said, "I'm going to kill that cocksucker, and it's not going to be an easy death. I'm going to take my time with him."

"What about . . .?" Jimmy nodded toward the front, where Steve's body rested.

"What about him?" Jack asked.

"Shouldn't we bury him? It's the Catholic thing to do."

"No time to dig him out of that shit. We'll have to do it later."

"But the animals—"

"They can't get to him under all that. Now let's go." He started down the path.

Jimmy paused, looking at the wreckage that covered Steve's body. He wanted to say something, maybe to even swear vengeance, but no words would come. A part of him wondered if maybe he should cry, but he felt too numb. Steve's death hadn't gotten through to him just yet. He wondered if maybe he was in shock.

"You coming?" Jack called out.

Jimmy glanced over to him. He knew he could do nothing for Steve. All he could do is ride out this exposè and hope it ended the way he wanted it to.

8

When they reached Jimmy's car, they were surprised to discover the tires were intact. "I thought that fucker would've shredded them," Jack said, "and I know he was here." He pointed to the single track of a motorcycle. "He probably figured us for dead."

Jimmy got into the driver's seat and unlocked the other side so Jack could get in. Only then did he remember that he'd puked all over himself. He hoped he didn't drip on the inside of his car, but when he looked at the filth on his chest, he knew he'd be fine. It had more or less dried, caked by ash and dust.

He jammed his thumb on the plate, but nothing happened. "Oh shit."

"What?" Jack asked.

Jimmy tried again. And again. And again. Nothing happened. The car didn't even chug.

"Stop," Jack said. "It sounds like the bastard did something to the battery. Looks like we're walking." He got out of the car.

"Goddammit," Jimmy said. He got out and locked the door behind him.

They began the long trek back to civilization, Jack carrying the bag of weapons, and Jimmy with his puke-stained trench coat flowing behind him like a low-class cloak.

CHAPTER 16

1

For the past half-hour, Stacy, Wayne, Randall and Kelly had been holed up at the Drake mansion. Gaining access hadn't been very hard. Luckily, Kelly had woken up before they had to climb the fence. They had to subdue a maid, but that hadn't been a big problem. She gave in meekly and let them tie her up and put her in the corner of the parlor, where they could keep an eye on her.

They settled in, waiting for the group that had been assigned to attack the Drake mansion, hoping to add them to their numbers. In the meantime, they watched the news coverage of the riot. They saw bodies strewn about everywhere. Riot police, punks and other looters, all dead in the streets. But the authorities were finally gaining the upper hand, and by eleven, the riot was pretty much over. Only a few stragglers remained.

They bandaged Kelly up as best they could, and shortly after, Wayne noticed that his pores had started bleeding again. Ordinarily, he'd let it go, since he usually lived on the street. Here, he excused himself and went to the bathroom to clean himself up and hope it stopped soon.

Stacy and Randall sat next to each other, watching as the cops arrested more rioters. The news showed footage of one guy who'd had his face stomped several times. The report identified him as Orville Anguson, but neither of them could have known he went by the name of Necro Cock. They still labored under the illusion that Skank's partner would eventually show up victorious.

Wayne came back, cleaned up again—for now—and joined them on the couch. Kelly sat in an easy chair, staring out into space, still dazed from the thrashing Skank had given him. No one said a word to anyone else.

Only two punks from the team designated to attack the Drake mansion made it, and one of them couldn't even stand on her own. A tall, gaunt man with a large, studded nose and a shock of purple hair pounded at the gate with one hand, and with the other, he held up a bullet-riddled woman against the bars, so she didn't fall. It was more a cry for help than a demand to be let in.

"I know that guy," Randall said. "How do we buzz him in?"

Wayne found a control panel by the foyer, and while he used it to unlock the gate, Stacy and Randall went down to meet the newcomers. Now the man carried the woman onto the property, blood leaking out from her in a steady spatter.

As they drew nearer, the gaunt man saw Randall and recognition lit up on his face. "What are you doing here?"

Randall tried to remember the guy's name, but he just couldn't. Instead, he glossed over it. "There's been a change in plans. Skank got killed, and now we're holing up and waiting for this mess to be over. Come on in. Is she all right?"

"Fuck no, man. Pigs shot her. We need help."

"Bring her in. Set her down on the couch. Wayne, get the first aid kit."

~

Elizabeth glared at the screen. "I paid five million dollars for that couch. It used to belong to the Princess of Tabutu. She died on it."

"And now it looks like this punk bitch is going to die on it, too." Edward couldn't help but smile. Serves the cunt right. He thought she should have done more to satisfy him than that five second handjob. Karma?

"They're getting blood all over my antique fucking couch."

Edward hoped the stain would never come out.

"Richard," she said, "I think we should send some of our guards out to my place and rout the scum."

Coppergate didn't even turn to face her. "I believe, Elizabeth-dear, that your request would not be very sporting. This is, after all, a game. We are not supposed to interfere unless in case of emergency."

"Oh? And what about Samuel?"

"Comparatively, Samuel is an extenuating circumstance. Although I despise our little hunter, even I must admit he can be entertaining. If we interfered, that wouldn't be very fun at all."

"Because of Samuel, we haven't been able to reward a winner in a long time, except for Edward. Doesn't *that* take away from the fun?"

"Only when he's performing poorly," Coppergate said. "So far, he hasn't exhibited a lot of creativity. Still, I believe this year will be a departure from tradition."

~

The gaunt man's name turned out to be Mange, and his female companion was his wife Cooze. As soon as he eased her onto the couch, blood saturated the cushions. Wayne produced the first aid kit, and Randall took it, getting ready to bandage her up.

"Wait," Mange said. "What about the bullets? We can't leave those fuckers in there. She'll die."

"I'm not a fucking doctor, okay?" Randall said.

Mange's face seemed to fold in on itself, and his eyes threatened tears.

Randall sighed. "Stacy doesn't know shit. Wayne has the Red Death. Kelly's not in any shape to do anything. Unless you've got an MD I don't know about, you're stuck with me. Okay?"

"She's my fucking wife, man," Mange said. "I don't want her to die on me." Finally, the tears spilled over his rocky cheeks.

"Look, I'm sorry. We can't do anything for her except make sure she doesn't bleed to death. We'll take her to the hospital when we can, but until then, those bullets are staying right where they are."

Randall found the remaining bandages and one by one, he pressed pads down over Cooze's wounds. There were three bullet holes and six pads, so he used two on each wound.

"Press on those tightly," he said to Mange. Randall took up the gauze and wrapped her up as best he could. "Just keep pressing down on those. We don't have any other bandages." Although they did have some tampons, if things got real bad. He thought it best not to mention that at such a tender time.

He checked the countdown. Fifteen hours to go.

Kelly mumbled something through his broken face.

"Huh?" Randall asked.

"He said he'll be right back," Wayne said.

"Where you going?"

"Buhfroom," Kelly said.

"Oh. Well, don't wander too far, and don't dally. You never know when the cops'll show up."

"Or worse," Stacy said. "That Drake woman is probably pissed at us being here. She might send someone to . . . get rid of us, I guess."

Kelly nodded and walked off in search of the bathroom.

2

As Samuel approached the east side, he saw a blockade in the road. Odd. What could this be about? He didn't bother trying to hide his weapons or the jet pack as he glided to a halt on the back of his motorcycle and waited for the cops to approach.

"What's the problem, officer?" he asked.

"There's a riot back there," the cop said. "I'm assuming you have a permit for those?" He pointed to the guns.

"Obviously," Samuel said. "Now, if you'll excuse me, I have to get through here. I live down there."

"Sure, buddy. And Richard Coppergate can dance the waltz. Get lost."

Samuel looked directly into the cop's eyes. Wordlessly, he flipped open his wallet, showing off his identification.

The cop jolted, as if he'd just been shown a license to kill. "I'm really sorry, Mr. Barnabas. I didn't know. You don't look like, well, you know."

Samuel ignored the fumbling apology and put his wallet back. "What's this riot all about?"

"A bunch of punks, sir. We don't know why, but this whole thing's almost over. There's just a few people still rioting. We've got it under control."

Skank. Of course. A very interesting tactic. But then, he laughed, remembering that she'd been killed.

"Are you all right?" the cop asked.

"I'm fine. Just fine. I'll be better when you move this barricade."

"Oh! Right. Of course. Sorry." The cop moved the barrier, scraping it across the pavement.

Samuel blazed past, driving parallel to the roadtrack as he zipped down the street, headed for his place. He thought he'd drop the motorcycle off and then walk to Elizabeth Drake's home, where he would finish everyone off. The walk wouldn't be long, and he didn't want them to hear the motorcycle. It was a sweet ride, but it made more noise than two cats fucking in a bucket of water. They didn't know about his wheels, of course, but better to be safe.

As he drew closer to his gates, he noticed something missing. The hydrant in front leaked water, as if the firefighters had just been here.

Then, he saw his gates, broken from their hinges. Beyond he saw what remained of his mansion: rubble. Nothing more. It had burned completely to the ground, and nothing would be salvaged.

A gnashing sound filled his head, and it took him a moment to realize he'd been grinding his teeth. He tried to force himself to stop, but he couldn't. Years and years of hard work, now reduced to dust. All his trophies, destroyed. The animal heads, nothing. The relics he'd collected over time, ash. All he owned he now carried on his person.

He didn't have to wonder who did this. He knew it had to be his . . . that cocksucker, Randall fucking Marsh.

When he found that fudge-fucker, he knew he wouldn't just kill him. No, he planned to tear his fingernails out one by one, and then he'd move on to Randall's teeth. He'd perform an autopsy on him before he died. He'd feed parts of him to dogs and make him watch. Then he'd cut off Randall's head, skin it, stuff it and put it on his mantle. No, wait, he actually wanted to skin Randall's head when he was still alive to feel it. And then he'd—

"No," he muttered. "Don't." He couldn't let Randall get to him. It would make him sloppy. He breathed deeply, hoping to calm down.

It didn't work. He still felt the anger burning in his head, searching for a way to steam out and kill something. Anything. He drove the motorcycle through the trashed gates and hid it behind some bushes. Then, he made sure his weapons were loaded, and he started walking toward the Drake mansion, eager to see his son once again.

3

By twelve-thirty, the news put a fork in the riot. They stopped showing footage and made no more mention of it. Outside, the sirens and gunshots stopped. They heard nothing but silence in the ravaged neighborhood.

Randall looked at the others. "I guess we won't be getting more reinforcements, then."

"I told you," Mange said. "None of my group made it. The cops got us a couple blocks away. Me and Cooze were lucky just to make it here."

"We'll need a new plan," Stacy said. "I don't think we alone could take on those rich fucks."

"We'll wait until the cops abandon the east end entirely," Randall said. "Then we'll take Mange and his wife to the hospital. From there, we'll have to start over again."

"We have fourteen and a half hours left." Stacy glanced over at Cooze, and she knew she didn't want to waste time with a hospital run. "We don't have much time left."

"We'll have enough. We'll have to."

"Speaking of time," Wayne said, "Kelly's been gone for a while."

"I'll look for him," Randall said. "I have to piss, anyway. Be on guard, okay? I'm sure he's fine, but you never know."

Stacy nodded as she patted the gun butt concealed by the front of her shirt.

4

Samuel slapped the switch on the jet pack, and he floated over the back fence of Elizabeth's property. He glided back down on the other side and turned off the switch. He knew that anyone who cared to look out the kitchen window would see him approaching, but by this point he didn't care. They only had a shotgun and a peashooter. Hardly heavy artillery.

He decided to enter the house from the top floor. They might expect an attack from the ground, but they certainly wouldn't expect it to come from above. Once again, he flipped the switch, and he flew up to the nearest third-story window, where he took out a pair of gloves, put them on and pressed on the glass. After a few seconds, the window weakened and finally broke inward almost soundlessly. Samuel quickly grabbed both shards before they could fall to the floor and shatter.

He then reached in and unlocked the window. He had plenty of room to ease into Elizabeth's bedroom. As soon as he shut off the jet pack, he breathed in deeply, getting a healthy whiff of Elizabeth's pleasant aroma. How many times had he fucked her on this very bed? One of his finest conquests. He almost wished he could mount her head and put it on display. But no, that would be a waste of good pussy.

He checked the LiveStreams and saw that a couple more punks had joined his prey. But he didn't find that nearly as interesting as the fact that Randall ascended the stairs, coming out on the landing of this very floor. He walked toward the bathroom—where Samuel had nailed Elizabeth in the shower every time they tried to clean up—and the bathroom adjoined with this one.

Quietly, Samuel approached the door.

5

After Randall realized how big the house was, he had no choice but to think Kelly had gotten lost looking for the bathroom. He called out Kelly's name.

He eventually found Kelly in the bathroom and asked him if he was all right.

"I'm taking a thit," Kelly said.

"A fine time for that," Randall said. "We're in the middle of all this danger, and you've got to pinch one off?"

"Man, thith one'th rough."

Randall sighed. "Just hurry up, okay?" And he went upstairs in search of another shitter.

He found one on the third floor. Upon entering, he noticed another door, and it probably led to the bedroom. He closed both doors and thought about locking them, but he decided against it. Who would want to watch him piss, anyway?

He unzipped his pants and fished out a dick almost as long as his forearm. He pissed, thinking about what they would do as soon as they got Cooze to the hospital. He lost himself in thought so far that he didn't notice the knob on one of the doors turn quietly. He didn't see his father slip silently over the threshold. Nor did he see the shotgun rise, aimed at his head.

Someone whistled behind him, and he whipped around so quickly he sprayed piss all over the bathroom wall. Then, he saw the shotgun, and his penis shriveled down to the size of a cocktail wiener.

Samuel grinned.

~

"No way will he do it," William said.

"Samuel's a savage," Charles said. "A billion dollars says he does it."

William nearly gagged. "That's . . ."

"Put your money where your mouth is," Charles said. "Or you can shut up."

"Silence," Coppergate said. "I'm trying to hear this."

Both of them whispered back and forth behind Coppergate, but they all watched the screen, intent on catching every single detail.

CHAPTER 17

1

After a mere two miles, Jimmy didn't want to go on any further. His body dripped with sweat, he couldn't stop breathing through his mouth and his feet felt damp with popped blisters. "We gotta' find a ride," he said.

"Fucking pussy," Jack said. "This walk'll do you good. You spend too much time behind a desk. You've been putting some pounds on. I don't want to see you get fat."

"I don't want to keel over and die," Jimmy said.

"Relax. We're almost to the mall. We can catch a bus from there."

"How much longer?"

"Another two miles."

"Oh fuck."

2

By the time they caught a bus headed for the city, Jimmy sat down and decided he would never stand again. Jack laughed at him. "Was that really so bad, Jimmy? You can't be that much out of shape."

Jimmy huffed. "Fuck. You."

"Maybe you should lay off the sauce. Or go to the gym more often."

"Fuck. Off."

"All right, live in denial."

Jimmy closed his eyes and dropped into an easy slumber. Jack watched the TV at the front of the bus. The news said something about a riot, and when they started showing footage of the east end, his jaw dropped. He slapped at Jimmy.

"What? Can't you let me get some sleep?"

"Look at the TV." Jack pointed.

Jimmy watched for a second, ready to dismiss Jack in an instant. And then, it sank in. The punks. Skank had to be behind this mess.

"We'll never get through the cops," Jimmy said.

"No, they said the riot's over now. They're just sweeping up the stragglers. We'll have no problem. But I think that goes to show that the others will want to be on our side."

Jimmy nodded. "Good."

"Better than good. It's starting to look like we might have a chance of coming out on top."

"So what will we do once we find them?" Jimmy asked.

"Charge Wingate's mansion, of course. Run in and shoot everyone in sight."

Jimmy grunted. "That sounds like an intelligent plan."

"It is. People don't appreciate the value of a guerilla attack. It's quick, efficient and no one ever expects it. We certainly didn't, when that bastard shot Steve and blew my house up. Besides, now that we'll have the numbers, we might be able to put up a decent fight."

Jimmy couldn't argue with that. In fact, he didn't want to. He just wanted to close his eyes for the rest of this trip. Something told him he would need every bit of rest he could get for the final confrontation.

CHAPTER 18

1

They stood like that for a minute, Samuel aiming the shotgun at his son's head, and Randall looking down both barrels, too shocked to so much as pack away his dick. Neither man so much as breathed.

Randall wanted to beg for his life. In all of his wild imaginings, he never thought he'd be the one on this side of the shotgun, and he couldn't believe it would end like this. Part of him hated the desire—no, *need*—to beg, but it didn't matter. One way or the other, he couldn't do anything.

Samuel's eyes narrowed, and his trigger finger flexed. Randall couldn't even close his eyes as he prepared for the impending blast that would send him into the next world. But then, no sound came. Had his father fired on an empty chamber? He hadn't heard a click.

And then, relief flooded his system. He wouldn't die tonight, after all. His father wanted to scare the shit out of him, that's all. Yet Randall still focused on the twin hammers, both cocked and ready to fire at any moment. Something slick moved in his belly, and he wanted desperately to turn away.

Samuel's mouth drooped into a frown, and something sparkled in his eyes. Not excitement, as it had a moment before, but Randall thought . . . could those be tears?

The double barrels drifted away from Randall's head until they aimed down at the linoleum. He felt tension melt out of him as he watched his father's chest start to hitch. Finally, Samuel said, "Why?"

Randall didn't understand. Why what?

"Why the fuck did you have to be a faggot?"

The word started something kindling in Randall's guts, and he had to remind himself that his father still had the upper hand and could kill him at any moment. He forced himself to remain silent.

"I brought you on camping trips," Samuel continued. "We hunted bear together when you were ten, remember? I showed you how to skin that fucker and cook the good parts. We put him in my den."

Randall didn't say anything.

"All those ball games we went to. Fishing. Remember I taught you how to bait your hook? You were scared to touch the worms, but you learned to do it anyway. These aren't faggot things to do. Didn't any of that mean anything?"

Randall's silence finally broke. "Yes, it did. You were my father. I thought you were the greatest human being in the world. I loved those trips more than anything else, and believe it or not, I still look back on them with fondness."

"Then why?" Samuel asked. "Why did you have be this way?" He struggled not to be too loud, but something inside his chest felt bigger than him, and he felt the need to let it out.

"What's so bad about it?" Randall asked. "It's not like I was nerve gassing children or beating the elderly. And it's not like I don't want women. I've been with plenty of them, too. I just also happen to like guys, as well."

"Don't give me that shit," Samuel said. "Packing fudge is packing fudge, and it just ain't natural. It's . . .you were my son, goddammit! No son of mine takes it in the ass!"

"Well, I've got news for you, *Dad*, I not only take it in the ass, I take it in the mouth, too. I sucked a cock just last night, before your goons kidnapped me."

Randall instantly regretted saying it. The shotgun came back up, once again aimed at his head. Yet . . . it wavered.

"Why do you say things like that?" Samuel's voice shook, and Randall saw his father's shining eyes finally start to drip. "And for Christ's sake, put that away!"

Randall forgot about his dick. He tucked himself back into his pants and zipped up. "Why were you so judgmental? You ask me why I say these things. I say them because you're the biggest asshole I've ever known. You disowned me, you fucking prick."

"God didn't make us like that," Samuel said. "We were meant to fuck women, not each other. We—"

"Tell me you've never fucked a woman up the ass," Randall said.

"Never." And he told the truth. He'd never think about putting his precious dick in someone else's shit hole.

"Liar. Guys do it all the time. It's not all that different from—"

"Unless you're taking it instead of giving it. Is that like anal sex with women?"

Randall thought about the gun he'd left behind in the flaming limo. He never wanted anything more in his life than to have that gun with him now. He even thought about Stacy's pistol. He gritted his teeth. "You'll never understand me. That's fine. I never wanted you to. I just wanted you to accept me for what I am, and what did you do? You disowned me. Sent me east of Eden, if you want to look at it from the Lord's perspective. We can still do all of those father and son things. All you have to do is get this archaic nonsense out of the way. I hate you for what you did to me, but you're still my father. The little boy who remembers the good times still loves you and yearns for the old days to return."

He'd told the truth in all of these things, but he'd said them mostly to get his father to wax nostalgic, to let his guard down. Part of him really did want another father/son outing. Maybe they could hunt another bear together. Or maybe just have a couple of beers and hang out.

But he also knew his father to be a monster. He knew, deep down, beyond all the dreams of the past, that he had to kill this man.

"You were supposed to be my heir," Samuel said. "I can't have a faggot take over the business and my name."

"I'm bisexual. I've fucked women, too. Don't you get that?"

Samuel grunted. "Bisexual. That's a laugh. That's what a faggot says when he's too much of a pussy to admit that he's a faggot."

"Can't you just let it go?" Randall said. "Do you have any idea how bigoted you sound right now?"

Samuel ignored him. "You'd destroy our reputation."

"Fuck that! Respectable men have been fucking other men since the days of Alexander the Great and before! Society looks up to someone who gets shit done, regardless of who he fucks!"

"The Barnabas name is a respected name." Samuel spoke in monotone, as if reading from a script. "We're world renowned. You don't run in the same circles I do. If people found out that Samuel Maxwell Barnabas, IV, takes cock in the ass, then they'd think twice about doing business with him. They'd think twice about his old man, too."

Randall roared and punched the nearest wall twice, cracking the tiles, opening up his injuries from earlier. He ignored the shooting pain in his split, bleeding knuckles. Instead, he looked at his father, his face red, tears running down his cheeks. "Goddammit, Dad, stop talking about that shit! You don't need more money! You've got more than you can spend in ten lifetimes! When are you going to think about me? When are you going to accept me? What the fuck do I have to do to get you to love me again?"

Samuel didn't answer. Randall punched the wall again, leaving four crimson marks the size of dimes to contrast with the ocean blue tiles, and he gave in to his sobs. As his eyes burned with tears, he couldn't believe it.

He'd meant to put on an act, but could he really feel this way? Could he really still love his father?

Samuel propped the shotgun against the wall near the window and turned away from his son. He let Randall cry for a while before he let out a tremulous sigh. "Why did you burn the house down?" He didn't turn to face his son.

Randall moaned. "Isn't it obvious?"

"That's kind of a stupid reason to burn a house down."

"Fuck the house!" Randall cried. "Fuck the house! You can always get another one! There's only one of me!"

They remained in silence again, and Randall rubbed the moisture from his eyes. In that moment, he noticed the abandoned shotgun leaning against the wall. He knew he could grab it and shoot his father, and Samuel wouldn't be able to defend himself. Still, after everything he'd gone through in the past day, he balked at the idea. Samuel could have killed him, but for some reason, he didn't. Could Randall's words have actually gotten through to his father?

He had to choose. He could either grab the shotgun and end this, or he could test the water. See if this bridge could be mended. The former sounded safer, but the latter? It could pay off a lot more, if it turned out to be genuine. Besides, he could probably still get the drop on his old man, just so long as he stepped between him and the gun.

Randall approached his father from behind. "Please. Tell me you love me, Dad. That's all I want."

Samuel spoke not a word.

"Father, tell me you love me."

Silence.

Randall grabbed his father's shoulders. "Tell me you love me, Dad." He turned his father around and couldn't believe what he saw.

Samuel Maxwell Barnabas, III, Alpha Male of the Highest Order, a Manly Man of many manly men, openly wept.

~

"I really hope we're recording this," Edward said. "I wouldn't believe it if I wasn't seeing it myself."

"Samuel's not a superman," Elizabeth said. "He sometimes cries during sex."

"That's . . . an interesting visual, Elizabeth. Thank you. I may never sleep again."

"Silence," Coppergate said. "I want to hear this."

~

Despite the tears, Samuel spoke lucidly. "Give Daddy a hug, Sammy."

Randall looked at his father, still unbelieving. No one had ever seen Samuel like this before. And Randall hadn't been called Sammy in a long time, not since before the incident with the scout leader. Yet it seemed so real, how could he not believe?

Randall forgot about the shotgun and embraced his father. He could feel Samuel's tears on his neck, and it felt more comforting than anything had since childhood. "Thank you, Dad. Thank you."

Samuel didn't say a word as they stood in each other's arms for the first time in years.

"I love you, Dad."

Samuel clenched his eyes shut and whispered, "Why do you make me do these things?"

Randall tensed. It felt like someone had jabbed an icicle up his asshole. Fear made him try to pull back, but his father's steel arms held him in place.

"What was that, Dad?" Randall asked. But he knew. He looked over to the shotgun and wondered if he could reach it from here.

Samuel didn't answer. Instead, he drew his knife and touched it gently to Randall's throat. The tip prodded his jugular.

Randall whimpered and tried to yank himself away from his father. He couldn't move.

Samuel, his eyes screwed tightly closed, snarled. "If I'd known how you'd turn out, I would have killed that childfucking scout master. And you."

"No—" Randall said.

He never finished his plea. Samuel pushed the blade into his son's throat, letting the juices flow freely from the deep wound all over his hands.

Randall gagged, and blood sprayed from his mouth and nose. His lips formed words that couldn't be given voice as he clutched at his father's hands. Tears oozed out from behind Samuel's closed eyelids as he listened to his son die in his arms. He could feel Randall's life saturating his clothes.

"Why do you make me do these things?" Samuel whispered. Then, his sobs turned into rage, and he roared. "Why do you make me do these things, you faggot?!" He pulled the knife from Randall's throat and stabbed him in the chest. Again, he pulled back and stuck the blade into his son again and again and again. Blood flicked off cold metal and dotted the entire bathroom. The walls, the floor, the ceiling.

Randall fell under the hail of his father's thrusts, most of his blood already voided from his body. He could barely hear Samuel's shouts, but he knew the words. Over and over again. "Why, faggot? Why? Why do you make me do these things?"

Samuel stabbed down again, but the blade didn't penetrate his son's body this time. He stopped and saw that the blade had broken off, maybe against the tiles underneath Randall's body. He cast the defective weapon away and grabbed for the one most readily available, the blackjack hanging off of his belt. Randall's bones crunched under the blows. His eyes puffed out and closed, popped behind the useless shields of their lids. Broken teeth pushed through his lips and littered the floor around him. Blow after blow, his head flattened just a little more as blood poured from his nostrils and ears. His obliterated skull finally started showing through skin too tattered to remain on his face.

Finally, mercifully, Randall died, and Samuel wept over his body, beating it again and again, slowly growing weaker. Then, he collapsed on his son's pulped chest and poured his tears into the knife wounds. "Why did you do this to me, Sammy? Why?"

2

It took a while for the tears to stop. When they did, Samuel straightened out and wiped the knife clean before returning it to its sheath. He then picked up the shotgun, ready to take on the other occupants of this house. He wanted to get this over with as soon as possible.

On his way out of the bathroom, he caught a glimpse of himself in the mirror. Covered in his son's blood, his eyes shot with red, snot in his mustache and the wild mess of his hair. He looked like an animal, yet his eyes were cold and focused, just the way he needed them to be.

Time to finish this shit.

~

"And that, friends and associates, is why I find Samuel occasionally entertaining." Coppergate smiled as he watched the screen filled with Samuel's puffy, tear-streaked face just before it dissolved into static.

"Wow," Edward said. "I didn't think he'd do it. I mean, the guy was Samuel's son. What kind of cold-hearted son of a bitch kills his own son like that?"

"We didn't think he'd do it, either," Charles said. "That's why we nominated young Sammy. We thought Samuel would draw the line with his own kin, thus bringing an end to his interference with the game."

"I never doubted him," Coppergate said. "I merely thought it would be entertaining, and I have been correct. As for eliminating Samuel's participation, never fear, Charles. We still have one hope."

CHAPTER 19

1

Toby took one final sip, finally killing off the drink he'd been nursing for two hours. He placed the empty glass quietly down on the bar, and the bartender looked over to him, his eyebrows lifted. Toby could tell the bartender didn't like him; after all, he'd been sitting in this bar for hours, drinking two whiskies, nothing more.

"Well?" the bartender asked. "You want another one?"

"No thank you." Toby flipped through the LiveStreams from the intranet Coppergate's techs had downloaded into his head. Only two of them were left: Stacy and Wayne.

"If you're gonna' sit there, you have to buy something," the bartender said. "This ain't a hotel."

Toby considered this for a moment. On one hand, he could have another drink while waiting for Samuel to arrive, but that could take too long. The hunter had apparently left Toby for last. Besides, he didn't want to have a buzz when it came time for their showdown. On the other hand, he could just leave now and finish this nonsense so he could fulfill his contract and collect an extra billion dollars in the bargain.

The latter seemed more practical.

"I'll be leaving now," he said.

The bartender snorted. "I give a shit." He turned to watch the TV mounted on the wall. It presented a classic show from 2170 called *Daddy Needs Love*, a stupid sit-com about a family in which everyone was perfect except the father. Daddy always tried to fuck other women, but his plans were constantly foiled by his do-gooder wife. Toby hated shit like that. All sit-coms were stupid, but *Daddy Needs Love* came from the absolute bottom of the barrel.

As soon as Toby stood outside, he paused, wondering where he should go in order to find Samuel. He supposed he could head to the man's house, but who knew when Samuel would go home? No, he had to find Stacy and Wayne, since they would be Samuel's next target. He'd let the hunter kill them first, and then he'd step in and work his magic.

He checked the LiveStreams and saw Stacy and Wayne were both in a parlor of some kind. He saw a nude painting on one of the walls, one he recognized from the meeting he'd had with Elizabeth Drake. It had been pleasure, not business. The young woman had clearly taken a shine to him because of his occupation. She seemed to love death, no matter whose mask it wore. He remembered fucking her on that very couch. Stacy sat where he'd fucked Elizabeth in the ass.

He looked forward to doing it again.

He checked the countdown. Fourteen hours. Still plenty of time. He walked up to the street and held up his hand. "Taxi!"

2

Jack and Jimmy took the bus to the station, where they called for a cab. It took a half an hour for the taxi to show up, and then they headed out to the east side. Jack gave Samuel's address as the destination.

"Shouldn't we be going to the Wingate place?" Jimmy asked.

"I want to see if the motherfucker went home first. If so, we'll waste him in his own house."

"I don't think he'll be there. He's still out hunting the others, remember?"

"It's worth a shot. Besides, his place is the closest. If he isn't there, we'll go on to Wingate's."

When they got to the east side, they heard nothing but silence. The riot had long since passed. The bodies and barricades had all been taken away, as if nothing had happened here. Of course, the burned out hulks of mansions and the crashed cars still remained, reflecting the sun off their dirty metal surfaces, testament to Skank's best attempt to avenge Nutsack.

They pulled up to the Barnabas mansion, both of them shocked to see what remained of it.

"What the fuck?" Jack said.

"What the hell happened here?" Jimmy asked.

"I guess he's not coming home, then." He turned to the cabbie. "Change of plan. Here's the new destination." And he recited Wingate's address.

"You already owe me fifty bucks," the cabbie said. "You sure you can pay me?"

Jack's nostrils flared. "You want to check my account?"

The cabbie waved him away before programming the new destination into his dash computer.

CHAPTER 20

1

Since the riot ended, they didn't find much worth watching on the TV. Wayne and Stacy sat on the couch together, watching the big screen, flipping past sit-coms, ball games and opinions shows that disguised themselves as news shows, all boring tripe that would melt the brain given half a chance.

Behind them, Mange paced back and forth. He'd been sitting on the other couch, the fancy one, with Cooze, but when he realized she wouldn't be waking up any time soon, he began wearing a hole in the carpet, his head down, his giant hands jammed into his pockets.

The maid, having figured out that these guys didn't mean to harm her, got tired of watching the television and closed her eyes. Wayne didn't think she really slept—could anyone tied up and gagged sleep like that?—but he didn't care.

Neither of them noticed that Randall and Kelly hadn't come back yet.

Stacy found her *Eightball Gabe* marathon and turned up the volume.

"Ugh," Wayne said. "Change it."

"Fuck no. I love this show. I love how it's told from the criminal's point of view instead of the stupid cops."

"This blows."

"Eightball's sexy."

"The guy who plays him couldn't act his way out of a torn paper bag, not even with a bottle of water and a knife."

"He's got a nice ass, though."

"He's thirteen years old."

"He's still got a nice ass."

And then, Wayne remembered Stacy was only fifteen, herself. He found it hard to believe, considering how she carried herself. Hypersexualized and eager to violence. He didn't know what had happened to make her this way, and he didn't want to know, but it had aged her at least a decade beyond her years.

Stacy laughed when Eightball Gabe beat the shit out of an old lady and started raping her. Yeah, she liked an edgy show like this, but her mind didn't want to follow the story. It kept reflecting on what had happened so far since she'd been kidnapped, and what might happen soon. She knew there couldn't be many fellow contestants left now. If they were going to go through with this plan to bring down the rich people, they'd have to do it soon. She checked the countdown and saw how much time had dwindled. Of course, it didn't matter much to her. If things got bad, she could always turn on her "friends" and earn a quick billion dollars.

Or could she? Stacy glanced at Wayne, who looked out a window, bored. Truth be told, she didn't know if she could kill him anymore, after all they'd been through together. Also, he was one of the few men she'd ever known who wasn't an asshole. Too bad about the Red Death. She probably would have fucked him by now, if not for that. Gazing at his profile—clean for the moment—she wished she'd met him before his diagnosis. She had no doubt he'd been handsome in his youth.

Why couldn't he have been a piece of shit? Why did he have to be such a nice guy? Why did he have to make this so hard on Stacy?

Wayne turned and caught her looking at him. His eyebrows raised. "What?"

No, she couldn't do it. Even though he smelled and looked like shit, she knew she wouldn't be able to kill him.

"Nothing," she said. "I was just thinking."

"About?"

Her mind stumbled, but she managed to snag a cover-up. "About you."

Wayne felt his skin tingle as he looked into her clear blue eyes. For the first time since they'd met, he saw past her hypersexuality and recognized something at her core, something he could almost feel attracted to. When he realized how he felt, he turned away from her, mentally berating himself. How could he think about her in such a way? She should be in high school, for Christ's sake! And what made him think she might be attracted to him in the first place? She'd seen what the Red Death had done to him.

He cleared his throat. "Me?"

"Yeah, you. How did you get to be a crusader?"

He laughed, and the sexual tension poured out of him. "A crusader? Me? No, I just see the chance to do something good before I die."

"You're a good guy."

"I don't know about that." He thought about David Nelson again and remembered the pulp of his face. "I used to be a mean bastard."

"You? I don't believe it."

"Believe it. Sometimes, I wake up and think that I deserve what I got, that the Red Death is payback for a life of being a piece of shit."

"No one deserves the Red Death," Stacy said. "Well, maybe those rich fucks."

"I did some pretty bad things to people who didn't deserve it. I guess it's just time to finally make up for it, to somehow balance the cosmic scale."

"See? You're a good guy."

"I hope so." He sighed. "I know you agreed to go with me on this because I threatened you—and I'm sorry for that, I really am—but if it's any consolation, I wouldn't have been able to do it."

"I know," she said.

"I understand that the money is pretty tempting, and everything, but . . . well . . ." He found that he couldn't come out and ask it. The thought of such weakness repulsed him, and he wanted to punch himself a couple of times in the head to jumpstart his brain.

"You want to know if I'm going to fuck you over for the billion," Stacy said.

"Well . . ." Wayne nodded. "Yeah. I don't mean to look a gift horse in the mouth, and I'm really grateful to you for saving my life back at the liquor store, but not knowing is killing me." He grimaced. "Ugh. Poor choice of words."

Shit. She couldn't get around it this time. She drew in a deep breath and let it out. Why hide it now? "I almost didn't save you. In fact, the only reason I went along with you was because two heads were better than one at finding the others. I was going to double-cross you and kill you all and take the billion dollars."

Wayne blinked, breathing through his mouth. He searched her face for a joke but couldn't find one. "You're kidding me, right?"

Stacy met his eyes with hers in a cold lock. "No."

Holy shit. He couldn't get his mind around it. She could have killed him at any moment. He wondered if, back when he'd been taking a shower and had been thinking she might kill him, had she seriously considered going into the bathroom and murdering him? Had their thoughts crossed in the ether like a data stream?

And then, he realized something else: it didn't matter to him. He only felt surprise because he hadn't expected something so Machiavellian from such a young girl. But he'd had the Red Death for a long time, and he really didn't have much longer to live, even if he survived this game. Of course, he didn't want to die, but he knew the grim reaper would be a break in his daily, painful routine. It would be nice to have no more worries, no more fears. It would also be nice to not bleed from his pores constantly, or to wake up in a puddle of his own diarrhea.

"Why tell me now?" he asked. "It sounds like a pretty good plan."

Stacy bit her lower lip and turned away from him. "I . . . I couldn't have killed you. At first, I thought I could, but not now, not after I've gotten to know you a little. You're too good a guy to kill."

"Shit. It's a good thing you didn't know me all those years ago. You would've killed me for sure if you'd known—"

"I don't want to know," she said. "All that matters is the man before me now." She smiled a little and gave him a sidelong glance. "Maybe if things were different, you and I could have gotten to know each other better."

Mange stepped in front of the television. "You know what? You guys are seriously fucked up. I've never, in all my life, heard a conversation like this one, and I've heard some fucked up shit."

Stacy and Wayne looked at each other and laughed. It felt good, better than either of them had felt in a long time.

2

Samuel stepped lightly on the stairs as he made his way to the first floor. He knew every step that creaked and avoided them, even though the others probably couldn't hear him. The TV blared, and he could hear the conversation they were having.

He walked along the wall as he headed to the parlor. Occasionally, he had to step around an exotic plant or ease around a large painting, but for the most part, he kept his trek straight and narrow. He wished this would end quickly. A bath, some relaxation and maybe some sex waited for him, but most importantly, he wanted to curl up in his bed and go to sleep . . . except he no longer had a bed, did he? Fuck. He'd have to stay the night in a hotel, then.

He reached the parlor and saw the wide-open door. Poking his head over the threshold, he saw Wayne and Stacy on one of the couches, their backs to him, watching the TV. Some stupid cop show. A tall, skinny kid watched along with them, but he sat on the floor next to the couch. On the other couch, the one Elizabeth prided herself on owning, a punk girl rested, not unlike Skank. They'd wrapped her in so much gauze she looked like a mummy. A mummy with a lot of blood stains.

Samuel saw a maid against a wall, bound and gagged, her eyes closed. She wouldn't be a problem.

The punk girl was the closest, and killing her would cause the most shock and confusion. He approached her with the shotgun aimed at her head, stepping with the silent ease of a ninja. The punk girl looked badly damaged, and he wondered if maybe he'd be doing her a favor.

He thought using one barrel would be sufficient, and it would probably be smart, since the others would react very quickly. If they had guns, they might be able to nail him. But he had more guns, and he knew he could draw faster than them. Besides, two barrels would have a much more desirable effect.

Smiling, he touched the shotgun into the girl's belly and prodded her. When she didn't respond, he pushed down into her gut harder, and her eyes shot open.

She moaned, too lost in pain to comprehend Samuel.

He smiled and shook his head, his eyes glued to hers, and he moved the barrels to her face. He gave her just enough time to realize his intentions, just enough time to draw a breath to scream, before he pulled both triggers, turning her head into a large, saturated smear on the remains of Elizabeth's couch.

3

Kelly heard the shotgun blast on the third time he flushed the toilet. He'd been unleashing a horrible bout of diarrhea—probably because of the greasy fast food he'd had for dinner—and he couldn't stop wiping his ass. As he gingerly wiped his burning poop chute, he wished he had a good snort of heroin to ease his pain, not just from the shits, but from the damage Skank had inflicted upon him. Hell, even a cigarette would help him now.

He thought one more wipe would do the trick when he heard the explosion from the parlor. If he hadn't just voided his bowels, he probably would have done so then and there.

For a moment, he sat on the toilet, his thighs numb, deathly afraid to do anything. A shotgun blast sure as hell couldn't be a good thing, no matter who pulled the trigger. Then, he remembered throwing the Molotov cocktail at the limo that had Skank and the others in it, making him responsible for the deaths of God knew how many of his friends. He had to do something to redeem himself.

He yanked his pants up and ran for the door.

4

Wayne jerked, and Stacy yelped, instantly wetting her jeans. Both turned their heads in unison to see Samuel standing above the split pumpkin that had been Cooze's head. They saw the shotgun, and both jumped to their feet, pressing their backs against the wall. Stacy wanted to go for her gun, but she knew she'd never make it. Samuel looked directly at her, almost daring her to draw down.

Mange froze in place, staring at the remains of his wife. Her jaw still clung to her throat, as did part of her nose. Everything above that, including her eyes, had been replaced by bloody mulch. That couldn't be his wife. She'd been lying on the couch, sure, but that couldn't be her. Cooze had an entire head, not that pulpy mess.

But he couldn't deny it any longer. Her death finally sank into Mange's head, and he screamed.

"She looks prettier this way," Samuel said. "No piercings, no stupid hair. Very nice. I'd fuck her."

"Cooze!" Mange screamed. He fell to his knees, tears streaming down his bony cheeks. Snot ran down his chin as his body shook, and he tried to call out her name again.

Samuel's smile vanished. "What did you call me?"

"You killed Cooze!" Mange howled. He lurched to his feet, rushing toward Samuel with his fists raised. "I'll fucking kill you, you mother—"

He never finished his sentence. Samuel casually dropped the shotgun and drew his .44, pulling the trigger in one fluid motion. Mange took it in the chest—in the heart—and his back exploded out, shredded flesh and bone spraying the wall behind him. He collapsed in a pile, dead before he even knew it.

Stacy saw her chance and reached for the butt of her gun, which poked out of the front of her jeans. She felt like a gunslinger, full of righteous fury, ready to put down the bad guy like a dog.

But Samuel was too fast. He whirled on her, and she felt her blood freeze. She couldn't move. She couldn't even breathe.

"I wouldn't do that," Samuel said.

"Why not?" she asked. Her voice trembled so badly, she sounded like a nervous kid trying to give a speech to his class. "You're gonna' kill us anyway."

"Maybe. Maybe not. Maybe I just want to talk."

All three of them heard loud thumping sounds as someone ran toward the parlor. Stacy and Wayne both looked at Samuel, but he didn't betray any notion that he'd heard the sounds as well.

The two of them looked beyond the hunter and watched as Kelly appeared at the door, holding what looked like a bar from a towel rack. As soon as Kelly's bandaged face had surveyed the scene, he began to creep up behind Samuel, holding the bar high.

They tried their best to ignore him as Samuel continued:

"It's been quite the chase, but you two are the last, aside from Toby Munger. Did you know that? You came this close—" He held his thumb and forefinger a half-inch apart. "—to getting the billion dollars. I have the power to make royalty of you paupers. Or I can make corpses out of you. And I'll be honest: it sometimes helps to beg."

Kelly stood directly behind Samuel now. He pulled his arms all the way back for maximum force, but before he could start the downswing, Samuel straightened out his free hand, and a Derringer popped into his palm. Without looking, he aimed behind him and pulled the trigger, sending a tiny bullet into Kelly's adam's apple. He gagged, dropping the bar, and he clutched his throat, trying to get the blood to stop. It only forced the blood down his windpipe, and he started choking.

Wayne couldn't believe it. How could Samuel be that good?

Samuel fired again, again without looking, and got Kelly through the eye. He dropped to his knees and fell to his face. He contemplated the bloody carpet for a moment before his life faded away like reception from a bad antenna.

Stacy didn't think Samuel could still be so focused on them in that moment. As soon as she saw him shift to draw out the Derringer, she yanked at the butt of her gun, ready to take advantage of the moment.

It wouldn't come out.

The sight! It had hooked up on her jeans. She reached her other hand down the front of her pants to unhook it.

Samuel, surprised by the audacity of this little girl, watched her for a moment, amused. Usually, when he shot a man behind his back, the move inspired fear and awe in onlookers, just like it had in Wayne. Not for Stacy Bartlett, though.

She freed the gun and brought it up, firing wildly.

Only once before had Samuel been shot, and that had been last year, when Edward had grazed his head with a bullet. Now, he felt another bullet, and this time it slammed into the left side of his chest, knocking him back a couple of steps.

~

"Holy hell," Edward said. "She got him."

"Don't count him out yet," Coppergate said. "I don't see any blood."

~

If this had been last year, Stacy's bullet would have killed Samuel. But this year, he'd worn Kevlar, just in case. It hurt like a bitch, but it wouldn't leave anything more damaging than a bruise. He also thought himself lucky. If he hadn't been wearing armor, the bullet might have punched through his body and gotten the jet pack. He didn't relish the idea of his insides decorating Elizabeth's parlor.

It took him a moment to catch his breath, but when he did, he saw that Stacy's chamber had opened. Her gun was empty.

"Oh shit," she said.

Samuel brought the .44 up and shot her in the chest, exactly where she'd shot him. Then, he shot her again on the opposite side of her breastbone. His bullets tore her tits to pieces, and that brought him some kind of satisfaction, destroying something so many men had sought to own.

"Stacy!" Wayne screamed.

She'd been blown back against the wall, and now she slid down, leaving a thick smear of blood on the plaster. He knelt beside her as she gurgled blood from her ruined lungs. He wanted to touch her, to soothe her in some way, but he couldn't. What if she survived? She might end up with the Red Death, and he couldn't live with that.

"Stacy, don't die. Please, don't leave me. Not now, not after all of this."

She looked into his eyes and tried to say something. Instead, she sprayed blood on his face from her lips. Her baby blue eyes, which had captivated him mere moments ago, were now wild and somehow empty, blind and trying to see.

He saw through the red and white prison of her ribcage as her torn heart beat erratically before finally stopping.

"No!" Wayne cried. Tears fell from his cheeks and onto Stacy's staring eyes.

Samuel took up his shotgun again, using it to brace himself so his quivering legs wouldn't collapse under him. When he knew he wouldn't fall, he dropped the .44 in favor of a lighter .38.

Wayne looked up and saw Samuel approach him. His eyes darted about the room, looking for an escape route. He wanted to kill Samuel for what he'd done to Stacy, just as he'd once wanted to kill Stacy for what she'd done to Old Shit, but he couldn't do anything without a weapon.

He only had one way out, and Wayne didn't hesitate; he ran for the nearby window and hurled himself through the glass.

He fell face down into the lawn three feet below. A puddle of broken glass surrounded him, and he could feel a few shards sticking into his body. He had no time for regret, no matter how much of his own blood seeped out of him. He felt glad to be alive, and he wanted to keep it that way.

His body wanted to remain on the ground in surrender, and to add insult to injury, he felt the Red Death kick in yet again. Blood oozed not just from his wounds, but also from his pores. It would have been so easy to just give in then and there, but he knew he had to get away. Carefully, he placed his hands between the pieces of broken glass and eased himself to his feet. He had no time to take inventory of his injuries; as soon as he stood, he staggered away from the house as quickly as he could.

5

"Goddammit!" Samuel roared. Without thinking, he slung a bullet into the maid's head, killing her in the blink of an eye. As if he didn't notice his split-second homicide, he shuffled over to the window and peered out as Wayne ran for the gates.

Samuel lifted his gun and took aim, but his hand shook, even when he tried to steady it with his other. Fucking Stacy. She just had to hit him, didn't she?

No, he didn't want to do it like this, anyway. He loved nothing more than to look into his victim's eyes as he killed them.

He kicked out the remaining glass in the window and slipped out. Once on the ground, he slapped the switch on his jet pack and blasted into the sky just as Wayne made it to the front gate. Samuel watched from above as Wayne slid through the open bars and nearly fell onto the sidewalk. Just as he started to lurch away, Samuel decided to descend.

He landed directly in front of Wayne. He drew the .44 again and aimed it at his target. Wayne skidded to a halt, and Samuel shoved the barrel of the gun into his gut, dropping him like a sack of shit.

"Hurts, doesn't it?" Samuel asked. He aimed the gun at Wayne's head. "Yeah, well, just imagine what it will feel like when I put this bullet in your head."

Wayne looked down the barrel and couldn't believe something could be so dark. So everything in his life led up to this moment, did it? The good times as a kid, the bad times as an adult, David Nelson, Old Shit, Stacy Bartlett, the whole fucking mess? He remembered being a teenager, wondering how he would die someday. He and his friends had tried to come up with something really cool they could say just before they died. Something witty. Maybe even profound.

Now, nothing came to mind. He couldn't even remember what he'd settled on back then.

"Think of it this way," Samuel said. "At least getting blown away by me is better than dying of the Red Death. I'm doing you a favor, here. Maybe you should thank me."

Wayne closed his eyes. At least Samuel was right. Getting shot would certainly be more dignified. He tensed himself for the blast that would inevitably come.

"Fine, don't thank me. And don't watch. But you're missing a lot. You bought the ticket, you might as well take the ride." He laughed.

"Just get it over with," Wayne said. He clenched his teeth and couldn't believe that in mere seconds, he wouldn't be in this world anymore.

Then, he heard the crack of a gun.

CHAPTER 21

1

Toby had the taxi drop him off a block away from the Drake mansion, just to be safe. He gave the cabbie a nice tip and began walking toward his destination. He'd been watching the LiveStreams, so he knew that Stacy had been terminated. He knew that Samuel tracked down Wayne at this very moment. He heard the crash of Wayne going through the window with his own ears.

About fifty yards ahead of him, he saw Wayne slip through the gates—something he couldn't have done if not for being so skinny thanks to the Red Death—and almost fall down. Then, he saw Samuel float down from the sky like a god of war, his hair tousled around his head like a dirty halo. Toby guessed the hunter wore a jet pack, which impressed him. Rich people got to have the coolest toys. Though he couldn't see it, he knew Samuel now aimed a gun at Wayne. Toby drew close enough to hear them talking.

"Think of it this way. At least getting blown away by me is better than dying of the Red Death. I'm doing you a favor, here. Maybe you should thank me."

Toby's body thrummed with adrenaline. His hands shook as he felt his senses sharpen. He could see every filament of dust in the sunlight, and he could hear even an ant tapping its legs on the sidewalk. He could smell Stacy's blood in Elizabeth's mansion, and he could feel air molecules skating across his skin as he walked closer to Wayne and Samuel. He drew out his hunting knife, staring at the back of Samuel's hairy, sweat-grimed neck. Usually, he did this for fun. This would be the first time he'd ever been paid to kill someone. He had no idea how Coppergate's men figured out he'd been the serial killer stalking the Sleaze Strip, but it didn't matter, did it? Fuckslingers and junkies didn't make for great prey. They fed the demon in him just enough to keep it sated. Taking on a hunter like Samuel, though, that was different. He could feel his need clawing at his insides, eager to draw blood, to feel its warmth on his flesh, ever so soothing.

"Fine, don't thank me. And don't watch. But you're missing a lot. You bought the ticket, you might as well take the ride." Laughter.

Toby lightened his step until it seemed like he walked on air. He stopped breathing, although it hurt to do so. His blood pumped too fast, and he feared Samuel might hear his near-orgasmic panting if he'd let himself breathe. His pulse beat too loudly as it was, and Toby knew from experience that sometimes, if one was attuned to the art of murder well enough, one could hear loud blood.

Now he could see the gun Samuel held on Wayne, and he supposed he could just let the former kill the latter, but what fun would that be?

"Just get it over with."

Toby wondered what Samuel would look like when he died. He didn't think the hunter would beg for his life, but his blood would feel erotic on Toby's skin, he knew that for certain.

He took careful aim with the hunting knife, pulled back his arms, and brought it down with all of his might.

2

Wayne heard the crack of the gun, but after a moment, when he didn't feel the pain that surely must come with being shot dead, he opened his eyes. He saw Samuel standing before him, but the gun pointed off at an askewed angle, far away from Wayne. Samuel's jaw hung open, and his eyes bulged.

Wayne opened his mouth, thinking to ask what had happened, but no sound came from him except a short whimper.

Samuel made a gurgling sound, and blood sprayed from his lips. He doubled over, trying to reach behind himself. Wayne saw someone standing back there, but he couldn't identify the person. A scraping sound filled his ears, and he ground his teeth as the person behind Samuel pulled the knife out of the hunter's back from just above the jet pack.

Samuel fell to the ground with a clank, and all of his weapons spilled from their hiding spots on his body in a clattering cacophony. Wayne could now see who had stabbed the hunter.

"Toby?" he asked.

"Hello, Wayne," Toby said. "Are you well?"

"You saved my life. Jesus, I've never been so happy to see anyone, ever." If he'd had the energy, he would have pushed himself off the ground and given his savior a hug.

"It wasn't a big deal," Toby said. He rolled Samuel out of the jet pack. "This thing looks pretty cool. I always wanted one, ever since I was a kid." Of course, when he'd suggested it to his father as a possible Christmas gift, his father had slapped him around and pushed him down the stairs, muttering under his breath, something about money and ungrateful brats.

Only six years after that, Toby had slit the old man's throat. Not out of some sense of revenge. It just felt pretty cool.

Wayne staggered to his feet. "It was a very big deal. If you hadn't shown up, I'd be as dead as him." He pointed to Samuel.

"He's not dead yet." Toby didn't even look away from the jet pack when he spoke. "He whistles when he breathes."

As soon as Samuel realized he hadn't fooled anyone, he tried to stand, but he had no energy left in him. His legs didn't want to respond to the suggestion of getting up, and he suspected Toby might have nicked his spinal cord.

Samuel crawled toward Toby, his hands stretching out to reach the young man's legs. His lips moved, as if he cursed the killer who had done this to him, but only a wheezing sound came out of him.

Toby placed the jet pack on the concrete and casually grabbed a handful of Samuel's hair, turning him so he could look in the hunter's eyes. In Samuel, he found something he'd never seen in a victim before. Usually, the last emotion his victims felt—he knew this because he always looked them in the eyes—was fear. Samuel's eyes were rock solid, marbles filled with fire and brimstone. Toby had no doubt that Samuel would have fought to the very last drop. Too bad he didn't have anything left.

"Sorry, old man." Toby tapped the tip of his knife against Samuel's left eye, ever so gently, just enough to scrape his cornea a little. Samuel flinched, but he didn't have the energy to scream.

Then, Toby eased the blade into Samuel's iris. The eye punctured and deflated slightly as the knife dug deeper, slowly, into the orb. Samuel wheezed and tried to flail away from Toby's grip. He didn't have the strength, and Toby pushed the knife all the way back into Samuel's brain, ending his life in an instant.

~

The room went dead silent. All eyes stared at Toby's screen, filled with Samuel's corpse, the hilt of a hunting knife sticking out of his head like a nail from a board. Blood eased slowly out of him, surrounding him like a chalk outline. Even in death, Samuel's face remained twisted into a murderous scowl.

Charles finally broke the silence. "He did it. I can't believe Toby actually did it."

"It's about time," Edward said. A grin shone wetly from his face, lubricated with whiskey. Finally, Samuel was dead. He would no longer call Edward "Eddie" or "Ring-Piece," and he would never belittle him again. Good fucking riddance.

Elizabeth sighed. "I'll miss him."

"In an odd way, so shall I," Coppergate said. "I hated him, but I truly loved to hate him."

"He could fuck like a beast," Elizabeth said. "Had a big dick on him, too. Couldn't get all of it in me."

Coppergate ignored her. "He interested me a great deal. He could be annoying during these games, but I did enjoy his presence. He was made from an outdated mold, and therefore could always surprise me. I've seen a lot of this world, so surprising me is no easy task. He, and others like him, will be missed."

"I hated him," William said. "I found him downright detestable."

"You chose your assassin well, Charles," Coppergate said.

"To be honest," Charles said, "I never would have thought young Toby, so small and ordinary, capable of killing a he-man like Samuel, no matter what my sources said."

"That's why he makes such an excellent serial killer," Coppergate said.

"He's worth every penny."

Coppergate smiled. "The game's not finished."

~

Wayne felt like gagging as Toby pulled the blade from Samuel's eye socket, letting blood and other viscous fluid flow freely from the wound. Toby got some on his hands, but he didn't seem to mind. In fact, as strange as it seemed to Wayne, it appeared that Toby actually enjoyed having blood on him.

Still, no matter how unpleasant Toby seemed now, he'd been the last of the contestants, and Wayne knew he had to stick with Toby, if they were going to take on the rich fucks.

"I guess it's you and me now," Wayne said. "The others are dead. Just before this guy killed . . . killed Stacy." He gulped, remembering. "He told us you were the last."

"Yes." Toby stooped down to pick up the jet pack. He slipped his arms through the straps and tightened them around his slender frame until they fit him. He tugged on them and smiled. "The other's are gone."

"Then we should come up with a plan," Wayne said. "We can't let these rich bastards get away with any of this. They're just as good as murdering us for their amusement."

"Great," Toby said. His voice sounded as neutral as a machine's. "Any ideas?"

"I hoped you might have some. We've been holed up at this mansion for the past few hours. Then, this bastard came along and killed us all."

Toby wiped the blood from his knife off on Samuel's coat. "You look like you're in pain. Are you all right?"

Wayne looked down at his battered and torn body. It hurt, all right, and he could still see glass sticking into his flesh. But it didn't hurt yet. It would probably cripple him later, when he had the chance to relax and let his body come down from the adrenaline high. "I'm fine, for now."

Toby nodded as he checked his gleaming knife for spots of blood. "How do you suppose I'd go about killing someone like you with a knife?" His eyes never left the blade.

Wayne had gone through too much to let self-delusion lead him astray. He heard Toby's words, and his soul clenched. "Come on, man. Don't."

Toby turned the knife over and over in his hands. "I saved you without really thinking. I thought it would be fun to rescue you and then surprise the hell out of you by killing you after. But I wasn't thinking. I forgot about the Red Death. If I get your blood on me, I'll get it, too, and the billion dollars wouldn't do me any good."

Not true, of course, but Wayne didn't want to disabuse him of the notion. He slowly backed away, his hands up, palms out. "Wait. I'm not the bad guy here. The people who put us in this situation, they're the bad guys. We should be thinking about taking them down, not killing each other."

"Oh, I'm a bad guy," Toby said. He advanced, matching Wayne step for step. "I've killed three hundred and twenty-three people—I'm sorry, Samuel is three hundred and twenty-four—and that includes women and children. Would a good guy do that?"

Wayne's mouth dried up, and he tried to think of something to say. He tried to find a weapon to use. He tried to not trip over his own feet as he walked backwards. He saw the scattered guns around Samuel's body, but he knew he'd never be able to reach them in time.

"Well?" Toby asked.

"No." Wayne's voice croaked so badly he could barely understand himself.

"I eat flesh and drink blood. Would a good guy do that?"

Wayne cleared his throat, and still his voice crawled out of his creaky throat. "No."

"When I have a lot of time, I like to hone my torture skills on my victims. I can be pretty creative, too. I once tortured an old woman for three days with a sewing pin, a bunch of balloons, and a pair of dirty underwear. Would a good guy do that?"

"No."

"I'm a bigger monster than any of those rich people could ever dream to be," Toby said. "Bigger than Samuel Barnabas. Bigger than Richard Coppergate. Why should I kill any of them? Certainly not because they're evil. Especially since they paid me to be here."

Oh shit. Wayne stumbled and felt his back come up against a light post. He couldn't talk Toby out of this. Suddenly, he wished that Samuel had blown his brains out, after all.

"You can't kill me." Wayne hated the sound of his own mewling voice. "You'll get my blood all over you."

"True," Toby said. "I don't want to live like you. I suppose I'll have to be a little crafty." He playfully flicked the blade at Wayne's gut. Wayne sidestepped quickly, but it didn't look like Toby had really tried to get him, just to scare him.

Wayne stumbled over his own legs, and he went down hard enough to feel a jolt go through his ass and up his spine. With horror, he realized that he couldn't defend himself. Toby had him at his mercy. Nothing would stop him from killing Wayne.

3

On the way to Wingate's mansion, Jack looked out the window of the cab and saw something interesting down the block. He nudged Jimmy's shoulder. "Look."

Jimmy, bored, glanced out the window. Then, his eyes sharpened, and he leaned forward. "Stop the cab."

"Here?" the cabbie asked.

"Yes, here! Now!"

The cabbie pulled a lever, and the taxi came to a halt.

Jack held up his hand. "Come on. Hurry!"

The cabbie leaned back, presenting his left hand, and Jack made the transaction as quickly as he could. He and Jimmy then got out and started running toward the Drake mansion.

There, they found Samuel's body, still warm with the fading remnants of his life.

"Motherfucker," Jack said. "I wanted to kill him."

"He killed my friend," Jimmy said. "You would have had to wait until I'd killed him."

"The fuck you say."

Jimmy grunted. "Who do you think beat us to the punch?"

Jack looked down the block and saw two figures by a lamp post. "Could ask them."

"Is that--?"

"Yeah, Wayne Richards. I think the other might be Toby Munger. It looks like Munger's going to kill Richards."

"What should we do? We didn't plan for anything like this."

"Well, considering Toby would kill someone to get that billion dollar prize, I've got to think he's an evil son of a bitch. I don't like evil sons of bitches."

"I know."

"On the other hand," Jack continued, "that killing mind frame of his would do us good, considering how we plan to kill sons of bitches more evil than him."

"It looks like Wayne Richards is too much of a pussy to fight back," Jimmy said. "I don't think he'll fit in with the whole evil-sons-of-bitches thing. If we let Toby kill him, we might also be, well, you know." He didn't want to say it again.

"Good point. But who's to say Wayne wants to help us out? What if he wants the billion for himself?"

"No, I don't think so. He's in the last stage of Red Death. I don't think he's going to need a billion dollars."

Jack nodded. He watched as Wayne fell over, and Toby approached his fallen body, drawing his knife back for a killing blow.

"Hey you!" Jack shouted. "Stop that!"

Toby turned to look at them. "What do you want?"

In that moment, Jack knew he had to kill Toby. Wayne could have very easily taken the opportunity to attack Toby with his back turned, but he didn't. "You shouldn't kill that guy," Jack said. He set down his duffle bag and started rummaging through it.

Toby held the knife by his side in a relaxed grip. "Why not? Do you know how much he's worth to me dead?"

Jack's hand fell on a shotgun, but he didn't take it out yet. "A billion dollars."

Toby's eyebrows lifted, and Jack had a good idea that the guy couldn't have been more surprised. "Did Coppergate send you? I wouldn't be surprised, now that I've finished my part of the bargain."

"The only one who sent me," Jack said, "was that dead fuck over there." He nodded to Samuel's corpse. "If not for him, I'd be sitting at home right now, eating chips and watching TV."

By now, Toby had gotten close enough to Jack to attack him, but he made no suspect move. He merely stood still. "Too bad. Maybe you should've stayed home."

"Nope. I don't have a home anymore—"

"No TV and chips, either," Jimmy said.

"—and worse than that, Samuel Barnabas killed Steve McNeil."

Toby smiled, but his eyes remained calm, as serene as a mud puddle. "I saw that. He never saw it coming. One minute, he was looking out across a field. The next, he was static. It brought me that much closer to the billion dollars." And then he recalled what Jack's house had looked like through Steve's eyes. He knew the magic word that would throw this man off his game. "It's all right, though. I wouldn't expect a nigger like you to understand something as beautiful as that."

Jack's jaw muscles worked like twin pistons next to his ears. Toby saw the anger flow into Jack's face, and he knew he had to make his move now, while emotions blinded his opponent. Toby whipped the knife up like a snake with one large fang jutting out from its front, and he aimed at Jack's throat.

Jack's body tensed as he pulled the shotgun out of the duffel bag. Quick, but not quickly enough. He knew that in the last second, but he still tried to defend himself, even though he knew it would do no good.

Jimmy still had his gun from Jack's armory, and as Toby flashed forward with his knife, Jimmy drew down and pulled the trigger.

The bullet only grazed Toby's shoulder, but it still knocked him off course. Instead of opening Jack's throat from ear to ear, the knife scraped across the sidewalk, bringing up sparks. Yet even though he'd been shot, he rolled with it and came up on his feet, his knife at the ready.

Jimmy didn't give him another chance. He fired again, this time nailing Toby in the upper chest. The bullet passed through him and punctured the gas tank of the jet pack. It erupted, sending flames up so high they lit the top of Elizabeth Drake's mansion. The explosion blew Jack and Jimmy back, and when they looked up, all that remained of Toby were two legs standing, their tops cauterized and smoking, leaning against each other for a split second before they toppled over.

~

Toby's screen fizzled out, and after a moment of static, it went dark. All eyes shifted to the final screen, Wayne's.

"Two years in a row," Elizabeth said. "Not bad."

"It's good to have a winner for a change," William said.

"Not a bad game this year," Charles said. "A bit quick for my likes. We still had thirteen hours left, you know."

"It was still pretty entertaining," William said.

"Speaking of, I believe you owe me a good twenty million." Charles held out his left hand.

"Hold on, Charles," William said. "Wayne Richards didn't kill Toby Munger."

"It doesn't matter," Charles said. "We didn't bet on who would do the killing. We bet on who would win."

"William, give him his money and be silent," Coppergate said. When they stopped bickering, he reached to the microphone on the control panel.

~

"That was fucking close," Jack said. He looked down at Toby's remains, and he couldn't believe the little guy had almost gotten him. "Thanks, Jimmy."

"I was point blank, and I still almost missed," Jimmy said. "I'm a lousy shot."

Jack clapped his friend on the shoulder and squeezed. "It was good enough. You saved my life, Monaghan."

In a near echo, Wayne said, "You guys saved my life. Thank you."

Both of them watched as Wayne limped toward them, covered in blood and shards of glass.

"I really hope you're not here to kill me," Wayne said. "I don't think I could take that again."

"Just don't be an asshole, Wayne, and we'll get along fine."

Wayne looked at Jack. "How did you know my name?"

"We're friends of Steve McNeil," Jimmy said. "We did some research on this whole . . . game, I guess you could call it."

"That's a good sign," Wayne said. "It sounds like you guys might have a plan."

"Hell yeah," Jack said. "First, though, we need to patch you up. You look like you swam in a pool full of broken glass."

Wayne didn't hear that last part. A sudden, loud flare of static exploded in his right ear, enough to drop him to his knees with a scream. He slapped a hand to his throbbing ear, and his palm felt wet. He didn't need to look at it to know it was blood.

A voice boomed inside his head loud enough to rattle his teeth. "Congratulations. You are this year's winner, Mr. Richards."

Wayne screamed again as everything in his head vibrated. "Stop! Please!"

Jack and Jimmy exchanged a glance. They would have thought Wayne crazy if not for the tiny sound of a voice—almost like a radio transmission—coming from Wayne.

"In a moment," Coppergate said. "I want you to wait where you are, and I will have someone pick you up and bring you back so we can remove the explosive from your neck. It should not take long. Then, you'll be awarded your prize."

Finally, the voice ceased, leaving what sounded like a bell ringing in his head. After a moment, the ringing faded into a deafening silence.

"You okay?" Jack asked. He offered his hand.

Wayne checked to make sure his right hand didn't have any blood on it before he let Jack pull him to his feet.

"What happened?" Jimmy asked. "You're bleeding from your ear."

"I heard some kind of transmission," Jack said. "Was that Coppergate? What did he say?"

It took Wayne a moment to get his bearings, but when he did, he explained everything.

Then, Jack said, "Cover your right eye and ear. I've got to tell you something."

"Uh . . . why?"

"That's how they've been watching you," Jack said. "I don't want them to hear what I'm saying. They probably can't read lips, but just to be safe, I need to cut off their visual, too."

"Okay." Wayne put his left hand over his right eye, and then he jammed his index finger from his right hand into that ear. It mellowed the pain, a little.

"We can't have anyone pick you up," Jack said. "We need to come up with a plan first."

"But what about the bomb in my neck?" Wayne asked.

"Never mind that. You still have a lot of time. We need to get sneaky."

"Oh?" Jimmy asked. "This coming from Mr. Guerilla Warfare?"

"Shut up, Jimmy. Time's important, and we've got a ticket into Wingate's mansion now." Jack took a deep breath. "We need to sneak into that place with you, and that's just not going to happen if they send guys to pick you up now. It's better than storming the mansion and hoping they don't have any guards with heavy duty weapons."

"How are we going to handle this, then?" Wayne asked.

"I don't know yet. That's why we need more time. Let's get going, and don't you dare take that hand off your eye. I don't care if they hear us or not, but they can't know where we are yet. Do you still have your credit chip?"

"I haven't had one in a long time. Traded it for booze a couple of years back."

"Thank Christ. I would hate to have to dig it out of you."

Wayne shrugged, happy that the burden of coming up with a plan had been removed from his shoulders. He would never be the smartest guy, or even smarter than average, but now someone smarter than him had happened along. Perfect.

He didn't even think about the billion dollars that he had coming to him if he just kept standing here. "Let's go, then."

~

"That could be a problem," Edward said. He stared at Wayne's blackened screen.

"I wouldn't worry about it," Charles said. "What's the worst they could do?"

"You saw the, uh, colored guy. He's got his arsenal with him. Not to mention that journalist. They could do us some damage."

"We're well protected here," Charles said, "thanks to Richard's mob connections."

"Still . . ."

"Have no worries," Coppergate said. "Never doubt the temptation a goodly sum possesses."

CHAPTER 22

1

The phone rang, and Bob Whiteman cracked his eyes. Not far enough to be blinded by the light flowing through the window, but just wide enough so he could see the clock readout in the corner of his vision. Ugh. Could it really be that late in the day?

Then he remembered how he'd spent his evening. As soon as he dropped McNeil off at Wingate's mansion, he'd taken his pay and had gone to a cunt club with a group of friends. He paid off his debts with Two-Finger Finney and then got absolutely hammered while watching women make things vanish into their pussies. Then, he'd gotten one of the masturbators to take a couple of Shifts, which made her look like Bob's favorite actress of all time, Joan Gabriella. He'd brought her back to his place and fucked her till his cock hurt.

He rolled his eyes slightly and saw a naked female form still in bed with him. He smiled, thinking he might want to go another round with her.

The phone rang a fourth time, and Bob accessed his cellular account. "Hello?" He mumbled, not wanting to incur the wrath of his hangover.

"Robert?" It was Richard Coppergate.

"Already?" He sat up and did a quick calculation. The contestants still had about twelve hours to go. No game had ever gone this fast.

"Did I wake you? Dreadfully sorry, Robert. I just need you to finish your obligation for this year. You're to pick up Wayne Richards."

Bob yawned. "But my guy is Steve McNeil. Didn't Victor pick him up? It should be Victor's job."

"Victor is apparently offline," Coppergate said. "We can't reach him. Since you're our most reliable employee, I hoped you would be available. For an additional fee, of course. Double your usual."

"Sure." Bob took a moment to light a cigarette. "Where?"

"We're not sure. We tried to locate him via his credit chip, but apparently, someone else uses it now. However, we will send over our intranet connection, so you can track him through his own LiveStream. For the time being, he's concealed his location by covering his eye, but we expect that he'll soon slip."

"You mean, you want me to drive around the city and hope I find him?"

"More or less," Coppergate said.

"That's ridiculous. Do you know how big the city is?"

"I pay you well."

"Yeah, but—"

"Excellent. I expect you to begin immediately. After, of course, you find Timothy."

Coppergate hung up before Bob could object. He didn't have a car. The van belonged to Tim, so Bob would need a taxi to get over to Tim's apartment.

The form next to him stirred. "Something wrong?"

Bob glanced over. The Shifts had worn off, and she now looked like herself. Too bad. She had a crooked nose, a lazy eye and her front teeth were obviously fake.

Still, she kept fit. He'd fuck her like this.

No, he didn't have the time. "You need to get out of here."

She blinked, her eyes looking in opposite directions. "Okay. But you didn't pay me last night."

Fuck. "How much?"

"A thousand."

"Shit on that. You weren't worth five hundred."

"You made me take Shifts. I know you liked that. It costs extra."

He wanted to argue the point, but again, he had to get moving. He held up his left hand and transferred the money to her account. When he saw how much he had left from last night's celebration, he couldn't believe it. Coppergate had given him half a million, and he only had a little more than five thousand left. Did he black out or something?

The woman gave him one last pleasure—a hell of a view while she bent over to pick up her clothes, showing off her puckered asshole and her fat, juicy pussy, all framed by her wonderful peach of a derriere—before she walked out of his life.

He tried to call Tim, but his partner wouldn't answer. Motherfucker. He then called a cab and hopped in the shower before it arrived.

2

Bob paid the cabbie and got out, standing in front of Tim's place, squinting against the sun. His hangover still lingered in his stomach and floated in his head, and the sunglasses he wore didn't do much to stop light from penetrating his brain.

He walked up to the second floor and hammered on Tim's door. When he got no answer, he knocked harder. "Come on, Tim. Open up. It's me, Bob. We gotta' go, man."

Still, no answer.

Bob tried the doorknob. He expected it to be locked, since it was not a very good neighborhood—not as bad as Bob's, but definitely not as good as the east side—but it turned in his hand. He shrugged and pushed the door open.

"Hello? Tim? Where the fuck are you?"

He walked through Tim's living room, noting its cleanliness and organization. Clean coffee table, not so much as a sweat ring. Dusted pictures hanging on the walls. Even the windows sparkled.

In the kitchen, there were no dirty dishes in the sink. The food in the fridge was all in plastic containers, even the butter. No crumbs on the counter. Bob thought about his own messy apartment and couldn't help but marvel at Tim's. Not bad for a dirty hippy. Tim probably didn't even drink from his milk carton.

He closed the refrigerator door after noting the lack of beer and moved on to the bedroom. As he cast his gaze around at the well-made bed, the carefully folded clothes in the dresser drawers and the orderly desk with its computer on it, he tried to think back to what Tim might have said last night. He knew Tim was a high school teacher in the daytime, but he couldn't have needed to be in class today. Who taught on Saturdays?

Then, he remembered Tim's disgust at how they'd kidnapped Steve McNeil. While Tim didn't know Steve, he knew that Bob had been friends with him back in the day. He'd considered kidnapping Steve an act of betrayal, which struck Bob as strange. He'd been working with Tim for eight years, and he'd never objected to any of their targets before. Not even when Bob accidentally killed a former contestant by hitting her over the head did Tim give him shit. Coppergate had, since they then had to find a replacement, but Tim didn't say a word about it. He'd even laughed a little.

Bob stared at a hamper for a while before he figured out its purpose, and then he checked the bathroom, where he finally found something messy. No, the toilet shone immaculately. The mirror didn't have any splash marks of toothpaste sputum on it. Even the floor sparkled.

But the bathtub was full of blood, almost to the very brim.

"Jesus Christ." Bob scratched his balding head. "Schoolteacher by day, serial killer by night." He chuckled, but he stopped when he saw something pale through the thick, coagulating blood. Bob bent over and squinted.

He saw someone's dick.

He could also see something else, but he didn't recognize it. He had a suspicion, though.

"Shit." He reached his hand into the tub and recoiled when his wrist touched something cold and stiff under there. He gritted his teeth and tried not to think about it. When he found the stopper, he pulled it out. Then, as the tub drained, he turned around and washed the blood off his arm in the sink.

By the time the surface of blood had lowered halfway, his suspicion was confirmed. He saw an entire body in the tub, and it had long hair.

"You stupid fuck."

He looked into Tim's blank, bloated face and wondered how long ago his partner had slit his wrists. Probably a while ago, maybe as soon as he got home. The corpse had curved in rigor mortis and now fit the bottom of the tub like an adjoining puzzle piece. Bob couldn't see through the red lenses of Tim's glasses, and he wondered if Tim had killed himself over something stupid like the McNeil situation.

Or had this been building up over the years? A schoolteacher had to have brains, more than Bob, at least. Bob knew he'd never impress anyone with his intelligence, but Tim had to have something more between his ears. Maybe his moonlighting job had fucked with him for a while, and McNeil had just been the straw that broke the camel's hump.

Sure, it had left a bad taste in Bob's mouth, but come on. It was just business. Tim should have known that.

Bob dialed up Coppergate, who picked up on the third ring. "Yes?"

"Tim's not coming with me."

"Why not?"

"He's . . . uh . . . dead."

"Is this a joke?"

"Nope. He slit his wrists. I'm looking at his dead body right now."

"Hm. Pity. Did you notify the authorities?"

Bob almost said, “Fuck no.” Then, he remembered that Coppergate didn’t like curse words, so he just said, “No.”

“Then don’t. Tim is dead. He can wait until we’re finished.”

“All right. But hey. Before you hang up, I don’t have a ride. I had to get a cab over to Tim’s.”

“Oh. Right. I’ll send you a replacement from another team. He’ll be there shortly.”

Coppergate hung up, and Bob looked one last time at Tim’s body. Eight years, down the drain. He’d never really liked Tim and his liberal bullshit, but the guy could be funny. Sometimes.

Oh well.

CHAPTER 23

1

Wayne, Jack and Jimmy went into Elizabeth Drake's garage and found a Lexus 2199 in there. Jack used his 'net connection to access a repair manual for that model, and he used it to hack the dash computer to bypass the need for a thumbprint identification. They then drove to the nearest grocery store. Jack and Jimmy went in while Wayne sat in the backseat and tried not to bleed to death. He'd removed some of the shards of glass from his body and managed to cover up those minor wounds, but there were a couple of big pieces still in him. Blood oozed from around the glass.

Jack and Jimmy came back, and they gave Wayne an eye patch and a set of ear plugs. Wayne, tired of holding a hand over his eye, eagerly put the eye patch on, and he put one of the plugs in his right ear.

"Good," Jack said. "Now we need to take care of your wounds. Jimmy, give me the bandages and pliers."

Jimmy did. First, Jack put on a pair of rubber gloves and formally patched up the smaller injuries. Then, he took a pair of needle nose pliers and used them to remove the bigger pieces of broken glass.

Wayne tried not to scream. He really did. But when he felt the sharp edges rubbing against his raw wounds, he couldn't help it. Jack pulled them as quickly as he could, but it still hadn't felt quick enough to Wayne.

After Jack rubbed some disinfectant into the easiest injuries, he bandaged them up. However, he stopped when he came to the biggest one of them all. "This one's going to need stitches."

"Yeah, well, I can't afford doctors," Wayne said, "so I'll have to do without."

"I could put them in, if I had sterile thread," Jack said. "So there's only one thing to do. Jimmy, go back in there and get us some duct tape."

"That doesn't sound very sanitary," Jimmy said.

"Nope, but it'll work, at least until this is over."

When Jimmy came back, he handed the roll over to Wayne. Jack said, "When you put that tape on, push your gash closed first. Then, as tight as you can, press that tape down and wrap it around your arm, as tight as you can. Okay?"

"That'll stop the bleeding?" Wayne asked.

"Yes. The blood will have no choice but to clot."

"Sounds like you've done this before."

Jack didn't answer him.

2

They had to find a place to talk things out, and they had to think about it for a moment. They couldn't go to Jimmy's place, considering that Coppergate had to know about him by now. Jack's place was too damaged to qualify for this, not to mention how long it would take them to get there. Jack thought Lenny's might be a good place to go, but Jimmy said that if Coppergate knew about him, he would certainly know about Lenny's, since he'd written quite a few columns that took place there.

High profile places were out, and they couldn't stay out in the open. They had no choice but to find the sleaziest bar they could.

At the end of the Sleaze Strip—across the street from Henry's Likkker, much to Wayne's dismay—they found a place called The Gutter. Anyone who walked into this place had to make their peace with the idea that they would be breathing SyntheSmoke instead of air. Peanut shells littered the floor, left there by customers who'd died fifty years ago. There were no decorations here, not even a neon beer sign. The splintery bar was actually a board nailed down to two other boards in front of a row of lopsided stools. The surface had sweat rings that could have been left by Methuselah.

The bartender might have been handsome, if he'd cleaned himself up a bit. His greasy dark hair hung in his eyes, which were hooded by the Wild Turkey he drank from the bottle. His yellowed undershirt looked like he might have rubbed cheese into it, and the dingy tattoos on his arms were almost concealed by grime and his heavy, wiry arm hair. A cigarette dangled absently from the corner of his mouth, and he took drags off it as if he were breathing. Ash fell all over the bar and his soiled shirt, and he never made a move to brush it away with his long-nailed fingers, which probably hadn't been washed in weeks, perhaps months.

There weren't a lot of customers. An old whore sat at the bar, nursing a beer and smoking much the same way as the bartender. An old man lay face down on a table, his head surrounded by a halo of puke. A group of burly men played cards in the back corner. No one seemed to care that Wayne, Jimmy and Jack had entered, nor did they give a glimpse to Wayne's blood-crusted clothes. Business as usual for the patrons of The Gutter.

Despite the filth in which this bar squatted, gentle jazz drifted from the speakers of the wall-mounted juke box. It seemed out of place, and it soothed the minds of everyone in here.

Jack went to the bar and ordered the best whiskey the place had.

The bartender gave him a quick glance and then wordlessly put a fifth of Wild Turkey in front of Jack. It had to be the only name brand in the joint. The other bottles lacked labels, for the most part.

Jack paid up and took the bottle and three glasses to the table where Wayne and Jimmy sat. He poured the drinks and said, "How much time do we have left?"

Wayne checked his countdown. "About eleven hours."

"Good. Still plenty of time. We need a plan and badly."

3

They talked, or more often, argued, for about an hour, trying to come up with a method of attacking the Wingate mansion. Jack believed in a sneak attack full of gusto, and Jimmy wanted to be low profile the whole way. Neither of them could come up with a plan to get into the building without alerting the occupants, though. Wayne didn't have much to offer, but he made it clear to them that no matter what, he wanted to kick some ass.

No one in The Gutter minded their conversation. In fact, it seemed that no one even noticed them, even when Jack's voice rose in anger. The bartender continued to stare drunkenly into space, the whore continued nursing her beer, the old man continued to snore in his own puke and the poker players continued playing their low-stakes game, lost in their own conversation about absentee wives, wishful fucking and wishful spending.

As the level of booze in the bottle lowered, Jack sat bolt upright, like someone suddenly inspired by God Himself. "I've got an idea. I should have thought of this sooner."

Wayne and Jimmy looked at him expectantly.

4

Wayne checked the countdown again. Ten hours to go.

Jack and Jimmy looked at him. He returned Jack's gaze, then Jimmy's, and then he took a deep breath. A hand went to his right ear and plucked the plug out. He threw it down to join the peanut shells on the floor. Next came the eye patch, which fell like a shroud over the ear plug.

~

The occupants of the room had mostly dispersed about the mansion by then, except for Elizabeth and Coppergate—and Coppergate's assistant, sitting unnoticed in the shadows—both of whom whispered gently to each other. Elizabeth lowered the blanket, revealing Coppergate's latest cock. She held it in her hand, stroking its thickness in accordance to her whispering cadence. Coppergate smiled, his mouth and eyes closed in rapture.

William had sent George home hours ago—the punks had miraculously not attacked it—after getting the boy's opinion on the whole game.

"It was interesting," George said. He pushed his glasses up his greasy nose. "I really liked it. I can't wait until I can start wagering with the rest of you."

William ushered his son to the car, and as soon as the driver had taken off, he joined Charles for dinner and drink.

Edward sucked the rest of his cocaine down his nostrils and now sat in the parlor, smoking a cigarette and tapping his feet in rapid succession.

Coppergate stiffened, and Elizabeth watched his lazy, blood-tinted seed ooze down her hands. Just as the assistant offered moist towelettes for cleanup, the sound of jazz popped into the room. The three of them turned in unison just in time to see the black screen with Wayne Richards's name on it fill with the image of a skuzzy bar and Jimmy and Jack.

Elizabeth stood and walked to the door. "It's back on!" she called out.

Edward came back first, his nostrils gaping and inflamed. He took his seat without noticing Coppergate's sticky nakedness. "It's about time."

Charles and William came back in, and Elizabeth finished cleaning Coppergate's dick off and had covered it back up. All of them paid close attention to the scene unfolding before them.

~

"That's the stupidest shit I've ever heard," Wayne said. "I'm sick of this goody-goody stuff. That Coppergate guy says there's a cure for the Red

Death, and now that I'm the last one of these poor bastards alive, I can afford it. All things considered, I've earned it. So, fuck you." He stood.

Jack's jaw muscles flexed, and his nostrils flared like a horse's. "Sit the fuck down, dickhead. I'm not done yet."

"No, I'm done. I don't know why the hell I wasted all this time. I don't have much left, you know. Maybe, if I thought we had a chance, I'd stick it out with you guys, but my head's going to blow up in a few hours. I can either hope losing my head in an explosion won't kill me, or I can get a billion dollars. Hm. Let me see. You know, I think I'll take the money."

Jack stood in a flash, nearly pressing his nose against Wayne's. "The fuck you say. Sit down and hear the rest of my plan."

"Your plan is going to get me killed."

Jack's face narrowed. He drew back an arm, ready to strike Wayne, but Jimmy grabbed his elbow.

"Don't," he said. "Not worth it."

Jack whirled on Jimmy, who flinched. "Why the fuck not? We've finally got a chance to fuck up some rich folks—like we've been planning for *ages*—and this Red Death motherfucker won't go along with us."

"You'll get his blood on you," Jimmy said. "Besides, there are other ways we can get Coppergate and his friends. I'm a journalist, remember?"

"Fuck that shit!" Jack yelled. "I should kill this motherfucker right now!"

"There ain't gonna' be trouble, is there?" The voice came from the bartender, who now held a shotgun. He didn't aim it at anyone, but it still looked menacing.

"No," Jimmy said.

"Good. I don't like trouble." The bartender put the shotgun on the bar and lit a new cigarette.

"Let it go, Jack," Jimmy said. "We don't need him."

Jack yanked his arm away from Jimmy and got back in Wayne's face. "Listen, you little shit. I'm going to fuck those rich assholes up, and then I'm going to come after you. Got it?"

Wayne didn't look very concerned. He took in a deep breath and prepared to say a word he hadn't said in years and never expected to again. "Whatever. Fuckin' nigger."

Before Jack could so much as move, Jimmy pulled him back. "Just get out of here," he said to Wayne. "Now."

Jack's eyes flamed, and the veins in his forehead pulsed wildly. Wayne shrugged and headed for the door.

~

"See?" Coppergate asked. "Did I not tell you?"

"Damn," Edward said. "You'd better get Bob to pick this guy up before the black dude tracks him down. I've never seen anyone so pissed off before. He looked red."

"I wouldn't worry too much about the colored man," Coppergate said. He turned to his assistant. "Send a man out to kill him. As I recall, his name is Jack LeCroix. Use footage from Steve McNeil's LiveStream to get any more details the man might need."

"What about the journalist?" Charles asked.

"As much as I would like to, we can't kill him," Coppergate said. "James Monaghan is not only a popular columnist, he's also syndicated. Were he to be murdered, there would be a high profile inquiry. I do not know if even I could keep my name out of such an inquiry. However, Mr. Monaghan is not paid well. Perhaps we can buy his silence."

"I doubt it," Charles said. "He may be a cad on the 'net, but he imagines himself to be a journalist of the old, noble school. You know, ferreting out the truth and telling the world. Such men are hard to buy."

"Regardless, I'm certain we can handle him. I do, after all, own the news outlet for which he works. In the meantime, notify the guards they won't be needed any longer."

"What about the colored guy?" William asked. "It sounds like he's still coming after us, and he looks pretty dangerous."

"The regular guards can handle him and the journalist," Coppergate said. "Three well-armed guards against a nigger and a pudgy journalist? Please. Besides, the mob guards cost more money every minute they're here." He turned to his assistant. "Pay them off with a nice bonus and send them on their way."

~

Even after Wayne had left, Jack felt his nerves bristling. He'd told Wayne to use the n-word, but he still found it hard to hear, even after all of these years.

"We'd better get moving," Jimmy said.

Jack forced his teeth to unclench. "We've got plenty of time. It'll take them a while to get a bead on him, and I'd rather not hang around their mansion, not where they might catch us."

"Let's just go. I'm sick of this place."

Jack looked around The Gutter and could understand. They finished off the bottle and walked outside to the car, where two young men lay dead by its side. They had to have been shocked by Drake's security system when they tried to strip it. A few others in the neighborhood eyed the car, more luxurious than any of them had seen in their whole lives, but after seeing what had happened to the others, no one dared to touch it.

Jack and Jimmy got in and drove away, headed toward the Wingate mansion.

5

Wayne strode as quickly as he could, but his sickness held him back. As he walked, he hacked wildly, coughing up blood and other gunk. His face started bleeding again, but he couldn't do anything about that. At least the wetness kind of cooled him off a little as he made his way to the City Centre.

His body ached, and he could feel his guts rumbling with the ever-familiar urge to shit. Finally, he knew he couldn't keep going like this, so he dropped his pants in an alley. He didn't even have enough time to squat down; just as he bent over to move his pants out of the way, his asshole dilated and blasted the brick wall with liquid shit. He groaned, bracing himself against the wall as more bubbled out of him and dripped down the backs of his legs.

When he finished, he realized that he didn't have anything to wipe with. He'd gone the last few years without wiping his ass, but now that he'd been using an actual toilet since last night, he found it hard to give up toilet paper again. He sighed and pulled his pants up, feeling the material cling to his ass and legs. He resumed his journey.

Jack had told him where to head, and about forty-five minutes after he'd left The Gutter, he found himself in the tourist area of the city, where the buildings scraped the sky and glorious restaurants and hotels dotted the land. Whenever a movie was shot in the city, they always used its distinctive skyline. Coppergate would have no problem tracking him down here, in front of the city's most famous building.

He hacked up more blood and wondered if he'd be able to make it. Wouldn't it just be fantastic if his illness finally killed him, here, at the very last second? He forced himself to keep putting one foot in front of the other as he made his way to his destination, hoping he could hold out for just one more mile.

CHAPTER 24

1

"We have visual."

Bob looked over to Keith, his new partner, and rolled his eyes. Tim could be an irritating bastard from time to time, but Keith downright sickened him. According to his social media, he was supposed to be a big shot hit man, but Bob knew after sitting with him for more than five minutes that Keith didn't have much between his ears. Whenever he opened his mouth to say something, he had to make it sound as if he'd just been discharged from the military.

They were at a stop light, so Bob checked out Coppergate's intranet connection and saw that Wayne's screen transmitted images once again. He saw a sleazy bar in the background. He saw a nigger and . . . wait, could that be Jimmy Monaghan? The columnist? Yes, he couldn't mistake Jimmy. His nose had to have broken at least once, and his face looked hard, like he'd taken many punches over the course of his life. Though age had softened him a bit, he still looked like a badass. Bob loved Jimmy's columns, especially the ones set in Lenny's Tavern.

Speaking of bars, Bob thought he recognized the one Wayne and Jimmy sat in. Yeah, he saw Brian, the bartender, wearing the same skuzzy shirt he'd had for years. Brian probably still hadn't taken a shower. Yet, Bob supposed Brian's slovenly ways weren't too bad; the dude still got plenty of pussy, and that was all that counted.

The Gutter. It was halfway across the city. It would take a while to get there.

He pulled into a McDonald's parking lot and turned the car around.

"Do you have a positive ID on his location?" Keith asked.

Bob resisted the urge to say, "Affirmative." Instead, he said, "Yeah. Used to drink there. I knew some guys who played poker there. Small time stuff, you know? Still, it was pretty fun. Then I fucked one of their wives. Forgot which one. She was pretty hot, though. Real dirty, too. She stuck her tongue so far up my ass I thought she'd tickle my prostate."

Keith turned away so Bob wouldn't see his grimace.

Bob caught it anyway. "What, you don't like it when a gal licks your asshole out?"

"Negative, sir," Keith said. "I like my women the old fashioned way."

What a fucking bore. "You're missing a lot, Keith. Anyway, I fucked her, and her hubby found out. Tried to beat me up, but I broke a bar stool over his fat fucking head. Fucked him up real good. They won't let me play cards with them anymore, though."

Keith cleared his throat. "May I speak freely, sir?"

"You're not in the army, Keith. Say whatever the fuck you want."

"I'd rather not talk during this operation. It's not in my job description, and I don't like you. You're filthy and insensitive. Sir."

Bob laughed. "That's pretty harsh, Keith. It hurts, you know? To be called filthy and insensitive. Jesus, is that the best you can come up with? You kill people for a living."

"I'm trying to be polite," Keith said. "Just because I kill people doesn't mean I have to be a jerk."

True enough. Bob kept his mouth shut as they headed for The Gutter.

"Target is on the move," Keith said.

"Where?"

"He's headed north, but it's hard to say more than that. He's still in the general area of the bar."

"Why the fuck would he go north?"

"The heart of the city," Keith said.

"I know that, fucker. But you saw the picture of him. How long do you think he'll last with all those high-and-mighty cocksuckers before the cops give him a taste of the long knuckle? He knows he's not welcome there. So why?"

"Too soon to tell, sir."

Bob sighed. He never thought he'd say it, but he missed Tim already. So much that he didn't know if he wanted to do this again next year.

2

It never failed to amaze Wayne. No matter how much he hated the city, he always felt enthralled by the skyline. The city contained some of the tallest buildings in the world. Even on clear days, their tops were invisible from the street. The offices on the upper floors were pressurized like the cabin of a plane, so the workers didn't have to wear masks. The city was truly beautiful; the people, on the other hand, sucked.

The buildings were all lit up despite the early hour, and cars flashed around him brightly. Pedestrians made sure to keep their distance, not just because of the blood on his face, but also from the horrid stench coming from his pants. He didn't see any cops, though. Most of them kept to their cars, anyway. Crime almost didn't exist in the City Centre.

Finally, after so much walking, he reached his destination and looked up. The Coppergate Tower rose majestically into the sky, where you couldn't see the spire at the top without a government grade telescope. It went so high that Coppergate had sold the rights to using the roof to the government, who planned to use it as an anchor for a ring they wanted to build around the entire planet. Wayne didn't know why Earth needed a ring, but he kind of hoped it would be used as a place to launch space ships into deep space without needing all that rocket fuel to break free from the Earth's gravitational pull.

He found a vacant bench in front of the building and sat down, waiting, hoping Coppergate's men would get to him before the police.

3

Wayne didn't have to wait long.

One moment, he sat, listening to the street musicians from a block down. The next, he saw a Ford Temptation parked by the sidewalk. A man in a crisp suit stepped out, looking directly at him.

Wayne stood up. "I take it you were sent by Coppergate?"

The man nodded. "Get in."

Wayne slid into the back seat of the Ford, and the fat guy in the driver's seat turned around. "How's it going, Wayne?"

"All right, I guess. All things considered."

"I'm Bob. I'm going to have to drug you so the doctors can get that bomb out of your neck."

"Okay," Wayne said. "Make it quick, though. I don't want my head to explode and ruin your nice upholstery."

Bob laughed. He liked Wayne much more than Keith. Too bad he had to stick Wayne instead. He pulled on a rubber glove and reached into the back seat with a needle. "Gimme your arm."

Wayne produced his uninjured arm and watched as Bob jabbed the needle in. In some distant part of his mind, he felt the burning pain of having metal penetrate his skin, but the other pain—not only from his crash through Elizabeth Drake's window, but also from his sickness—overshadowed it.

And then he felt himself drift away into the fog.

4

“That was easy,” Keith said. “What did you need me for?”

“Back up,” Bob said. He stowed the needle away and programmed the car to go back to Wingate’s place. “You never know with some of these guys.”

~

Edward went back to the bathroom to see if he could get anything else out of his empty vials. He stuck the open end of each into his nostrils and sniffed for all he was worth. He got a little bit, but not much. Not enough for the rush.

Dammit. He’d had too much whiskey. He felt wiped.

Defeated, he went back to the observation room and saw Wayne’s screen had gone black again.

“He didn’t bug out on us again, did he?” Edward asked.

“No,” Coppergate said. “Mr. Richards has been drugged, and he is on his way here with Robert and Keith.”

“Good,” Edward said. “I’m getting kinda’ tired.”

CHAPTER 25

1

Jimmy and Jack never knew how lucky they were. Just fifteen minutes before they arrived at Wingate's mansion, the mob guards had left. Only three remained. Two stood side by side at the enormous front door, and another made his rounds on the property. They wore flowing red cloaks which concealed submachine guns strapped under their arms. A decorative rapier stood out from their waists, but they weren't good for actual violence. They just looked pretty.

"I thought there would be more guards," Jack said. "I can see only two from here."

"Maybe they have attack dogs," Jimmy said.

"I don't see any."

"Could be in the back."

"Besides, I don't see any signs. It's a law. If you have attack dogs, you have to post a warning at the gate."

Jimmy smirked. "Yeah, and these guys are pretty good at obeying the law."

"All right, fine. You've got a point. But check that out." He pointed.

"Check what out?"

"Those sensors. If anyone with an unauthorized chip passed those things, alarms would go off. I don't have one. What about yours?"

Jimmy held up his hand, tapping a ring on his pinkie finger. "This is my chip. Since I'm a journalist, we have to be able to disguise ourselves. By law, we don't need a chip implanted. We can wear them on a ring."

Jack couldn't help but grin. "Aw. I was looking forward to cutting yours out."

"Fuck you."

"I guess you're going to have to ditch the ring then."

"But—"

"No buts. I don't want to get my ass shot off because of your vanity."

Jimmy scowled, pulling the ring off. He set it down in the grass on the very edge of the property, fully intending to retrieve it when this was all over. "So, what do we do now?"

Jack pointed to the bushes. "We hide and wait for Wayne to show up."

2

After waiting for nearly an hour, Jimmy said, "I'm getting mud all over my clothes."

"Me, too," Jack said. "Your point?"

"I'm sick and fucking tired of waiting here. I'm getting dirty, my legs are cramping up from kneeling and I'm hungry."

Jack grinned. "Bitch."

Jimmy ignored him. "How much longer can this take?"

"I don't know, but you should shut the fuck up. It's not like we're playing war games with water guns on a hot summer day. This is the real thing. We fuck up, we die."

"I understand, but couldn't we find a better hiding place? I mean, this really—"

"No, we can't. This is the closest we can get to the gate without being seen. The instant these guys show up with . . ." He trailed off, squinting his eyes. "Shut the fuck up. They're here."

A car pulled up in front of the gate with Bob and Keith inside. They could see Wayne's unconscious body leaning against a back window. Bob reached out and punched in a code. The gates parted slowly, just enough to let the car in.

"Quick," Jack whispered.

The two of them got to their feet, and Jack slipped easily through the gate. Jimmy lagged behind, his legs prickling over with pins and needles from kneeling for so long. He stumbled forward, unable to feel his feet. The gate started closing as he approached.

He gritted his teeth and gave it everything he had. He barely got through the gate before it locked shut behind him. Ahead of him, Jack ducked down behind a row of bushes. Jimmy threw himself at the ground directly behind Jack.

"Follow me," Jack whispered. "And whatever you do, don't lift your head."

Jimmy, panting, felt a burning stitch slice through his side. "Fuck, man. Wait a minute, Jack."

"We don't have a minute. We gotta' go now. Hop to it, Monaghan." Jack slithered forward on his belly as quickly as he could, and Jimmy groaned. He forced himself to follow suit, but he just couldn't keep up with his friend.

The car went much faster. Jack found himself falling behind quickly. He slipped across the grass like a ferret while Jimmy fumbled behind him like a crippled duck.

"Come on!" Jack hissed. "We're almost there!"

The car parked in front of the garage, and the door eased up, revealing a couple of people waiting, both dressed in doctor's whites. They stepped aside, letting the car in.

"No," Jack mumbled. He watched the door descend. He leaped to his feet and ran for the garage, hoping the guards at the door wouldn't see him break cover.

The door closed five seconds before he reached it.

"Fuck," he moaned.

Jimmy appeared next to him, panting like a dog. "Those guys almost saw us, Jack. What the fuck?"

"We needed to get in that garage," Jack said. "Now we have to face the guards and hope they don't die loud."

"I'd just be satisfied if they died without killing us," Jimmy said.

Jack took a deep breath and opened the duffel bag, which had been slung over his shoulder. "Take some guns. We're going to use them as a last resort. We'll try to use knives on the guards, but they're armed. I saw some big motherfucking guns hanging under their capes. I highly suggest you take something."

"I have a gun," Jimmy said.

"I don't mean the handgun. Take something bigger, like a shotgun."

Jimmy picked it out of the duffel bag, surprised by its heavy weight.

"It's loaded, so be careful. And grab some ammo, just in case. The big red ones."

Neither of them noticed the camera watching them. Yet they lucked out again, since no one would watch the footage until much later.

3

Since Wayne Richards's confirmed capture, the people in the observation room had convened to the parlor, where they awaited the winner. Coppergate sat at the center of the room with his assistant standing behind them. Everyone else sat on the couches. Charles and William shared one, talking about the wagers of the day. Charles had won most of them, but William managed to be a good sport about it. Edward had a couch to himself, as did Elizabeth.

Edward looked at the time. He'd been up for an entire day and change without sleep. The coke definitely helped, but now that he didn't have any more, he could feel himself coming down. He wanted nothing more right now than his bed. He didn't know how everyone else managed to stay up this long. Maybe Coppergate had some kind of drug, but the others had steadily been drinking over the course of the day. They should all be haggard.

"I should like to stand for this momentous occasion," Coppergate said to his assistant. "Give me my legs."

The assistant knelt on one knee and opened the suitcase on the floor. Coppergate's mechanical legs shone from within. No flesh-colored, lifelike appendages for him. Nope. He tried to go as far as possible when it came to intimidating people.

He pulled back the blanket that covered his lower body. His dick hung limply but thickly between two skinny leg stumps. The scar tissue around these and the base of his cock were sickeningly reminiscent of spilled milk gone sour, and everyone in the room found something else to hold their attention.

The assistant, however, had a cast-iron stomach. She took one of the robotic legs and knelt down before Coppergate, pushing his cock to the side so she could fit the metal cinch around a leg stump. Once attached, she jammed some electrodes and other probes onto and into Coppergate's flesh through scars that already existed. These connected to Coppergate's nerves and activated the leg. Once done with this, she moved on to the other one before dropping the blanket back over his lower body.

At this point, Coppergate prepared the billion dollar transfer and waited.

4

Bob and Keith watched as the doctors dragged Wayne's unconscious body out of the back seat and onto a gurney, which they then wheeled away. A third doctor came out, holding up his left hand. "Payment in full, authorized by Richard Coppergate."

Keith took his payment first and watched the amount in his bank account go up a thousand dollars. Not much, but still, not bad for just a couple of hours of work.

Bob watched with the glee of a child on Christmas Day as the numbers of his bank account climbed considerably more than Keith's. As far as he was concerned, it wasn't money. These numbers represented booze and fuckslingers and poker games.

"Nice doing business with you," he said. "Give my regards to the boss."

The doctor nodded.

Bob called up a taxi to take him away from here while Keith saw a guard walking around the back of the house. "Hey, I know that guy. I served with him. I'm going to say hi. I'll see you later, Mr. Whiteman."

Bob didn't listen to him. He just watched as Keith took off out the back door of the garage to see his old army buddy. Still on the phone with the cab company, he stepped out of the garage and started down the drive to the gate.

5

Jack held his shotgun in one hand and the knife in the other as he did his best to step lightly. Over the years of dealing with trespassers in the woods, he'd discovered how important stealth had been to his own survival. He'd had plenty of occasions to practice it, and now he moved without a sound toward the door guards.

Jimmy, on the other hand, had shoes with hard soles, and he breathed heavily as he walked. Twice, Jack had to turn to face Jimmy with a finger to his lips.

The two guards stood on the porch, but they left a lot of room between them and the door, which gave Jack some space to sneak up behind them. They talked to each other quietly about the chicks they were banging. It sounded like bullshit to Jack, just a couple of guys lying about the trim they've gotten over the years. Maybe if they'd paid more attention to their surroundings, they'd get the chance to actually get more pussy.

Jack stood directly behind one of them, and he waited patiently for Jimmy to get behind the other. He saw Jimmy holding his breath, and his face turned beet red.

Jack nodded and reached around his target's neck with his knife hand, yanking it across the man's throat. Blood gouted from the wound, but since Jack knew well enough where to cut, he made no noise, not even a gagging sound, as he clutched at his open wound. Without hesitation, Jack turned the guard around, plunging the blade into his eye, dropping him like a sack of bricks.

Jimmy didn't do quite as efficient a job. When he tried to slit his target's throat, he didn't get it right because the guard saw Jack out of the corner of his eye and turned his head. Instead of getting the windpipe, Jimmy cut the guard's jugular and carotid. Blood poured down the guard's body like a red waterfall, but he could still make noise. Worse, instead of grabbing for his wound, he reached under his red cape for the gun.

Jimmy panicked and jabbed the blade at the guard's throat again, this time getting him just under the adam's apple. The guard fell down the steps of the porch and thrashed wildly, but he couldn't make any noise from his throat.

Jack looked down at Jimmy's work. "A bit messy, but not bad. This your first knifing?"

"Yeah." Jimmy watched the guard's movements as they slowed to a creep, like a wind-up doll running out of juice. He thought about shooting Toby, and he realized that his second killing hadn't bothered him in the slightest.

"Now let's get inside and fuck some shit up," Jack said. He knelt down next to his guard and riffled through his pockets. He found the keys in no time and turned to use them in the front door.

"Hey! You! Stop!"

Jack and Jimmy turned to see who the newcomer was, both holding their shotguns at the ready.

6

The older doctor set up the ray carefully and stood back, watching it with a smile. They'd already implanted a new chip into Wayne's left hand so that Coppergate could make the final transaction. Now the other doctor, his protégé, stood by, waiting for an explanation.

"Mr. Coppergate is adamant that we not actually remove a bomb from a subject's neck. Never. However, we are supposed to neutralize it. Considering Mr. Coppergate's situation, he is justified in his thoughts. It really is necessary that he retains the ability to detonate the subject's head if said subject becomes unruly."

"How do we neutralize it?"

"A simple procedure with this ray. It eliminates the timer set in the bomb and turns it into a transistor that responds to a pulse emanating from a control only Mr. Coppergate has access to. It is set in one of his teeth. The one all the way in the back of his mouth."

"Brilliant," the apprentice said.

"I'll bet they didn't teach you *that* at Harvard."

"No, sir."

7

Keith met up with Jenner, the guard he'd known in the army, and they shot the shit for a bit. Jenner was on guard duty, so he asked Keith to walk with him as he made his rounds. They talked about the last place they'd been stationed together, where one of their friends had hooked up with a local fuckslinger and his dick had fallen off.

"I don't know whatever happened to him," Jenner said.

"As soon as he got back home, he got an implant," Keith said. "Nothing like the real thing, but it worked, I guess."

"You'd think with all these ridiculous drugs these kids have today, like the one that lets you transmit your tattoos and body mods to other people, you'd think that we could get something that would grow a dick back."

"Maybe they're working on something now."

They rounded the corner of the house and came out in front just in time to see two people take out the door guards. Keith froze and realized he recognized both of them from Wayne Richards's LiveStream.

A set up. They'd been set up.

Jenner brought up his gun at the ready, and the two of them approached the front door. Keith whipped out his own gun from under his arm. "Hey! You! Stop!"

The two on the porch whirled around, and Jenner opened up on them. Keith pulled the trigger of his gun twice, but surprise had thrown him off. He knew his bullets had gone astray without checking.

Jack and Jimmy dropped to the ground, hiding behind the marble porch steps. Jimmy hyperventilated, never having found himself in a position like this in his life. Jack, on the other hand, had been in many violent situations in his years, from his first beating at the hands of peckerwood third graders to the day his parents had been murdered by racist fuckers in their very own home. Jack knew what to do, and he did it quickly.

He whipped the shotgun around the stone steps and fired it at Keith. He'd loaded up with scattershot, and it turned Keith's head and chest into bloody gruel. Some of it even caught the other guard, but he acted like he'd merely been stung by a mosquito. He kept firing. Jack took cover and waited.

"Jack! What the fuck are we going to do?"

Jack ignored him. When he heard Jenner's gun click, and he heard the clip being ejected, he popped up again and fired the other barrel.

Jenner joined Keith on the grass. Their blood mixed together and soaked into the ground.

"So much for subtlety," Jack said. He hopped up on the steps, ran up to the front door and kicked at it with all his might.

He bounced back with a yelp and nearly rolled down the stairs. He cursed loudly, holding his foot.

Jimmy went to his side and helped him up. Jack gingerly stood on his injured foot and leaned against Jimmy. "Fucking door's metal. We need one of the guards to open it up. Drag him over here." He pointed to the closest guard.

Jimmy grabbed the corpse under its arms and dragged it to the door. Jack took its hand and placed it on the panel just below the door bell. The front door eased open, and they finally entered, guns ready and reloaded.

8

Bob nearly reached the gate when he heard loud popping noises coming from behind him. He peeked over his shoulder and looked back toward Wingate's mansion. He could see the guards on the porch, or at least what had happened to them. He saw another guard and Keith with their guns out, going up against a pudgy white guy and a nigger. Keith and his army buddy did not win.

A part of Bob thought he should probably go back and check on things, see what's going on, and to perhaps aid his employer. But at the same time, they didn't pay him nearly enough for this kind of thing. He knew they'd probably give him more than a hardy thank you if he went back and saved the day, but why bother? They had guards. More would probably come out and handle the situation.

In the end, he decided not to step into someone else's department. He went through the gate, locked it behind him, and waited for his taxi to show up.

CHAPTER 26

1

"What the fuck was that?" Edward stood suddenly, but his legs didn't want to cooperate. They quivered a bit too much, maybe because he'd been sitting for a while, but he thought it more likely that he'd been unnerved by what had to be gunshots. He didn't even notice that he'd cursed in front of Coppergate.

The old man ignored him. "I think I may have been too hasty in sending our guards away so soon. I'm sure Charles's guards can handle it."

Charles jumped up and ran to the window, looking out over the front of the property. "Uh, I think the guards are dead, Richard. And, um. I think I see that hitman you sent out with Bob. He doesn't look too good."

Elizabeth joined him. "Yes, they're dead." For the first time Edward could remember, he saw something other than cold disinterest in Elizabeth's eyes. A touch of fear? Edward, who considered himself an expert on the subject, thought it likely. He thought about putting an arm around her to comfort her, but he didn't want to risk an ass kicking.

Coppergate turned to his assistant. "I hope you have your weapon on you."

She reached under her suit and unsheathed a rather large .45.

"Excellent," Coppergate said. "Charles, how about you?"

"I have rifles in my study," Charles said. "I used to go hunting with—"

"Retrieve them. Quickly."

Charles nodded, but before he could move, an explosion rocked the room, and his head turned into a red mist.

2

Once inside, Jack stopped Jimmy. "Listen, there's something we need to be clear on, okay?"

Jimmy, under the impression that they'd been in a hurry, thought now might not be a good time for a conversation. But he saw the look on Jack's face, and he knew it would be better to roll with it. "Yeah?"

Jack took a deep breath. "Wherever we find these rich bastards, they are all guilty, okay? No matter who they are, what they look like, anything, they are guilty as fuck. You must not hesitate to kill all of them. Even if they beg for their lives. Understand?"

"That's a bit cold-hearted," Jimmy said. "I mean, if they're begging—"

Jack couldn't mince words, not when they were this close to the end. "They are all responsible for Steve's death. They might as well have killed all those people themselves and God knows how many others over the course of the years. They must all die, even if there are children."

"Oh, now that's ridiculous," Jimmy said. "I'm not going to kill kids."

"That's fine. I don't think there are any here. If there are, I'll take care of it. Nevertheless, everyone must be killed, even if there are women."

"I don't know . . . I mean, women? I really don't like violence against—"

"As far as I know, there should be only one woman, and she's just as guilty as the others. No matter what made her that way, she's an evil fuck. If we don't take a scorched earth policy with these people, it'll come back on us. Are we clear?"

"I . . ." Jimmy sighed. "Fine." He knew he wouldn't kill women or kids, and he wouldn't let Jack do it, either. He hoped that it wouldn't come to that.

"Good. I call dibs on Coppergate. I want him to know why he's dying, and I want to take my time explaining it to him."

Jimmy didn't want to know what his friend meant by that. Instead, he followed Jack down the majestic corridor, guns at the ready. As they went, they stopped to investigate each room, hoping to find their enemy.

The parlor was the third room. Jack peered through the door and when he saw the occupants, he couldn't help but grin. Jackpot.

He poked the shotgun in, took aim at Charles Wingate and fired without hesitation. Wingate flopped to the ground, minus his head. Only his scalp remained intact, and even in death, it remained well groomed.

Jimmy saw one of them, a burly woman dressed in a suit, had a hand cannon, and she brought it up, aiming at Jack. Jack, reloading his shotgun, didn't notice. Instead, he glared with hatred at Richard Coppergate. Jimmy whirled his shotgun around and aimed it at the woman. Still, he didn't think he could pull the trigger.

He hoped it would scare her. "Don't!" he shouted.

She didn't scare easily. Instead, she shifted her aim to Jimmy.

Time oozed down a molasses stream, and in that extended moment, Jimmy knew she would shoot him if he didn't shoot her first. Yet, he hesitated, his finger frozen on the trigger. His mind screamed at his body to take some kind of action, anything, before she gunned him down.

Then, instinct finally kicked in, and his hand acted on its own. He pulled the trigger a second too late. They fired at the same time. Coppergate's assistant, peppered with scattershot, flailed back, her chest perforated in a hundred red places. As she died, Jimmy felt something bite into his own chest. He looked down, surprised to see a hole under his right nipple. He tasted blood in his throat as his legs lost all power and folded beneath him. Jimmy hacked up a crimson knot on the floor.

"Shit!" Jack snapped the shotgun closed and pointed it at the assistant, making sure she was dead.

Edward thought it might be time to leave. He had no doubt that Coppergate had some kind of trump card up his sleeve, but he really didn't want to wait around for it. He broke for the door into the living room, which would lead him out to the hallway and toward the front door.

Just then, William saw the assistant's gun on the carpet, and he dove for it, his muscle memory recalling his time in the war. Not that he'd seen any action, of course. His money made sure he stayed far away from any military conflict. But he remembered hours of drills, and it came back to him in his moment of need.

Jack didn't know who to shoot. He didn't want Edward to get away, but then again, he didn't want William to have a free shot at him.

Fuck it. He turned on William and opened up on him. William's chest exploded into mush, and he had no idea what hit him. His organs, visible through the ruin of his broken ribcage, quivered like the cogs of a dying clock before they stopped.

Jack whipped the shotgun up, hoping he could get Edward before he escaped. Nope. He was gone. Not that it mattered, since Jack had used both barrels on William.

He took this moment, while he reloaded, to look down at Jimmy. The journalist's eyes were closed, and his wound bubbled with saliva. Jack could hear Jimmy's wheezing breath and knew that his friend would die if he didn't do something quick.

Jack felt something sharp connect with the side of his head, and he reeled, sparks flaring up in his vision. The shotgun leapt from his grasp and thumped to the floor. He blinked and watched stupidly as Elizabeth swooped down on him with another kick, this one aimed at his face, her high heel on course with his left eye.

~

Richard Coppergate watched Elizabeth jump into action and smiled. He wished he could stick around and watch her wipe the walls with her opponent, but what if she lost? Then, who would be next?

No, that wouldn't do. Coppergate flipped the blanket aside and stood on his robotic legs. A jolt of pain went through his body as he did, but he had expected it. He only wished he had something to cover his swinging dick. He liked this one the best of all that he'd collected over the years, and he didn't want it to get snagged on something, or shot off.

He blocked out these thoughts as he ran for the door Edward had used mere seconds ago.

~

Jack slapped her foot away just in time to save his eye. Elizabeth whirled around and almost lost her balance, but she managed to use the momentum to come back with another kick, which Jack easily deflected. This time, he grabbed her leg and pushed her down to the floor.

She rolled back onto her hands and pushed herself hard, flipping back to her feet like a ninja. She growled and moved at him again, this time with such a flurry of blows that Jack had never seen before. He managed to parry the first few punches and chops, but she was too fast. His eye swelled up and closed on him, and his nose, brow and lip started bleeding.

Elizabeth dealt a hard knee to Jack's balls, doubling him over, giving her a nice target to kick. Her foot connected with his jaw, knocking him back to the floor. He spat up blood and one of his teeth.

The pain didn't register with him, not yet. Fury blinded him to it. He roared and kicked out, connecting with one of her shins. She yelped, falling first to her knees and then to her side, clutching her leg.

No more time for games. Jack whipped out his handgun and fired into her body, not stopping until the hammer clicked several times on empty chambers.

She stared up at him for a moment, unable to comprehend what had just happened. Six holes gleamed in her, four in the chest, one in the belly and one in her face. Her jawbone hung only from one corner of her mouth, and blood gouted from the other.

Finally, she understood. A single tear rolled down one of her cheeks. Then, her body unraveled from the sudden lack of tension, and she died.

Jack forced himself to his feet, and while his head swayed back and forth from the dizziness, he reloaded his handgun as fast as he could. Then, he looked up and saw that Richard Coppergate had left them. He could have only gone through the door into the living room. He wanted nothing more than to track the old man down and fire every single bullet he had into his ancient head. But in the deafening silence, he could still hear Jimmy's labored breathing.

Jack glanced once more at the gaping door. He cursed and rushed to his friend's side.

3

The doctors both led a semi-conscious Wayne Richards down the hallway toward the parlor when they heard the gunfire begin. The doctors stopped in their tracks, holding Wayne up.

His eyes popped open all the way, and he struggled through the mist of the drug Bob had used on him. It took him a moment to figure out what was going on, but when it clicked, he felt adrenaline rush through his system.

The doctors had done a pretty good job of patching him up. He could feel the stitches in his previously duct taped arm, and bandages covered up a half-dozen wounds. Still doped up a little, he didn't feel anything yet. Good. He had no idea what the day had in store for him.

He rushed toward the parlor, hoping he could help his newfound friends end this thing, once and for all.

The doctors exchanged a glance. The protégé said, "They paid you, right?"

"Of course. I always insist on being paid in advance."

"Good, because I think it's time to quit. Let's get out of here."

"Agreed."

They turned in unison away from Wayne, hoping they could get to their cars and out of there before the police showed up. Both had lost their licenses due to malpractice, and neither of them wanted to add jail to their woes.

Just as Wayne drew close to the parlor, he saw someone run out of the door to the living room. He glanced down the hallway and saw Richard Coppergate hobbling toward the back of the mansion on . . . were those robotic legs?

"Hey!" Wayne yelled. "You! Motherfucker, don't you move!"

Coppergate glanced back, but he did not stop trying to run away.

With a roar, Wayne hurled himself down the hallway. Though still handicapped by his injuries and the drugs, he managed to move faster than the old man. Wayne felt like he was in high school again, playing on the football team. He launched himself at Coppergate, tackling him to the floor.

The two of them skidded along the waxed, gleaming tiles. Before Wayne could pin Coppergate down, Coppergate rolled and threw a metal knee into Wayne's gut. Wayne lost his air and fell backwards.

Coppergate, his arms too weak in his old age, tried to push himself to his feet, but he couldn't. "You fool," he said. "You could have had it all. Why didn't you take the money?"

Wayne managed to stand finally, breathing heavily, and he moved toward Coppergate. The old man tried again to get to his feet, but Wayne kicked him in his sinewy, emaciated chest, knocking him on his back.

Wayne slumped down on Coppergate, straddling his chest, planting his knees on the old man's arms. He drew his arm back, aiming a fist at Coppergate's gleaming mouth.

"No!" Coppergate screamed. "You don't—"

Wayne brought his fist down, cleaving Coppergate's brittle jaw in two at the chin. His knuckles plowed through the old man's razor-sharp teeth, mowing them down like blades of grass from his weakened bone structure.

And then his fist, now fully in Coppergate's distended mouth, struck the tooth farthest back, and the world erupted into blood red agony.

4

Edward huffed, nearly out of breath, as he ran for the front gate. He could hear more gunshots behind him as he fled, but no one followed after him. Holy shit, he might actually make it!

He slammed against the gate, desperately trying to open it up. No good. It was locked. "Fuck!"

The control panel stood by the gate, and he started pressing buttons at random, hoping to hit the correct combination by pure luck.

Nothing happened.

It had been a long time since he'd done something physical, and he wondered if he could make it over the top of the gate. One way to find out. He put his hands on the bars, and just as he braced his foot below them, ready to boost himself up, he heard something click in the back of his neck.

"What the fu—"

His head erupted, spraying his brains on the bars and between them. His body staggered back for just a moment, as if it didn't realize his head had been blown completely off, and then he fell to the grass, leaking the remainder of his blood out onto the ground.

5

Bob thought it was one of the most fucked up things he'd ever seen. In his time, he'd seen a horse fuck a guy to death. He'd seen a woman shove her arm up to the elbow into a fuckslinger's pussy. He'd even seen a young couple gakked out on Berserker cutting each other up while they fucked each other.

But he'd never seen a dude's head explode for no reason at all.

He watched Edward Bridges die, and it took him a second to realize that some of Edward's brains had splattered on his shirt. Grimacing, he picked off the smoking meat and let it fall to the sidewalk.

The taxi finally arrived, disengaging from the track long enough to park in front of Wingate's mansion. Bob took one last look at Edward's corpse and shivered, thankful that he hadn't gone back to check things out.

He got into the taxi. The driver turned around. "Where to?"

"The nearest bar," Bob said. "I feel like getting laid tonight."

EPILOGUE

1

At first, he only knew darkness, and he wondered if at long last he'd finally died. When he found the energy to open his eyes, he saw he wasn't in hell, as he'd expected. Instead, he saw the cracked and burned ceiling of Charles's hallway.

Richard Coppergate shifted his eyes down to examine the damage. A good deal of his flesh had been scorched away by the explosion, revealing his reinforced bones and machine organs. His metal heart thrummed strongly, and despite the loss of his cock, he felt thrilled to be alive.

Near his feet, he saw what remained of Wayne Richards' body. His head had been blown to pieces, leaving his spine, poking out through the ragged stump of his neck. His shirt had also disintegrated, showing his charred, scrawny chest. Blood poured from Wayne's body and it pooled on Coppergate.

He grimaced. Sure, he'd been lying about the cure for the Red Death, but he knew scientists were very close to figuring it out. Of course, such a cure would only be available to people with lots of money, so Coppergate didn't worry about it too much.

The grimace squirmed across his broken teeth, turning into a slippery grin. He'd survived. Despite the sudden turn of events, he'd survived as all the others died. His body had been ravaged by his enemies' best efforts, but they'd failed, as they always would. Who knows? Maybe his body would heal in a particularly gruesome way. Nothing would please him more than adding disgust to fear.

Drool oozed down his mangled jaw and cut a trail through blood until it slopped down onto his blasted metal-reinforced ribcage. Disjointed giggles fell from his mouth as he struggled to get to his robotic feet.

2

Jack treated Jimmy's injuries to the best of his abilities. He'd found a straw on the minibar, which he used to drain Jimmy's punctured lung, easing the sucking chest wound that would have undoubtedly killed him within minutes. He heard the explosion from the next room, and as he finished patching Jimmy up, he remembered Wayne. At first, he wondered if maybe they hadn't made the deadline, but when he checked the time, he saw they still had a few hours on the countdown. It couldn't have been Wayne.

He stood and took his shotgun with him, reloading as he walked. In the living room, he could see smoke drifting through the open door to the hallway, and he could smell meat cooking. Carefully, he ducked down and peered over the threshold.

When he saw Wayne's corpse, he felt his stomach sink. Sure, Wayne knew what he'd gotten into, but he didn't deserve to die like this. Jack thought him very courageous, and he found that quality lacking in almost everyone in this modern world.

And then he saw the metal and burnt flesh contraption that was Richard Coppergate. Little more than bone and shiny steel, he still tried to escape, crawling on his skeletal hands and robotic feet.

Jack couldn't believe such a creature could live. He'd read plenty of science-fiction over the years and had a pretty good idea of what today's technology could do, but androids? He didn't think it possible. How much of Richard Coppergate was still human?

His skull, some of which peeked through his tattered scalp, looked ordinary enough, but the rest of his bone structure had been reinforced so much he couldn't possibly be human. None of his organs were made of flesh. Jack wondered if he even had a human brain still, or if it had been replaced by a machine.

He pointed the shotgun at the back of Coppergate's head. "Hey, motherfucker." His voice reverberated throughout the hallway, and Coppergate, using the greatest effort he could muster, turned and faced Jack.

Coppergate said something, but it came out garbled, a mixture of human and a malfunctioning phone.

Jack wanted to walk up to the creature and blow him away point blank, but what if Coppergate had a reserve of power left? No, he couldn't take any risks.

Still, Jack wished he had more time to enjoy this moment.

He pulled both triggers of the shotgun, sending buckshot into the remains of Richard Coppergate's body, denting his organs out of shape, punching through his skull and shattering the eyes that had inspired so much fear over the years.

Jack noted the human brains leaking out of Coppergate's shattered skull and thought he should have known better.

The contraption of flesh and metal that used to be Richard Coppergate folded in on itself like a dead spider, and after more than two centuries, he finally died.

Jack smiled and took a moment to admire his own handiwork before he ran back to Jimmy.

3

By the time Jack got back, Jimmy had woken up. He couldn't talk, and he could barely breathe, but for the time being, he was conscious. Only then did Jack realize how badly fucked they were. The cops would be able to access the rich fucks' LiveStreams, and they'd be able to see what really happened here. He'd been hoping to set up a believable story and then hack into their systems to erase the truth. He just couldn't do something like that without his equipment at home. In theory, a dead man's LiveStream could be hacked, but to the best of Jack's knowledge, it hadn't been done. Maybe the cops had a way that they haven't made public yet, but he knew for certain he couldn't do it without his pills.

He didn't feel very concerned for himself, since no one really had any records concerning him, and his face would be blanked out of any footage taken of him, but he felt very worried for Jimmy. Now, as he looked down at his wounded friend, he heard sirens in the distance. He couldn't even drag Jimmy out of here to take him on the run. Fuck.

He knelt down by Jimmy. "I can't stick around here, so you've got to listen closely. This is the story, all right?"

Jimmy nodded.

"You came here to meet with Richard Coppergate concerning some story you're working on. Something about, I don't know. You think of something. You'd know better than me. With me so far?"

Jimmy nodded again.

"In the middle of your meeting, all these crazy fuckers armed with shotguns—maybe some leftover punks from that riot—showed up and screamed something about death to all rich fucks. Maybe they had some kind of agenda, like the environment or the class war, or whatever you think the cops would believe best. These punks, they started blasting everything to hell, you included. Okay?"

Jimmy nodded a third time.

"Good." Jack grabbed the gun from Jimmy's hand and scooped up the rest of the weapons he'd brought with him. He'd have to destroy them later, but he couldn't worry about that now. "The story isn't going to hold up when they check Coppergate's LiveStream. I just hope they hold off on that long enough for me to get back home and hack the system. Try to stall them if you can."

Jimmy hacked up a blood clot and croaked for a moment. Finally, he said, "Thanks. For saving my life."

Jack forced a grin on his face. He felt bad, knowing that he'd just lied to his best friend. He couldn't possibly succeed at hacking the system. "I'm going out the back. I'll visit you in the hospital. Get well."

He rushed for the back door, thinking about anything he might have touched in here. The only thing he could think of was the front door, but he'd kicked that open as soon as the guard's dead hand had unlocked it. No, he hadn't left fingerprints behind.

Jack pushed his way through the back door and started running toward the stone wall at the rear of the property. He didn't have to put forth much effort to scale over it, and just as he jumped down to the other side, the police showed up at the front gate, where they started torching through the bars, guns at the ready.

4

When Jimmy opened his eyes, he saw the stark lights above him and knew he was in the hospital. He blinked the fuzziness away from his vision and looked around. His wrist was attached to the sidebar of his bed by a set of handcuffs. Big surprise.

Someone had left the TV on, and he watched the news. The newscasters told the world about something they called the Wingate Murders, and they talked about who had died and why this would be a great loss to not only society, but also the economy. A group of banks wanted to get together and build statues of the fallen in a semi-circle around the tourist area of the city. A man-on-the-street piece showed a lot of crying citizens, as if they'd lost a national treasure.

It sickened Jimmy.

Not as much as the next tidbit, though. When he heard the next part, he knew Jack hadn't succeeded. They listed Jimmy Monaghan as a mad dog killer, and though they didn't have much of Jack's information, they had his name from Coppergate's LiveStream.

Fuck.

The door opened, and a slouched over man with a day's worth of stubble and messy hair entered. He showed Jimmy a badge. "My name's Mike McCannon. I'm with the city's anti-terrorism unit. And you're James Monaghan, but if I were you, I'd think about changing my name to Dogshit."

Jimmy didn't have the energy to respond.

McCannon lit a cigarette and blew a cloud of nico-fresh into Jimmy's face. It had the desired effect. Jimmy wanted nothing more than a cigarette. "By now, you've had a look at the news. You know we got your LiveStream, so you know how royally fucked you are."

Jimmy waited.

"We also got the LiveStreams from Coppergate and his dead buddies. They were into savage shit. Pretty crazy. None of us at the precinct could believe it."

Jimmy felt sudden hope bloom in his chest. Maybe things weren't so bad after all. Maybe this guy saw these rich fucks for what they really were.

"Of course, we always knew something was up with those guys. They sure pay us enough to look the other way every year. I got a shit-ton of alimony to pay, and they helped me get out from under that. I gotta' say, they might be sickos, but I got nothing against them."

Fuck. Jimmy looked away and sighed.

McCannon leaned in. "Relax, Monaghan. It's not all that bad. We're open to negotiation. The guy we really want is Jack LeCroix. He's a dangerous motherfucker, and we need him off the streets. I won't mince words with you. We're going to put that son of a bitch in the ground and salt the earth over him. But if you give him up, we can cut you a deal. How do you feel about doing a couple of years instead? Technically, you only killed that guard outside. The other guy was obviously self-defense. The D.A. is willing to go as low as manslaughter for you. What do you think?"

Jimmy didn't favor him with a response.

"Come on, if you don't take the deal, you'll do life without parole. You can't want that."

Jimmy said something, but his voice had atrophied in his time in the hospital.

"What was that?" McCannon leaned his ear in close to Jimmy's mouth.

"I said. Fuck. You."

McCannon sat back and rubbed his scalp through his dirty mop of hair. "Fine. Don't play ball. You should think about it, though. Two years doesn't have to be two years. There's good behavior and parole. You could be out in a half-year, if you're lucky. And by then, someone will want to publish your life story. They'll want to know what would drive a popular columnist to murder. Who knows how much you could sell such a book for?"

The door opened, and a male nurse came in, a surgical mask over his face. He rolled a cart in. "I'm here to get some blood for his daily test," he said.

McCannon nodded. "Go ahead."

The nurse wheeled the cart over to Jimmy's bedside and started preparing a needle.

McCannon said, "You get life with no parole, that's it. You look like you used to be tough, but right now, you're a frail, pudgy fuck. I don't think you'll last long behind bars. You might be dead before the year's out, especially if I send a care package to some of my connections on the Inside."

"Fuck off," Jimmy said.

McCannon snarled and drew in close to Jimmy again. "Listen, you fuck. I'm giving you a ticket out of this mess, and you disrespect me like this?" He turned to the nurse. "Stick it in good. Make it hurt."

"You're the boss," the nurse said. He stabbed the hypodermic needle down like a knife into McCannon's neck and pressed the plunger down. McCannon gagged and jerked back, yanking the needle from him. Blood oozed down his shirt in a thin line, and he went for his gun. Too late. The sedative already coursed through his veins. He had just enough time to sit down before he passed out.

The nurse pulled off his mask. "Come on, Jimmy. We have to get you out of here."

Jimmy stared into Jack LeCroix's face, unbelieving. "What are you doing? They're after you, and you walk into a place like this?"

"I couldn't leave my friend behind. But we've got to hurry. They won't miss you for very long. I have the nurse's rounds timed. She'll be here in about fifteen minutes."

Jimmy sat up, and the world spun a little. "I'm kind of out of it, Jack. I'm going to need help."

"That's what I'm here for." Jack ducked out the door and pulled in a wheelchair. He then pulled McCannon's clothes off. "Get in these. And put these bandages on your face."

Jimmy, still a bit groggy, followed orders. "Where are we going?"

"I don't know, but we're hitting the road. The city's too hot for us. We'll probably spend the rest of our lives on the run. Sorry I couldn't get to the LiveStreams in time."

Jimmy tried to envision living a life without being a journalist, and it hurt him a little. It had been a part of his identity for so long, he didn't know if he could survive without it. He supposed he would find out, though. As soon as he'd dressed up and disguised himself, he sat in the wheelchair and let Jack roll him past a sleeping guard—with a hole in his neck—and out of the hospital.

5

The next afternoon, five hours before Jimmy Monaghan's escape made the news, Bob Whiteman sat in a bar on the Sleaze Strip, his head aching from the monumental drinking—and his body aching from the monumental fucking—of the night before. As he poured beer down his gullet in an attempt to kill his hangover, he watched the TV on the wall. It flashed with the biggest news in the city: the massacre at Charles Wingate's mansion. The talking heads went on and on and on about the big names who had perished in the slaughter, noting only two people who had survived: Clark, the butler—who had been found hiding in a closet—and local columnist Jimmy Monaghan. They listed Jimmy in critical condition at the city hospital.

Everyone speculated that terrorists had done it. Others called it a new breed of justice, happy that someone had finally struck a blow against the über-rich. The majority thought the rioting punks had been responsible. However, according to the police statement, they were examining the LiveStreams of the dead and piecing the story together.

"Fuck," Bob said.

The bartender raised his eyebrows.

"Nothing." But it did mean something. Next year, Bob wouldn't have this plum job, and that bummed him the fuck out.

He finished his beer and sighed. He had plenty of money, but it wouldn't last him through the rest of the month. Soon, he'd need another job, and no one paid better than Coppergate and his friends.

Still, he knew things would be all right. In a city this big, there were plenty of questionable people who needed unscrupulous acts committed, and they always paid well. Getting another job wouldn't be a problem. Nope, no problem at all.

-THE END-

Made in the USA
Monee, IL
23 August 2022

12385673R00148